Fall of the Republic

by **Jim Hicks**

Alston Books
1112 Rogers Road
Graham, NC 27252

http://alstonbooks.xyz/
Second Edition
January 2013

Printed and bound in the United States of America

Library of Congress Control Number
2013931641

ISBN 978-1-795333917
Fall of the Republic
By James P. Hicks

"All that is necessary for the triumph of evil is that good men do nothing."

Edmund Burke

This book is dedicated to the people of the United States that sacrifice their lives, fortunes, and sacred honor to the preservation of liberty and self-determination found in the great American experiment. Our founding fathers warned us to guard against an overpowering central government establishing itself master-of-destiny over the fates of diminishing individual freedoms. If left unchecked, the avarice nature of mankind to dominate his brother, would wield a power through the federal government too formidable for the individual to resist. The U.S. Constitution provides limited governmental authority by adhering to the rule of law in opposition to the rule of an aristocracy or a dictator. Even well-intentioned authoritarian power wielded through legislative or judicial means, directly conflicts with individual liberty. Freedom is embedded in the words of our Constitution.

Author's Note

Thanks to God for giving me the opportunity and ability to tell stories. Without God, there is no freedom for man.

Thanks to my wife for putting up with my writing late at night, endless revisions, and editing. To my high school typing teachers, I share the blame with you. Thanks to my minister for providing his expert editing. I will replace your red pen as soon as the old one quits smoking.

This book is a work of fiction that asks the reader to consider possible outcomes of current events as the future reveals itself. What will your grandchildren ask you about the times we are living through now? Could the outcome of today's actions set up a cascading series of events that usher in a new era of collectivism? This book takes a lot of historical events and puts them in the context of how those same events would look and feel to us in the U.S.

Let us trust that providence holds the reigns of our destiny, and drives us to seek freedom instead of tyranny. Let human history be our warning.

Prologue

My 17-year-old Grandson asked me a few questions that got all this notion of a book started when he asked, "So Grandpa, what happened back in the Second Civil War? You fought during the war, didn't you? What was it like back in those days?"

I've tried to put those memories out of mind for the last 40 years. So when he asked me to explain what I knew, I hesitated. Reflecting on those days would be painful because I was witness to the brutality of mankind at its worst. How could I tell my story well enough to pass on the things I witnessed? Would I be able to make anyone understand what we went through?

I leaned back in my chair and considered his request. Perhaps it was time for someone from my town to chronicle what happened back then. In the past, I always tried to keep my involvement in the war something of a mystery to my family. Whether it was shame for killing people, or taking part in such a brutal conflict itself, I always tried to deflect the questions about my involvement. But if I don't share my stories, how can others learn from those events?

So, I collected my thoughts and told my grandson a few stories. You see, I was a sniper in the North Carolina 3rd militia during the war and was known by everyone as, "Huck". Right then and there my grandson wanted to know more; he wanted every detail. He was eager to hear my perspective and I wanted to share my history before my advanced age robbed me of my memories.

This book is a collection of old stories seen through my eyes. Most of my friends from that time are long since gone, so I felt it necessary to preserve their memory in my accounts. There are still a few of us around though. My life-long friend and fellow militia volunteer, Fred, was a great help in recalling our adventures. However, I am not ready to give out people's real names. You will find I refer to my brothers in arms by their code names.

Some say the Second American Civil War was where we fought ourselves for the second time and God willing for the last time. I hope my Grandson never has to face the same hardships that I went through during those dark days.

Spring

"Fall of the Republic"

Chapter 1
How America Fell

A spider saved my life one time. Yep, honest as I sit here today in this very chair, a spider saved my life. How can a little bitty spider save a man, you ask? It was way back in the days of the second American Civil War. I was on a sniper-recon patrol with two other men. O h, it was a sweltering summer's night. It felt like you were breathing in a sauna. We slowly crept through some of that thick underbrush you get on the edge of the woods, when my AR-15 sniper rifle caught on a mass of honeysuckle. I pulled free, only to have briers scratch my skin through my camouflage pants. How could little things like that, hurt so much?

Silently, I looked back to see my two teammates sweating out every step. Like me, they tried not to make *any* noise as we crept along. Just ahead of us, lay an open two-lane roadway on the other side of the fence. The moonlight shone partially on the pavement with the yellow and white lines barely visible in the dark. We had to cross that road to get to our objective another two miles away, before dawn. A pair of cedar trees formed a natural pathway on either side of the narrow game-trail I followed.

I raised my left leg to step over the fence's top barbed-wire when I glanced up and saw it. A great big wolf spider, suspended in its web, hung between the trees blocking my path. Condensation reflected the moonlight on the web's strands. The dark outline of the spider's body contrasted against the star-filled night's sky.

I slowly lowered my boot trying to keep my balance. I sure didn't want to get that big hairy spider crawling all over my face. The thought of that spider's legs on me made me shudder. Out of habit, I looked again at the roadway before continuing to cross the fence. When I looked right, I saw a roadblock not 40 yards away. I could see two uniformed men standing guard by a patrol car. Their weapons were at the ready. They were watching the road in our direction, thankfully, not yet alerted to our presence.

If the spider had not stopped me, I would have led my team right out in front of the enemy. From that distance, most of us would have likely been shot like fish in a barrel. That is how a spider saved my life.

I've got a million of those stories. I've seen a lot of things in my time. I sit here by the fireplace in a little farmhouse on the edge of town where I was born almost 80 years ago. My travels have taken me all over the place, but I still call our little farming community in central North Carolina home. My 17-year old grandson, Jake, is with me since this book-writing business is all his idea anyway. Jake has been my inspiration for writing down my old war stories. He is curious how life was before the war, and what part I had in it.

So, I will start with the very first questions he asked me, *"Grandpa, you were around back in the days of the Second American Civil War, what do you remember? You were a part of the fighting, weren't you?"*

Yes, I can still remember those days. I was a telephone engineer back when the electricity was on everywhere. Gas was available in every station, and every family had at least two or three cars. Grocery stores had thousands of choices in pre-packaged, pre-cooked meals for people always on-the-go. At any time we could turn on the TV and have our choice among hundreds of programs like sports, workout videos, movies, sitcoms, shows on floor cleaners, and every stupid thing in between. Life was real easy. Easy, led to complacency.

We got our first inklings of real trouble as our financial markets started to crumble. It seemed our nation kept spending to the point where we couldn't borrow any more. Failing European socialist economies didn't help either. All we could do was watch as our money became worthless in just a matter of weeks. Banks showed our electronic savings plans turn into digital dust as electron-based money mirrored the disintegrating value of paper money. We assumed foreign oil shipments stopped because of the financial crisis, but we were otherwise preoccupied. Our life savings were dissolving into oblivion. People were really scared.

Then the unthinkable happened. Someone, I don't know if they ever figured out who, got a nuclear device into Washington, D.C. and set it off. I reckon the people that blew up D.C. figured a take-over would be easier if all the leadership of a heavily centralized government was out of the way all at once. Most every elected official was in Washington for emergency sessions hoping to avert further financial meltdown. Then the bomb went off. The President along with all his department czars and cabinet were consumed in the blast. Only an event like the market crash would bring everyone into Washington all at the same time and afford someone the opportunity to strike the U.S. like that. Someone took full advantage of the situation.

Our television and radio stations covered the events non-stop, 24 hours a day. Everyone with a microphone or a camera was on the news with images of Washington, D.C. in ruins. Talking-head reporters debated the succession of civilian authority. Arguments raged on who was leading the country. People throughout the east coast panicked over the potential for radioactive fallout. Martial law was imposed in most large cities. Estimated casualty figures along with predictions for long-term ecological damage were the news of the day. Work came to halt. People wondered what was going on and who was responsible, but there were no answers. We sat horrified by the images on our TVs.

For everyone outside the Washington beltway, life continued for a short while as if we were insulated from those astonishing events. The lights were still on and grocery stores still had food. We waited for things to get better because they always had in the past. We hoped we had witnessed an event that was now passing into history. But we were to find out that the worst was yet to come.

The first signs of real riots started in the major cities. The communist protest movements had been active all over the country for a year or more by then. The largest gatherings in New York and Oakland were foremost in the limelight as protestors occupied city streets and parks. Other protests in major cities were fairly small, keeping the illusion that the protests were largely just an opportunity for new-age hippies to have public sex and crap on police cars. In the early years of the 21st century, the communists in America were considered nothing more than the children of fringe radicals left over from the 1960s anti-war movements. These modern protestors were comical to watch parading around spouting incoherent anger-filled hatred toward America and how capitalism was the blight of the world. They wrapped their environmental fanaticism around the old anti-war rant, but none of it made any sense to anyone for the most part. Claims of corporate greed were spoken through expensive cell phones and written on top-of-the-line laptop computers, so the overall message was generally ignored by the greater public. The outrageous hippie rants garnered so much publicity that they hid the existence of the People's Planetary Revolution (P.P.R.). Who knew their plans included a takeover of the U.S. from within?

Oh yeah, there were some people warning us before all this stuff happened. Some radio talk-show hosts had been telling us for years to watch out for these new-age communists making their way into the mainstream American culture. They told us how radicals were influencing legislation or funneling foreign money into certain political party officials. Yet, the majority of people in the U.S. largely turned a blind eye to the formation of socialist or communist movements. Senators and congressmen praised the protestors on their initiative and spirit while ignoring the blatant radical anti-American messages delivered on the streets at every protest. Radio hosts pointed out the threat of these radicals, but the American public only took moderate notice.

Polls showed forty percent of the country agreeing with the biased nightly news coverage. Of course, the nightly news only showed over-educated college protestors chanting clumsy meaningless slogans. The TV anchor people of the time underplayed any sense of real *danger*. Why worry about a bunch of young idealists, frustrated with student loans? America was busy trying to make it through seriously hard financial times. Harping on some college students protesting was not a top priority for concern.

These protests continued a couple of weeks, after the market crash, before they turned violent. The last we heard of independent TV studios, was when the People's Planetary Revolution (PPR) took over the responsibility of broadcasting. They replaced every TV personality we had ever known. Some say the TV people were executed, but it was hard to say. There was already so much violence in the big cities. It was ironic how the very TV broadcasters, who convinced the American public to look the other way, were some of the first people to experience the reality of the PPR first hand.

What was left of television news was consolidated under a strange new branch of government oversight. Some bureaucrat, in some government office, directed the content of every program. It was a level of control our free press had never experienced. The American public was left with only radio, or the web, to get non-governmental information. It all happened so fast.

Conservative radio hosts were personally targeted during the beginning of the violent riots. The FCC imposed new tolerance guidelines on their shows, and tried to shut them down. Some hosts started underground web-based programs, but they were instantly criminalized under new unauthorized broadcasting laws.

The World Wide Web was the only remaining venue for information without direct control of government oversight. However, the more you watched, the more it seemed that the web was being monitored or outright manipulated. Web sites were flooded with disinformation and propaganda. Search engines only pointed to government sites.

Every piece of video, every blog, contained unverifiable information. The American public did not know what to believe. Since there was still electrical power in most of the country, people watched their TVs and listened for bits of real news. However, every day we saw programs going off the air one by one. Things began to "change". Little did we know what that change would mean to us all.

It was hard to tell what was true, as the reports came in. There were new laws on public speech, new laws on public gatherings, church registrations, and new politicians in office. Heck, even new federal and state branches, nobody had ever known existed, were now in charge. Entire state governments were fundamentally transformed in days with people in power whom no one had met before. Elections certainly weren't being held. Yet, there were fewer and fewer reporters on the air pointing out these unbelievable changes. Pretty soon, the few TV news programs spoke of the glorious revolutionary new age and how people would need to get their new state ID cards. Registration with the state was mandatory.

I remember the night we heard the news about registration cards. Several of us sat in the town diner watching the broadcasts, listening for details. We sat among stainless steel napkin holders and Formica counters where a thin layer of grease made the place smell homely.

My best friend, Fred, sat beside me as we took in every word from the TV. Fred was my age. We grew up together and were inseparable since kindergarten.

Television reporters debated on the size of the nuclear device used. Was it a suitcase nuke? How did it get into the country? Nobody had anything but guesses.

"Can you believe this?" Fred asked me again as he stared at the TV screen.

I too gawked at the TV, and answered with a dry mouth, "Nope."

During a break in the report, we noticed two elderly sisters talking in the booth behind us. They looked to be in their late 80s, and were discussing the new environmental laws.

"It's just like back when we were kids, Clair. Do you remember?" one of the ladies asked.

"I don't remember. I was too young. All I remember is the camp," her sister responded.

"Well, I do. It started just like this. They told us we had to register. Then we had to go work for them. They always had an excuse for sending more of us away somewhere."

Fred and I turned in our stools listening without trying to keep our interest a secret.

The same lady continued, "Back then, *WE* were the problem. Now, it's everyone who uses gasoline or wants to drill for oil. They choose somebody to blame and then use them as an excuse for what they do."

Fred interjected into their conversation, "What do they do?"

"They give you these," each woman stuck out their forearm showing a row of tattooed numbers.

We were sitting next to a couple of women who had survived the Nazi death camps. The hair on the back of my neck stood straight up. These women really knew first-hand what it meant to suffer under the will of their government.

"Do you really think these guys are as bad as the Nazis?" I asked.

The little old lady looked at Fred and then the TV, "Same people, just a new story. You will know it when they show up in uniform looking all official. But by then, it might be too late though." Both women looked sad. I'm sure they were remembering their childhood experiences in one of the Nazi occupied countries.

Others in the diner completely discounted the notion that our government was undergoing a *fundamental transformation*.

"You guys are making a mountain out of a mole hill," some claimed.

"Aw, what do we care what they do?"

"That's in the big cities. There's no protesting here."

"This will pass, boys."

"Everything will settle down soon."

"These new laws don't mean nothin. Don't worry yourselves too much about it, fellas. What can you do about it anyway?"

These and other statements tried to calm those of us who voiced concern how our country looked more like the old Soviet Union of decades past. I guess some people just could not handle the fact that our government was changing in front of our eyes. If they recognized the changes, they would have to do something about it. Those of us concerned were mocked.

Fred and I walked to our homes that night not really knowing what to think. All we knew was what we heard and saw on TV. Refineries were shut down, people in the armed service were let go by the thousands, and money was no longer worth the paper on which it was printed. Something had to be done, but what?

As time went on, America, once known as the beacon of freedom in the world, was going communist. John Q. Public simply could not believe that radicals and communists were now in charge of prominent public offices. Some people were blissfully ignorant as they watched the remaining government-controlled TV news. They failed to realize that power had shifted to the officials of the PPR. The public had no clue how unseen forces were determined to reconstruct every aspect of American life.

Fred and I commented several times how even Hitler feared the communists beyond anyone else. We were just beginning to understand why.

All the discussions were academic until about a month after the market crash and nuclear attack. Then, the power went out. Everyone remembers where they were when the streets went dark. When the power went out, it was like someone hit a reset switch on the whole country, and everything changed.

We all expected the power to be restored any day. But night after night of darkness drove people into a frenzied panic. TV, radio, and now the web, were completely shut down. It was a complete news blackout. Except for a few H.A.M. radio operators spread across the country, there was no communication between cities.

When the big cities went dark, it was bad, I mean real bad. People literally tore their towns apart. Even if someone could have flipped a switch and generated power up in New York, it would have changed nothing. Power poles hung in tangled ruins, substations were completely wrecked, and wiring was destroyed. People actually stole electrical transformers just to steal something. I mean, what in the world do you want with a transformer, for crying out loud?

Bedlam that America had never known, even during the darkest times of its birth or previous Civil War, ensued. Well, maybe Sherman's burning of the South, was close, but *this* was a complete breakdown of Western society across the entire country. Most city and suburbia dwellers absolutely panicked when the local fast food places and grocery stores ran out of food. Everything with the slightest value was looted from stores as mayhem spread throughout the country. In desperation, people actually peeled up floor tiling from Wal-Mart after the shelves had been picked clean. Police forces were overwhelmed with looting and open gang warfare. Drug lords consolidated power and removed rivals. Society shed its thin veil and we descended into complete anarchy. People died by the tens of thousands every day.

The question for those of us in rural towns across America was "*Why?*" and "*How?*" did all this happen? From what we could tell, the largest cause of the power grid failures was fuel shortages of diesel and gasoline across the boards. The fuel embargo had been in effect for a month now. There was not enough domestic production to keep the nation going. Environmental regulations had kept the oil companies from drilling new wells for years. Gaining a drilling permit was a lengthy process costing billions. By the time we realized the need for emergency domestic drilling, there was simply not enough time to get production up and running. And from what we heard, the new government offices stood in the way of re-opening the refineries.

The effects of fuel shortages took out the crucial tractor-trailer trucking industry which was the central backbone to supplying our country. Every business depended on our extensive trucking system to supply our every need. Once one system breaks, it cascades onto the next industry until the whole system grinds to a halt.

Some small oil refineries managed a limited amount of gas output. I think that kept us from completely shutting down as soon as we might have otherwise. Power generation is definitely one of those areas that absolutely rely on fuel. You see, coal-fired and nuclear power plants don't directly need gasoline to generate power. But every train that delivers coal, or every bull dozer that moves coal, absolutely depends on that precious diesel fuel. It did not take too much of a fuel disruption to cripple the operation of those power plants. Wind power and solar panels only accounted for 2% of the power generated in those days. They were overwhelmed immediately and offered no help to the masses. The fuel embargo sent whole regions into darkness as the power grids failed one by one.

We initially thought foreign crude oil shipments stopped because financial markets were in shambles. We later found out that Islamic fundamentalists had gladly risked financial ruin for the opportunity to bring the great Christian nation to its knees. So many Middle Eastern countries were poised to be influenced by the PPR. We should have known the dangers since we had Muslim Brotherhood foreign affairs advisors working for the White House. The PPR enlisted the top oil producing Arab nation's support for the oil embargo months before the market crash. Our demise had been carefully orchestrated by the PPR. Their claws were in every continent.

With American armed forces preoccupied, there was no stopping the Arab nations from attempting to wipe Israel from the face of the earth once and for all. That was what they thought anyway. Damn, I would have loved to have seen their faces when the Israelis pushed the button on Iran's, Syria's, and Egypt's capitols. "BOOM!" The use of tactical nukes was their only way to keep a billion Arabs at bay. It worked too. What surprised everyone in those days was the speed at which the Israelis realized their situation. They reacted immediately to the Arab threat. It wasn't their first rodeo when it came to fighting off all their envious neighbors; Israel had learned from its history.

The uncertainty of America's future sent Europe's economies and streets into complete anarchy while the world followed suit. China seemed to cut off all communication from the outside world and tried to handle their people the only way they knew how. Stories leaked out that China was taking a hard line on control within its borders and there were a lot fewer Chinamen to feed after they were done. It seemed China was going back to hardcore communist rule.

India became only interested in their regional neighbors as they attempted to keep their billion plus people happy without going over to complete Islamic rule.

Commerce at a global level stopped dead. The seas were thick with pirates without fear of retaliation from superpowers. Africa was on fire as every tribal warlord took advantage of the crisis to settle old scores with rivals.

Russia became a powerhouse in Asia as well as Eastern Europe. They were not expanding their territory militarily as far as anyone could gather. But they didn't need to roll tanks into old Soviet republics to regain power. All they needed to do was promise food and aid for which the people gladly traded their inedible sovereignty. They won control with bread instead of bullets—at first anyway.

It also became apparent over time that the PPR and the drug cartels of Central American countries had formed informal "understandings". Parts of the American Southwest would be under cartel control upon collapse of the U.S. government. We found out those relationships the hard way and only after a lot of bloodshed. The Mexican drug cartels had such control over southern California, Arizona, and New Mexico that they took the opportunity to seize authority over most of the cities bordering Mexico. Border patrol agents were no match for masses of cartel armies plotting for overthrow for the last 20 years. A lot of people sneaking across our southern border were quite accustomed to staying out of the way of the drug cartels. Scattered border agents with pistols were no match for cartel armies with RPGs and machine guns. They simply rolled over our borders and into our cities.

Functional governing control of the southwest was shifting from the people of the U.S. to drug lords that had been waiting for this opportunity. Funny how little cash it takes to shift power while people are frantic to hang onto bits of paper that used to represent a mode of trade. The new economy was to be based on bullets rather than pictures of dead presidents.

From what I understand, the least affected state was Texas. Like Israel, Texas realized early the need to beef up its border to keep the cartels out. The Texas legislature disregarded the federal laws preventing them from securing their own border. With their local Army, National Guard, and Reserve units helping them stand guard, Texas managed to stand alone. The Texans also had most of the remaining domestic oil drilling and refining capacity, so they were able to keep cars and trucks on the road longer than most other states. However, there was no way Texas could provide enough fuel to keep our trucking infrastructure going throughout the entire continental United States. It was only a matter of time before fuel shortages crippled every major industry.

We thought our military was invincible, and we were right for the most part. PPR officials influenced the remaining American civilian authority to release masses of soldiers from active duty. De-activation of troops eradicated our military from within. Our soldiers simply received messages informing them that their service contracts were terminated. Allow troops to go home and protect their families during these troubling times, was the mantra. Soldiers were told to go home and work on co-op farms and other odd things. Entire commands were erased off the books without so much as Congressional oversight. The speed by which all this happened added to the confusion factor as divisions of soldiers were sent packing.

I don't recall ever hearing that we lost a battle at sea, but I do remember that our navy was stranded all over the world. Our ships were unable to resupply fuel stores in overseas ports due to the embargo. Food supplies in port cities were non-existent. Nuclear powered ships made it back to U.S. ports, but upon arrival, they found our cities in complete chaos.

The Air Force went the same way. They could not be defeated in the air, but could not continue to operate with such a limited fuel supply. Our strategic oil reserves were going towards critical domestic needs and the Air Force was informed that they were placed on a lower priority for fuel. Someone in our new government chose to release most of our experienced pilots anyway. No amount of fuel would help pilotless planes. The Army and Marine bases were so intertwined with civilian support companies for food services, water, and electricity that a lot of bases lost their ability to function. The infrastructure was simply no longer able to support the masses.

We also guessed that the commanders left in command, after losing the Pentagon top brass, decided to support the leadership of the new state governments no matter who was in charge. Military leadership was accustomed to taking civilian orders, and this was no time to question the chain of command. The remaining units were so depleted of troops and officers that they no longer stood as a fighting force. By the time they were done, the U.S. military posed no threat to PPR plans for bringing a communist form of government to America. The news blackout kept the dismantling of the military a mere fragmented mystery to the public.

Those of us concerned for our country, state, and communities started the militia, as it became apparent we needed to band together to fight for our own survival. We viewed the PPR as a domestic enemy that seemingly erased our constitution overnight. I was a young man of 28 when the PPR introduced the political party we commonly referred to as the green shirts. The militia was not about to accept a communist form of government in the United States. We all knew our resistance to this new collectivist tyranny would be considered treason. We viewed it as a civil war.

Chapter 2
Introduction to the Green Shirts

All these events played out in front of us as we listened to the hand-crank radio every night. You see, the reason we listened at night was because the atmosphere is clearer and allows radio signals to be heard at greater distances without as much interference from the sun. A lot of people sat around their radios hearing those reports night after night and kept the information close to their hearts. As incredible as it sounded when you said it out loud, we had to come to the conclusion that there was an actual revolution in progress.

Just about every state seemed to have new people in charge of new government departments. Stories of radicals taking office were all over. There were no elections, no transition of power. It was hard for us to understand. America was not supposed to be run this way. You don't just assume power and command obedience to your will. Yet, that was happening every day. Radio operators told us of new offices now in charge of all sorts of things like the media, public safety, even public speaking.

No, not everyone saw these changes as a problem the way we did. Some people just rationalized the new laws and believed in the phrases like "social order", "public good", and accepted "new government authority". These nice-sounding phrases were being used to mask the radical changes to our form of government which had guaranteed freedom and liberty since our split from England. Several arguments broke out as those opposed to the changes were challenged by people frantic to believe that the government was going to fix everything and get the power back on again. Some people found the news to be just too outrageous to be true, so, they simply chose not to believe what they were hearing. Soon we would have our own stories to tell.

I remember when the new State Church Registration Office came to our small farming community and set up in my church's parking lot. We were in the midst of a soup service to help feed those waiting for the grocery stores to get resupplied. These guys rolled up in regular police cars but they were wearing some new dark-green uniform none of us had ever seen. It resembled something like a parks and recreation getup.

"Where is your preacher?" one of the officers demanded.

Someone replied and pointed, "That's him over there by the door."

It seemed kind of odd, but hey, what didn't seem weird or out of place with the power out, food supplies running low, and riots in the streets? Once the minister talked with these "officers", he was escorted to one of the squad cars which left right away. The remaining officers explained that there was an emergency which needed our town's ministers or some such excuse. After our minister was gone for an hour or so, they introduced us to a new green shirt preacher assigned to our community.

"What? Has anyone heard where they took Darin?" People kept asking, but there were no answers. People looked confused and concerned, but did not know how to respond.

Meanwhile, the green shirts started to issue ID cards under the excuse to track people needing food supplies.

"If you don't have an ID card, you don't get to purchase food with your state credits," some green-shirted official told us. We barely noticed how they collected a lot of personal information on us as we applied for food aid. They asked us where we worked, our professional skills, marriage status, and all sorts of other things that should have nothing to do with a simple identification.

We didn't know what any of that meant. What happened to the dollar? We watched as green shirt information boards were going up in the church's fellowship hall. These billboards were filled with new regulations and new laws that nobody understood. People stared at the boards in disbelief.

"What does it mean that you have to be *"certified"* to speak publicly? I don't need anyone to certify me to speak my mind."

"The state now holds my mortgage and I am not allowed to sell my property? I have to fill out a housing permit to make a claim to live in my own house?"

"Just who is in charge of these new state offices?" people asked. "What does the Department of Recycling have to do with anything right now? Why is that department so important when I don't even have running water?"

"In order to have secure and safe streets, we can only have registered firearms approved by the state?"

"Local police forces and sheriff's offices are now directly rolled into the State Public Safety Offices. All officers must report to the office in Raleigh to re-register as law enforcement officials before they can continue in these roles? How do they get there with no gas? With our police out of action, who is in charge?"

After watching this for a while, Fred and I shared some *"What-the-hell?"* glances and walked over to see what these green shirts were doing inside our church. Just what do they mean by all this? They have no business putting all these billboards in a place of worship.

I didn't notice them shadowing our moves until I started asking questions. As these green-uniformed officials gave us a few bull-crap answers that included a lot of code-words like "responsibility to public welfare," I told them to get the hell out of our church. Fitting words I thought, until the green shirt on my left unleashed his baton onto my left temple. The last thing I saw before losing consciousness was Fred with arms and legs flailing as the two other green shirts wailed on him.

When I woke up, it was the first time I realized this would not just go away or get better on its own. Of course, a few people believed the official story that I had been trying to start a riot in the foyer of the church and had attacked one of the green shirts. It was genuinely hard for some people to ever accept the fact that the new government was all about power and control with no room for a contradictory opinion or personal freedom. Freedom of person or property was replaced with "sense of community" and "public duties."

Some business owners had it worse as they watched green shirts simply issue papers that somehow shifted their businesses to some new state government office. You see, our youth were not taught in school about the Nazis of the 1930s and communist revolutionaries in Russia around 1917. Our people had been lulled into a false belief that communism or socialism was somehow a fairer or more equitable form of government for *ALL* the people. Who doesn't want fairness and equity and social justice? Those things sound fine if you don't know what a communist means by them. Justice has a different meaning if you're a communist. Justice means getting even with people like landowners or business owners perceived to have too much wealth. Social justice means that everyone must have their wealth redistributed among all the people in order to have equity from person to person. Personal freedom to own property has to be restricted or re-distributed to make things fair.

Every time communism has been tried, millions have died in order to reduce the surplus masses of mouths to feed. This happened in the Russian Bolshevik revolution when the farmers were killed because they were considered "rich" land owners. Then the new government-appointed farming officials ordered the planting of crops in snow-covered fields. When the new crops failed, the new farmers were killed because they followed orders that resulted in public harm. It always struck me as amazing when the communists could justify killing their own citizens for the "public good." "People dying is just a part of life," they claimed.

These new green shirt officials must have studied how the Jews were rounded up in Poland by Hitler's brown shirts. The Jews getting on the train to the concentration camps thought that they were simply being relocated to new settlements or work camps. Little did they realize the ovens awaited them at the end of those railroad lines. We were looking to our government to help us restore order and electricity. The PPR and green shirts kept deflecting the public's questions on lost liberties. At the same time, they promised a more sustainable form of public order. We just did not grasp the depths by which communism had already taken root in our public offices. History was our warning, but it takes people to recognize when history is being repeated in order to stop the dreadful chain of events.

America had fallen asleep as collectivism crept into our thinking. By the time you are asking the state for "permission", you have already lost the battle for self-determination. In a communist government the state will decide for you and those decisions can come dressed in some pretty flowery expressions like environmental awareness, social justice, and duties to the public. When stuff started happening to our community and in our houses, those of us who recognized the danger started to organize the unregulated force of citizen soldiers known as the militia. I joined the militia the day after I woke up from my baton injury and Fred signed his application with his arm in a sling.

Chapter 3
Organizing the Militia

You see, militias were not regular army by any stretch of the imagination. Most of the ranks were filled by people that have never served or were never law enforcement officers. Our militia took both men and women that were willing to resist an all-powerful government hell-bent on forcing us to bend to their will. Some of the volunteers had talents that translated well into the teams while others were not physically able to carry out combat operations. Physically unfit people were not denied service, but rather given jobs that offered them a chance to support the fighters. It takes a lot of logistical support to keep troops in the field for any amount of time. Our philosophy was to never turn away intelligent people.

Man, you don't know the effort it took to organize random people from all walks of life and give them a common focus. I had never been in the Army, but I had been a competitive shooter and was well-versed in rifles, pistols, and shotguns. I could also teach, and that ended up being the reason I was able to help structure the early militia and make it a potent fighting force. Oh, we had ex-Army, Marines, and so forth, but most of them needed as much training as a new recruit because they were not accustomed to waging guerrilla warfare with irregulars like militia. Most Marines measure an engagement by the number of tons of ammo they shoot. We had to teach these guys that ammo was to be treasured and only expended when absolutely necessary. We could not count on artillery support or close air support. We simply didn't have them. Those concepts were worlds apart from anything they had ever known, but we made it work. Army types found it hard to work in small teams without a lot of direction. They tended to get hung up on "mother-may-I" kind of stuff which stemmed from typical modern Army training. Individual thought is not tolerated and literal interpretation of orders is all consuming. In the militias you have to make up a new plan on the spot and keep rolling to get the mission accomplished.

Getting equipped was one of our first core problems. Most people that came to join the militias did bring their own rifles or what-not. Some had real good equipment like AR15s and assault vests while others had their dad's double-barreled shotgun with a pocket full of shells. We knew right away that we would have to make a real effort to capture as much ammo and weapons as we could. Some guys didn't even have a holster for their pistol and had no way to carry enough rifle ammo for a fight lasting more than 2 minutes. You can't be very effective unless you can bring enough bullets to a fight and get to them in a hurry. Your enemy will overwhelm you with their firepower until you are completely wiped out, if you cannot do it to them first.

Some of the early militia units fell to this fate, but we learned by the mistakes of others early in the 3rd. We had to get as much gear as we could without raising too much attention. You see, you have to do things quietly so as to not draw attention to yourself. If you try to do too much in the same area over and over, you develop a pattern for the bad guys to find you. So we had to be damn sneaky. In some cases we stole from the feds themselves. Remember that sporting goods stores were well-looted early on by gangs. Nothing was available there or in your local big-box stores anymore. We could not go out and buy anything anyway because money was worthless at this time and people were still freaking out in the major cities. We had to scrounge what we could and we had to think unconventionally.

There were some 1st and 2nd militia guys at our first organizational meeting. Since our 3rd militia leadership core was only ten people strong, we needed outside guidance. Our leadership had only met a couple times previous and was just starting out from scratch. The only paperwork they had was the sign-up sheet where Fred and I wrote our names. They had a dry erase board and were making plans as fast as they could write. That first meeting was in Mr. Clayton's barn if I remember right. Mr. Clayton was an older farmer who had a dairy farm just outside of town past a housing development. That was an easy place for us to get to without drawing too much attention to ourselves.

Dozens of men gathering out in the open would have been our first and last meeting. The green shirts would have had us rounded up and in jail almost immediately if they knew what we were up to.

Several people had covered the windows of the barn and lit lanterns so we could have a good long talk. I remember that we started by everyone sharing stories and information about what was happening and what people were hearing from HAM radio guys in other towns. The 1st and 2nd militia guys were sharing ideas on how to organize and where to find equipment. After we talked for a while, the 3rd militia Colonel got up and spoke. His speech was inspirational.

"We must preserve the dignity of the people and we must serve to protect our family and communities by re-establishing a freedom loving form of government. We must always be aware that we are not to become the enemy of the people, and we will only use our power to free ourselves from those who seek to remove our liberty. When we are not fighting, we will be directly serving the people of this town. One of the core principals of our militia is to use the force of arms on a limited basis and never for selfish gain or profit. We will fight for what we believe in and never surrender."

Afterwards, he said he appreciated everyone showing up and suggested we break up into specialty groups so that we could get our units up and running. The Colonel said that everyone wanting leadership roles or to work in intelligence should see him. He then pointed to one of the other officers and said that everyone with information on explosives was to meet with him. Another officer was appointed to be in charge of communications/maps/codes and so forth. Another group was in charge of the firearms training programs. I talked with him first because I had gear and expertise to offer. The fourth group was medical. They would handle all our first aid and medical needs. The last department was logistics.

Logistics were the guys that were our scroungers and builders. All the other departments would come to the logistical group for the things needed to make our teams operational. Logistics would also include transportation and fuel which had been all but used up. These scrounger teams had to be some of the most creative people I have ever met. They could make a nuclear bomb out of a paperclip and a pack of chewing gum.

After several hours we had a pretty good idea of what we needed to get accomplished and who would be doing what until our next meeting. The hard part was trying to decide how to communicate the next time we would meet without phones or the internet working. We had to keep our militia a secret, but find a way for everyone to be notified of our next meeting. One of the code guys suggested that we meet in this same barn; and on the day of the next meeting, he would hang a flag at the post office flagpole. The best plans are simple ones.

I had been assigned part of the firearms group. That meant we were the first trainers for the most part. Things were still pretty new to us back then. I left the gathering and was already eagerly anticipating the next meeting. This organizing was right up my alley. I loved the planning; I wanted our group to be the best trained and best equipped militia in North Carolina, bar-none. Our meeting resulted in some homework assignments for me and the other guys in our team. We decided that we would try to get most of our teams equipped with AR15s since they offered the best firepower and matched government troops, bullet for bullet. It was vitally important for us to be able to share rifle ammo in a firefight and have the ability to use government ammo when we could capture it. As for pistols, we decided that we would let team members choose and carry their own, as long as they had a good holster. We anticipated we would have non-conformists when it came to our standards. It was only matter of time before volunteers balked at our decisions.

So, we decided to form teams of fighters that were really dedicated to their AK47s or whatever. Similarly equipped units could share magazines and ammo wherever possible. We did not have enough people in the ranks to be too hard-ass about what they carried at this point. We needed all the people we could get, and it was my job to come up with a covert way to train everyone. We needed our volunteers to be born-again shooters while maintaining operational security. We couldn't simply walk out back and start shooting or else they would get wise to our cooking up plans for armed resistance. We didn't have the ammo to waste training either. A real firefight takes *LOADs* of ammo which we didn't have. This meant training was going to be limited and creative. We would have to use as much dry firing as possible to get the basics down pat. Most gun owners had only a couple hundred rounds in their garage at most. It would take all the bullets we had to make our first few armed scrounges and still have enough left over to protect ourselves. I was already working on a shopping list for the scroungers in the logistics group.

Fred signed up for our codes and maps department because he loved maps. But Fred was no code-man. Fred was not what you call a math wizard, you see. Fred's talents were direction and map reading. He could look at a map and walk four miles right to the darn place in the pitch dark without taking a wrong turn. That was rare among even outdoorsmen in my generation. Many of us were not accustomed to long walks. We drove everywhere we wanted to go. Gas stations had been picked clean of snacks and drinks, so Fred had taken the only things left—city maps. Those maps proved to be some of the best tools for planning our first operations.

Chapter 4
Our First Mission

By the time of our third meeting, my team had about ten men. Our firearms officer was kind of like a project manager instead of a hard core military authority figure as some people would have imagined. He was a good man because he did not try to push his opinion to win on every situation. It was that kind of man we needed most to lead volunteers from differing backgrounds. Without the formal obedience training soldiers get in boot camp, we needed our volunteer's loyalty to obey orders. Some orders would push loyalty pretty far indeed.

The logistics group swelled to about 20 people working non-stop to get us the things we needed. I put what looked like a small book in front of the beleaguered logistics officer, detailing the things we would need in order to manage ourselves in the field. We required a mode of transport to haul away as much gear as possible away from our first scrounge in order to make a quick getaway. The logistics guys had a couple of ATVs we could use, but by this time fuel was real scarce so we had to make every trip count. You see, people had continued to drive their cars after the fuel supplies had stopped coming in. All the fuel left in the gas station's tanks had been pumped out after the power went out. We were just so used to our cars and trucks that we used them until there was simply no gas left. It was stupid and wasteful, but there we were.

Our goal was to get the militia ready to fight. We wanted quick engagements whose objectives allowed us the best chance for obtaining the supplies we needed. The firearms training group was not as weak as you might think. We were not military by trade, but there were some guys with real talent. We gathered all our own personal gear and found that we had enough serious shooters and equipment for two six-man squads. Our training, to date, worked out a few standards on how to patrol as teams and work together during the darkness of night. But we had not fired our first shot in anger and were untested. We drilled every available night and met secretly whenever time permitted. Training to be soldiers in secret was a big challenge for people that had never worked together or never served in the Army. Fred came over to help with maps and compass work while we planned for our first recon missions.

My first mission plan was pretty straight forward. The nearest town of any size was about five miles away. We knew there was a National Guard Depot on the north side of that town but what we did not know was if it was still there or not. It may have been burned down in all the riots for all we knew. Nobody had left our town in weeks due to fuel shortages. Radio reports were few and far between now. So, our first mission was to see if the place was still intact. If so, we were to gather as much information as we could for a future raid. We were given the go-ahead from the Colonel and headed out that night.

Since this was a recon, I took my sniper rifle and five men who trained as a squad together during our first meetings. Logistics gave us an ATV and a Kawasaki Mule for transport in the hopes of making our trip as fast as possible. We were armed and eager to find out about towns outside of our own small community. The night was cool and clear with a starry sky. The moon was about one quarter on its waning cycle, so we had enough light to run the edges of fields while staying off hard pavement. There were reports of roving gangs on the roads, so we wanted to steer clear of them if possible. Our team was accustomed to ATVs because we were comprised of what others might call good-old-boys from the country. This meant that getting wet and dirty was not a real problem for these guys. They were fairly tough compared to city types. We got about three miles down the road before we saw a few lights way out in the distance. Funny how these lights seemed out of place after we had gotten used to no electricity, no street lights, nothing other than occasional oil lamps in farm windows.

We approached our objective cautiously and stayed close to the edge of the woods as best we could. We knew better than to drive right up to any place without giving it a good once-over first. Reports of fighting in the bigger cities made us cautious. I climbed down off the back of the ATV and motioned for the team to sit and listen. While they waited, I crept over the hill and bellied down. The National Guard depot was bathed in light and I could hear a diesel generator running over on the other side of the main building. The slight hill I was on provided me a good vantage point where I could oversee this side of the main building with a fair view of the surrounding lot. However, I could not see the other side of the fenced-in compound very well.

I went back to the team and we split up in two groups. I took Fred while the rest of the guys were to do a left hook around the other side of the compound to see what they could see. I reminded them that this was just a recon and we did not need to engage anyone. The plan was to meet back at the ATVs in 1 hour. Heck, we might find that this place was a soup kitchen or a Red Cross station. The team headed out as Fred and I went back to the ridge. Fred looked nervous as he started to map out the place.

Looking through the Leupold MKIV scope of my AR15 sniper rifle, I noticed there had been some fighting here at some point. The doorways had bullet dings around the frames and a lot of the windows were broken. Most of the Humvees looked like they were half-trashed, and those were the good ones. One of the old self-propelled guns that used to sit out back was now half blocking the street in front with its gun raised. I noticed that conex boxes now seemed to be arranged closer to the main building with their doors facing the open bay of the depot.

The first guy I saw in the compound came from the building with some cardboard boxes in his arms. In the yellow halogen lights of the parking lot, he opened one of the conex boxes and went inside. The storage containers housed rows and rows of furniture along with massive stacks of cardboard more boxes. Another couple of guys came out and headed to the next conex box. With a small UPS cart all loaded down with what looked like liquor cases, the men rattled the boxes into storage. These guys were definitely not National Guard since none was dressed in any type of uniform. These guys looked like a pretty tough biker gang that had made this depot their new home. It looked like they were plundering town and were using the depot as their own little fortress. The Depot was fairly secure with a fenced-in parking lot and its own generator.

We stayed for the whole hour taking notes before our suspicions were verified. Right about the time we were packing up to leave, an old pickup truck left the depot with a couple of guys in the back yelling and screaming like a couple of Barbary pirates. One of the gang stood up and fired his shotgun as the truck careened around the corner towards town. Otherwise the night was silent except for the spring crickets.

It was coming up on time for us to return to the ATVs when something caught my attention. As I was pulling my rifle up off the ground from the bipod, I heard a commotion and noticed movement from outside the fence. I could see my three-man team openly sprinting back towards my ridge on their way to the rendezvous point and our ATVs. At the same time a gang member with a shotgun ran to the back of the compound where he could get a shot at my guys. He stopped at the hood of one of the derelict Humvees and blasted away. I plopped back down on my belly and shouldered the rifle. While he pumped his shotgun I pulled the stock firmly into my shoulder and took aim for the man's upper torso. His upper body was all I had visible from my vantage point. The compound was well lit, so I was able to see my crosshairs on the dark figure against the tan painted truck without straining. I had the scope set to its lowest setting of four power. My thumb flicked the selector counterclockwise to *fire;* making a faint metallic click in confirmation. I took the slack out of my two-stage Jewell trigger. When the man's silhouette centered in my crosshairs, I fired. I barely remember the report of the rifle as I watched through the scope to see if I had hit my target.

At the time I was fully engulfed in the shot and wanted to make sure the target was down before I looked away. I watched the figure slump over the hood of the Humvee. I felt Fred pulling at my field-shirt harder and harder until I acknowledged him. He motioned that now would be a good time to leave. We hastily packed up our gear and headed for the ATVs.

Our team was back under cover of the surrounding woods, and the once quiet depot now looked like a giant ant hill with swarms coming out of every door. Our team met at the ATVs and we departed without a look backwards. Gunfire was heard pounding the stillness of the night behind us.

The trip back to our meeting barn was fairly uneventful and we used that time to gather our thoughts. We took care to hide our tracks and not leave a trail for others to follow. We absolutely did not want to lead anyone back to our homes. After what seemed like hours, we finally arrived back at our meeting place and concealed our ATVs. Once inside our makeshift bunker, our team gathered in what we had made the conference room table where the Colonel's team usually worked. Everyone there stopped what they were doing and gathered around to hear our report on what we had seen. I relayed my part of the story to the Colonel who was listening intently. Then I asked the other members of my team to relay what they saw from their perspective on the other side of the depot.

They had gone around the other side of the depot and peered through the fence. They saw a bunch of high-end cars like Porches, BMWs, and Mercedes, lined up beside military trucks. They saw gang members loading a variety of plunder from household items to cigarettes as well as something more disturbing. There were several prisoner transportation busses from the federal penitentiary sitting outside the parking lot. We all stopped and looked at one another.

You could see that everyone was thinking the same thing. What are these guys doing with those busses? Are the prisons compromised? Are these gangs made up of former prisoners now on the loose? Is this gang using busses as armored personnel carriers or are they rounding people up? Fuel was a rare commodity now. Whatever the gang was doing with the busses it must be important.

After about an hour of debriefing, we began to break up so we could all head home quietly. Our team gathered one last time for the night and we talked amongst ourselves. The mission had shown some serious need for more intense training. Although we were all good with firearms, we had not shown enough caution and had gotten too close to our objective. Getting too close led to some of the team being spotted and that was something we had to avoid. The reports we gave were sufficient, but not detailed enough. The three-man team had run directly for the rendezvous point after they were engaged by the biker with the shotgun. This mistake would have led our enemy right back to the rest of the team if my shot had not persuaded them to stay inside the Depot's fenced-in area. We all agreed that we would iron out all our standard Operating Procedures (S.O.P.) and we would not make the same mistakes twice. To a man they agreed that it was my team now and I was promoted to sergeant.

Only on my walk home that night did I realize that I had just shot someone. As a man of faith I knew I would have to make the decision on whether or not to join the militia. Joining likely meant that I would have to kill someone sooner or later. That night I killed to save my teammates because I felt responsible for them. I felt guilty for the life I had taken even though my target was definitely a criminal of the worst kind. But at the same time, I realized that by doing so, I had saved the lives of my men, Fred, and perhaps even myself. My prayers that night were heartfelt. I trusted solely in grace and forgiveness for my eternal soul as well as the man I shot. My friends assured me that I had saved the lives of countless townspeople from all over the county.

Chapter 5
Disarmed

A few days later, the green shirts returned to our quiet community. We knew this could be trouble, but we were fairly naïve back then. The next few hours allowed us to witness the green shirt attitude towards free-thinking people. Six police cars, two SWAT vans, all followed by several empty busses, pulled into town. We had stationed some guys to watch out for gang activity along the road leading into town. To our dismay, both sat in the back of the lead squad car as it pulled up to the fire station. Out of the cars came the same green shirts we saw once prior in our church.

As the town's people gathered around, it became clear that these green shirts were here for something in particular. The green shirt in charge was being pelted with questions from the people, but it was becoming evident that the questions were bothersome to him. Mothers were giving him the "Oh you need to answer me" with crossed arms that people of all ages understand.

"Are you here to protect us?"

"Where is our minister?"

"When is the power coming back on?"

"We need gasoline, when are we going to get some around here?"

One of the green shirts responded to this question immediately. He spouted some crap like how the environment could not sustain the rapid re-introduction of fossil fuels. He informed us that fuel supplies were limited to government vehicles *only*! We needed to walk or bike wherever we wanted to go. But he strongly suggested we should not travel between towns for safety reasons.

Someone asked, "What are our guys doing in the squad car?"

The lead green shirt said these men were arrested for possession of unauthorized firearms and would be prosecuted under new state law. Outrage was clouded by complete shock throughout the crowd.

I could tell immediately that the green shirt in charge was not here to give us information; he was here to get something from us. As the crowd got louder by the minute, I could see the green shirt's frustration grow.

Finally, the green shirt in charge announced, "You people are on the list for services and supplies. But now that you have shown violence in this community we cannot send in aid with all these dangerous firearms just floating around." The crowd did not comprehend as they continued pelting them with questions.

At that point it dawned on me that these guys were here to remove our ability to protect ourselves. They wanted us completely obedient to their will and the only way to do that was to confiscate our weapons. Weapons in our hands were considered dangerous to the "public welfare" or something similar. I started backing away from the crowd and signaled as many of our militia as I could to come with me. There was still a throng of townspeople allowing most of my men to slip around the corner and get a block down the street where we stopped to talk.

Everyone was in complete shock because we had hope that there were still some people looking out for us in state government. But that hope was fading fast.

I looked everyone in the face and said, "We need to tell as many of the militia as possible to go home and get their gear tucked away and hidden. These green shirts are here in force and will be coming door to door going through our houses. Our only hope is to get our stuff in hiding before we have nothing left. And guys, you need to leave them something to find. They cannot go through your house and find an empty gun cabinet because that will tell them that you hid your guns. We will have to leave out some of our non-warfare weapons we cannot use anyway just to act as camouflage."

"Now run home and tell everyone to squirrel away as much as possible. We will not resist because they have too many of our people surrounded up there at the fire station. We don't have enough militia here to do much against all those SWAT vans. And hey, be courteous to these green shirts when they come knocking. Act like you don't like what they are doing. But tell them you understand the need for civility and are willing to work for the public good or whatever you can come up with along those lines."

About that time we heard screaming from the street in front of the fire station. My fears were coming true, the green shirts started using pepper spray on the crowd in order to get the upper hand and start the arrests.

I ran home which was a couple of streets over. Winded, I bolted through the front door and ran to my garage/office out back. My militia gear was already packed in a single bag which I kept ready to go at a moment's notice. It held my AR sniper rifle, Glock 19, and my load bearing equipment including a small daypack. I grabbed a couple of backpacks I had used for camping in the Boy Scouts and started chucking everything of use from my closets. I had cleaning kits, first aid kits, batteries for flashlights, bullets, holsters from my competition days, magazines for the AR, and a host of other things that I knew I could never replace if they were confiscated. The bags weighed around 70 pounds each after everything was crammed into them. I had packed everything and was running out the door of the garage not 5 minutes after I entered.

There were woods out back of the house which bordered a small tobacco field. Hiding places were few and far between, so I stashed my gear in the top end of an old weed-covered derelict hay bailer. The thing had been sitting for the last 20 or 30 years. I knew all barns and structures would be searched and I was not about to lose all my stuff to some green shirt.

By the time they came to my house, I was ready. I rearranged my garage so you could not tell there were empty spots where things used to sit. The green shirts came in and started asking where my guns were. No pretense, no discussion, they simply were there in force and were not asking permission to give my home a thorough once over. And they did just that. They tore the place apart even after I told them I had guns in the garage and was willing to turn them in.

"This is how its' done; now back away," was their only retort.

I complained just the right amount, but did not make them angry. I was not about to give them any excuse to arrest me. They got my dad's old shotguns as well as some older revolvers lying in the cabinet. After the green shirts left, I cleaned up the house and waited for them to leave town. They left late that night, having gone through every house, every shed, and every barn within two miles. My prized gear was waiting for me in the old bailer.

Not all of us were as lucky though. Two of the militia guys were arrested in the crowd in front of the fire station. They had not seen our discrete departure and had gotten too focused on giving the green shirts a piece of their mind. They ended up losing every bit of their gear and their houses were boarded up and condemned. A couple more guys were not as good at hiding their weapons. Several men had nothing left but empty hands. Some guys forgot to hide their bullets which made the green shirts search harder until the hidden weapons were found. Men were confronted with the arrest of their wives if they did not hand over every gun, bullet, and pocket knife they had ever owned.

About 20 people in our town were arrested and carted off to God knows where. Anyone who showed the least little opposition to green shirt authority was arrested. Our minister was still missing from the green shirt's previous visit. We did not know when we could expect to see anyone again. It was a real dark time for many of us; but the next time the militia met, our ranks tripled.

Chapter 6
Carver Street Battle

It was about 10a.m. the second day after the green shirt firearm-raid when things changed for our little rural community. Some called it the "Carver Street Battle" because that is where a gang came across our newly-formed 3rd militia for the first time. Our town was small and rural so the gangs had not been very motivated to come out our way. We simply didn't have liquor stores or car dealerships to plunder. Our poor farmer reputation kept us safe for at least a while. We called these roving bands of thugs, "gangers". They looked like men straight out of a prison movie or some cop TV show. They were brutal people without fear and full of hate.

We knew our area would become a target when the city dwellers ran out of food someday. But we were not expecting the gangs to come our way so soon. We didn't understand what prompted the raid at that time. In some respects, we were pretty naïve back then.

We were alerted to the raid by shots from the southern end of town. Carver Street was our main thoroughfare because it had both our traffic lights. The gang reached the edge of town and started going door-to-door shooting and ransacking anything that looked valuable.

Those of us in the militia quickly grabbed weapons and ammo when the fire station's old air-horn sounded. The Colonel had the old fire horn as our call-to-arms signal in case of emergencies requiring a rapid muster. I don't think people in town knew the old siren still worked. It was a shock when the old droning horn echoed through the streets.

We gathered at the fire station until we could get enough people together to make up a complete squad. Townspeople were standing on their porches in the morning sun peering down the street. Most people simply did not have the fear of gunfire that they should have.

Most of my squad was at the fire station so we let our team leader know we were heading down to the sounds of gunfire. He could look for us there. He said he would gather teams and send them our way to help out as soon as they were assembled. We mustered in groups of six so we could keep track of our people easier and direct movements quicker. The team leader handed me a hand-held GMRS radio that had a range of 20+ miles depending on terrain.

"Report back when you have something. Now, go find trouble," he ordered.

My team started down the street. I passed several people running from the sounds of the gun fire.

"They are shooting everyone!" a man I knew named George screamed as he ran passed me towards the fire station. His shirt was splattered with blood.

George lived at the end of Carver Street and I knew him to be a well-mannered church-going man that would never hurt a fly. We approached the sounds of gunfire and screaming. I could see we were facing what looked like a gang of about 25 of the meanest, most deranged characters I had ever seen. They were going house-to-house pillaging everything in sight. Their pickup trucks rolled right down the middle of the street as their shotguns and pistols blasted at everything that moved. You could see the men in the background coming from each house loading panel trucks. It looked like they had done this sort of thing before.

With this many bad guys and only my team in the area, I decided we would find a defendable position where we wait until backup arrived. There was an old concrete-block building on our left that used to be a garage. I directed the team inside with hand signals. Luckily, we were not spotted. I had my AR sniper rifle, while others had their standard M-4s with dot sights. Some guys had low-power scopes like the ACOG, while others used the Eotech red-dot sights. All the ranges were going to be short, so I made sure my scope was set to its lowest magnification setting. I set up an overwatch position on the 3rd floor where I could see the street below. My longest visible shot would be only 150 yards down the road. We spread out and took up positions covering the street as well as the stairs leading to the first floor. I radioed our team leader and gave him a quick assessment.

I radioed, "Sir, this is Huck. I have 20 to 30 gangers raiding every house along the southern end of Carver Street. I see at least four bodies on the sidewalk. They are shooting everybody, over."

"Where are you Huck?" he asked.

"We are in the old concrete building just short of the Donner Street stop light, on the left," I told him.

"Good, I will send the next team down the right side and have them set up opposite of your position."

"Roger that, I will hold here," I said. All the time I watched the gang trucks get closer and closer.

My team leader said he would send another squad a couple of blocks off to our west, have them pass us, and get to the western flank of the gang. That would give my squads a chance to block Carver Street while our other teams could flank from the right and put the gangers in a cross-fire. This would be like a standard "L" ambush pattern.

It sounded like a good plan to me and I told him we would make them holler when all the teams were in place. The second team arrived about three minutes after we got settled in our hide. They found a good spot to watch the street and we settled in for our first gunfight. The team leader called me back and said they had the 3rd and 4th squads in position. We could spring our trap as soon as we were ready. I told the teams to hold their fire until the gang got within 30 yards of our position. Our guys were new at this, and fire discipline would be an issue in our first engagement. I knew we had to make hits on our first strike and never let up on the pressure.

The gang got to the end of the block where Donner Street crosses Carver under the stoplights. Our teams were in hiding on both sides of Carver. Nerves were tense. The intersection provided us an open field of fire as the bikers approached. I radioed the other teams to start up when I fired the first shot on the lead pickup.

I checked everything one last time before the crosshairs centered over the driver. I squeezed the trigger until I felt the rifle lunge backward in recoil. Milliseconds after my shot, it sounded like the street erupted in 5.56 fire. Those gangers must have thought the world was coming down around their ears as five of their people dropped in the first second. The roar of gunfire was earth shattering. The truck I shot veered onto the sidewalk as the driver slumped onto the wheel with his foot still on the gas. I saw gangers from the street run into houses, and I saw gangers who were in houses, run onto the street. They were completely taken off guard and confused. It was resistance to a level they had never expected in their wildest drunken dreams. They had shotguns for the most part and the rest seemed to be carrying pistols. In contrast, our teams used AR15s that fired 30 rounds before reloading. Most shotguns will only hold 5-8 rounds before a lengthy manual reload.

These gangers were not used to actual gun battles. They kicked in doors on old ladies and shot unarmed townspeople. These rough and tumble guys were running all over the place completely disorganized as we decimated their ranks. Our two teams on Carver killed at least half their number in the first two minutes. I kept them from escaping to their trucks by targeting the driver every time one tried to get behind the wheel. Pickup trucks littered the street along with dead or dying men. Some lay with their booty still clutched in their arms. The remainder of the gangers was continually off balance without a clue where to run next. After another two minutes of fire, I radioed the team leader and told him that the squads to our west could head east to Carver.

Thirty minutes later we had complete control of the streets. Once quiet, our town started picking up the pieces.

Two of our militia had been killed. Another four had gunshot wounds, but were expected to make a full recovery. Our medical teams took care of our guys' first-rate and got them stabilized. The gang paid dearly for the twelve people they killed in their incursion of our quiet community. Of the estimated 25 enemy, we found 22 dead with at least one of their pickup trucks managing to find its way through to a back street. Trees lining the street must have covered its escape. We buried our dead, contained house fires, and consoled those who had lost family and friends. The 3rd militia had its first real engagement. It would become a legend for old men to recount for years.

Chapter 7
Training for Real

The next militia meeting was postponed several times after the gang raid on our town. We were pretty sure the green shirts would be back sooner or later, and we didn't want to face them yet. The 3rd militia Colonel wisely chose to wait nearly a week before calling our next gathering. This time we changed the meeting place and used a new meeting signal just to keep anyone outside our unit guessing. We set traffic cones around the storm-water drain beside the fire department curb. This alerted members of the militia of a meeting that night.

Turn-out for the meeting was incredible. Anyone that had been on the fence about joining the militia had shown up. The Colonel greeted the crowd and directed the volunteers to the departments we had previously set up. It was as if we were starting all over. New people needed to be oriented on how we did things. New security protocols for keeping our organization secret were implemented. We started weapons training for real. Our engagements at Carver Street taught us the need for good communications between teams. Militia ability to coordinate firefights was our key advantage. The goal was to always stay one step ahead.

Something else happened that I was not expecting. I was starting to develop a reputation. As we were all organizing in the barn, I overheard some new guys talking to one of the volunteers from my squad.

"He was nailing those gangers left and right. Every time one of them got to a truck, BAM! He dropped him. He must have cleared half the street himself. Some of those guys still had their loot in their arms."

"What's his code name?" one of the new guys asked.

"They call him, Huck. We use code names all the time so outsiders can't identify us for real," the volunteer explained. "I was with him on the mission to the National

Guard Depot. That ganger was blasting away at us and Huck dropped him from way up on the hill. And the dude was behind the cover of a Humvee as well."

I didn't make much of it until the team leader and the Colonel wanted to meet with me. I had a sinking feeling like a kid being sent to the principal's office.

"What can I do for you, Colonel?" I asked waiting for a dress down. He offered me a seat as he spoke to me.

The Colonel started, "Huck, I hear from everyone that you are a natural leader and all the men in your team respect you. I see now that we are going to need a real sniper program. These street brawls are going to draw too much attention from the green shirts. If we are going to make a difference, we need the sniper's ability to gather intelligence and make accurate reports. We need to act like a scalpel instead of a blunt force object. What do you think?"

I told him, "I see what you mean. I could offer some suggestions on getting started."

The Colonel laughed and ordered me to take a dozen fighters from the firearms group and start a proper Sniper program.

"Let me know when you are operational," was the last thing he said to me.

I was shocked that I was promoted to team leader and not in trouble at all. My brain was fuzzy as people shook my hand congratulating me on my promotion. Once the news spread, every guy with a rifle thinks he has the capacity to be a sniper. Boy, the selection process was fun! I meant that sarcastically by the way. I left the meeting with a list of volunteers for the sniper squad while the poor logistics guys were crying over my new wish list. Glad I was not in their shoes. Those logistics guys were working non-stop to equip all the new volunteers.

But in true logistics group fashion, they came through with flying colors. Two meetings after the creation of sniper squad, I had data sheets on bullet ballistics, training manuals from the Army and Marine sniper programs, maps with waterproof cases, compasses, a few laser range finders, and promises of ammo. I luckily had saved a bunch of my gear when the green shirts had come, so I was able to use my own equipment. As we started up, I found a diamond in the rough in an ex-Marine Gunnery Sergeant that had been part of the sniper training cadre in Quantico. Gunny was one of those guys that retired with 20 years' experience and had done a bit of everything which included combat.

Unfortunately, he was unable to walk missions anymore due to foot and leg injuries he sustained in Iraq. In true Gunny fashion, he was not a cripple by any stretch of the imagination. His experience brought authority to our training program with a fierceness only found in Marines. I recruited him into the sniper squad about 20 seconds after meeting him. The Gunny tended to think of me as a 2nd lieutenant fresh out of ROTC. I tried to get his attitude to soften towards volunteers. After all, we were not hardcore Marines coming to his school in Quantico. It was a match made in heaven. We got along like a couple of school boys playing guns. By the time we had our new militia sniper school ready, I had my "dirty dozen."

Anyway, we started with camouflaging techniques, map reading, first aid, orienteering, and used team competitions to hone our observation skills. We gave the recruits a list of common items to look for while they peered through scopes or binoculars. Twenty minutes later we took up their notes and graded their answers. We taught range estimation through mil-dot scopes and how to judge distance at night with or without optics. Ghillie suits were made in class and dirtied through practice stalks. Recruits spotted by referees during these practice stalks were punished with extra log PT designed by Gunny. Goodness, he must have studied medieval torture in school or something. Guys that did not perform up to Gunny's expectations were thoroughly straightened out in true Marine fashion.

Finally, the logistics group found enough passable sniper rifles to equip our team. We started the shooting portion of our training as ammo became available. Shooting was tricky to keep quiet without suppressors. We decided to use long range patrols outside of town as our training venue. Fred came up with several orienteering routes for recruits to hike 4 or 5 miles away while observing roadways and other points of interest. These missions ended up along power line easements where you could see maybe a mile or so. Power line towers offered long range shooting opportunities where our guys could practice a few long range shots without attracting too much attention. Once they got their practice in, they would sneak back to our own community.

We had to keep our existence a complete secret or else risk an anal exam by the green shirts. That motivated our guys to do their best to stay hidden during these training missions. Some guys brought back observation reports that were useful in tracking the movements of the green shirts. One of our guys came back from one of these training missions with news that a town eight miles north had been visited by the green shirts the previous week.

Our man found out that the green shirts had rounded up some people and were confiscating firearms. This town had the misfortune of being visited by a gang after the green shirt raid. This meant that the people of that town were completely at the gang's mercy. There seemed to be no mercy from what we heard. The gangs had killed maybe 30 people and burned most of the buildings in town. Some of the outlaying road traffic was gang oriented, and it was becoming clear that the gangs were not being intimidated by the green shirt presence. It was starting to look too convenient that the gangs were able to operate so openly. The green shirt's ignoring the gangs scared us more than anything we had seen so far. The only thing we knew for sure was that there would be more trouble.

Chapter 8
News from Neighbors

We were not getting as much information as we would have liked from outside our community. You see, when the green shirts raided a town for what they called "contraband", they often seized home radio units. Not enough HAM operators knew to or could hide their radios in time to save them when the green shirts came. In some cases the operators were taken off the air as they were broadcasting. Some keyed their microphone on VOX which would allow us to hear the sounds of the scuffle as they were being arrested. Those radio transmissions were tough to hear. It always made us wonder if the person being arrested would ever make it home again. It also meant one less source of information.

Apart from the Ham radio guys, we may have never known what had transpired down south in the Pittsboro area. The volunteers of 1st militia made the grave error of trying to openly resist the green shirts when they showed up to collect guns. From what we heard, the green shirts showed up in force and the 1st militia took more than a little offense. The problem was that the 1st militia decided to fight back even though they were outnumbered. They tried to stop the green shirts in an open street brawl. What 1st militia did not realize was how willing the green shirts were to call upon heavy firepower and just plow through anyone standing in their way. About the same week we were fighting the gang at Carver Street, 1st militia was engaged in a three-day fight for the outskirts of Pittsboro.

We still don't know how many they lost, but the stories that trickled back to us were horrific. From what we could gather, 1st militia had been all but wiped out. The green shirts took heavy losses at first, but were able to call upon armored personnel carriers and mortars to rout the militia. There was even a report of a helicopter used in the battle. That was a rare thing since fuel was in such short supply.

Even the green shirts had to conserve fuel resources. This meant the battle was given a high priority.

It's not like there were any news organizations reporting anymore, so the green shirts were not worried about the story of the battle getting out. They must have wanted to teach the locals a lesson. Stealthy reporting from a HAM radio operator was the only way we even knew the battle took place. Pittsboro ended up under martial law, but it was hardly necessary since there was nobody left to resist. The conflict had the effect of fortifying our resolve. Fear was our constant companion because this could happen to anyone.

As these events played out, we had interesting things going on at home. We figured out pretty quickly that the green shirt preacher-guy was kind of like the old "political officers" the Soviets used in their churches back in the 50s. He was young and impressionable, which is why they sent him to a small town to "preach" his social justice, green living, and public works version of religion. We also realized that the green shirts would most likely be getting information about our community from this guy. You see, he didn't live in town, but rather came on a bicycle every Sunday morning just to run the services. What he taught had nothing to do with God, so the town was fit to be tied with him.

The militia took the opportunity to make the best use of this "preacher boy." Our intelligence group devised a whole plan around giving this guy false information. They pumped him full of bogus stuff about the town so that his handlers would think our town was on its last leg and barely hanging on. The fake information included our real efforts to plant the fields; but we exaggerated how we were near starvation. We talked in front of him about how none of us had a single gun left. We complained about gas, but threw in some crap about how the environment was getting better without cars. This guy must have reported back that we were some of the biggest saps in the world, and that is just what we wanted.

Our small town was rural, but we still depended on electricity to provide our fresh water. Even if someone had a well, there was no electricity to run a pump. Most people in town used city water which ran off electrical pumps for purification and delivery. That meant we had serious water shortages in our homes pretty soon after the power went out. No water in the sink, no water to flush toilets, no showers. People were down to collecting rainwater. Lucky for us this was a town of farmers, and farmers can always find inventive solutions. It's a shame farmers never get the credit for their ingenuity until you work with them for a week or two. You find that farmers are some of the most creative people around. They see solutions to problems utilizing whatever material they have on hand.

To solve the water problem in town, our farmers came up with a way to build up a small dam across the Branson Creek about a mile away. Since that part of the creek was several feet higher in elevation, we were able to get the water to naturally flow down our irrigation piping. We didn't have enough large diameter pipes, so we used smaller diameter pipes closer to town. This smaller pipe section increased the water pressure at the tap, which made filling buckets quicker. People still had to haul buckets of water home, but they were happy to have it that close. The militia kept right in the middle of the project and supplied both manpower and engineering assistance. We wanted to make sure we could conceal parts of the piping as well as the source for our town's water supply. Few things could make life worse than running out of water if our irrigation system was taken out of service.

The militia was also involved with limited power generation. We had a few generators but very little gasoline. We organized charging-sessions for rechargeable batteries used in defibrillators, EMT flashlights, and the like. A small refrigerator stored critical medicines. We worked together and asked people to donate materials for these projects. That was the difference between us and the state. Making community claims on people's property was not how we were going to operate. Our goal was to keep everyone's freedom versus taking their stuff and forcing them to "share." Forced allocation of resources is not sharing; we left that to the green shirts.

Chapter 9
Sniper Squads Go Active

About a month of training was all we needed to get the sniper squads up to speed. The men I chose had experience of some sort, while others just took to sniper training like butter. There was no TV to distract us from training. So, we spent all our spare time doing town projects or honing our sniper craft. At the next meeting I talked with our Colonel and told him we were ready to get to work. The Colonel was glad to hear it and put us to work immediately. I had men all over the county just about every other night. We were bringing back enough information to overwhelm our intelligence group. The problem was the picture we were developing was pretty grim. Most towns were now at the mercy of roving gangs. Sooner or later we would be visited again by some unsavory characters. It was time for us to get sneaky and see if we could keep the gangs out.

Part of our sniper training included something not in any Army manual. We trained to hike between towns all decked out in camouflage which kept our movements a secret. We also instructed the sniper teams to carry civilian clothes so that once they got into an area they could blend in like anyone else. Intelligence gathering was an important aspect of our role and required some special skills to pull it off. Our people were cunning as they walked through towns and talked with people to find out what everyone knew and thought. We made some great contacts during those first few weeks and discovered some amazing things. One sniper two-man team came back from a hike to a local town of about 2500 people and gave us all a brief upon their return. Everyone gathered around because this was our first visit to a town so large.

Here is what they reported:

"It took us about half the first day to hike into town. We kept to the east of town, according to plan, but we had to take some extra precautions. There were green shirt traffic stops set up on almost every major road. It seems they wanted to keep people from walking down the roads or going from town to town. Once we got past the road blocks, we changed clothes, stashed our cammies, and walked down the main street."

"The 200-year-old courthouse, restaurants and all, are burned down. People mill around the town square waiting for the green-shirt soup trucks about midday. When the green-shirt trucks arrive, they come with armed escorts either in squad cars or SWAT vans with about 20 troops. While the people eat, the green shirts set up a bullhorn on a stage and preach to them about public work projects. They drone on about the lack of justice in democracy, how the rich screwed everyone, and how the new regulations are meant to provide some meaningful social justice. Isn't that a load of crap?" Men commented in the background as the room descended into conversation. After a few minutes, he continued his story.

"While this is going on they start recruiting. Anybody that looked good to them, they grabbed and loaded onto buses. These look just like the ones we saw at the depot a few weeks back. Now they have a new green paint-job with PPR printed on the side and something about public works. We nearly got pinned when we were asked for ID cards in the soup line. We made some wild excuses about just getting back from the doctor and used the confusion to get the hell out of dodge. Even though we hoofed it straight back to our stash, we almost got dinged by a green shirt patrol that was sent looking for us. We crossed roads only under bridges, crawled through ditches, and kept to the woods at every opportunity. Getting back here took a day and a half," he concluded between sips of water.

We took in all that information and followed up with some questions. It looked like that town was under complete green shirt control. There seemed to be no local police authority. The green shirts were using the people for who knows what under the guise of what they called "public works". Our Colonel called a team leader meeting so we could share information and think about what to do next.

Chapter 10
Escape Plans

We knew it was a matter of time now before the green shirts or some gangs would come for our community. We resisted at Carver Street and that was bound to attract attention. Our little rural township was wide open for the most part, so we needed an escape plan where we could get everyone out at a moment's notice. That was a tall order when you think we would have to move 345 folks with their supplies. The 1st militia proved that without heavy weapons, fighting in your own town only destroys your home. You will end up losing a totally defensive battle.

Plan A: Our plan needed a way to cut access to town giving us time to get everyone packed up. The explosives group was pretty sure they could take out one of the small bridges over Johnson Creek which was the most likely route into town. They placed a sealed 55-gallon drum full of their "special recipe" under the bridge and camouflaged it. They ran the detonator wiring a good 300 yards up into the woods were us snipers had set up an observation bunker to watch the road. The plan was to blow the bridge from the hide which would signal everyone in town to pack up and leave. We still needed some evacuation transportation, so our plan was to use our own school buses. The problem was fuel. There was a shortage of diesel because our farms had been using tractors to prep and plant our spring crops. The school buses had only what was left in their tanks after the schools stopped operating. We needed more fuel to make this plan work.

After discussing Plan A, we discovered that finding a place for us all to go was the real issue. None of the surrounding communities could support us for any length of time and Texas was too far away. There was no way for us to get by the green shirts through town after town over a thousand miles away and make it to the relative security of Texas. It was doubtful they would take us anyway, because we heard their border was closed. Many times we debated where we could go, but each time we came to the same conclusion, nowhere. There was simply no place to move all the people to safety; so when you can't move, you have to hide yourself. So we came up with plan B.

Plan B was the building of several secret bunkers strategically located throughout town to house people during raids. We built underground bunkers big enough to accomplish two things at once. We could use the bunkers as our militia meeting places and we could house the townspeople in emergencies. Building underground bunkers from a supply perspective was a major challenge for that timeframe. There were no supplies sitting on shelves, you had to scrounge for everything. Not to mention trying to build secret bunkers all over town without every Tom, Dick, and Harry knowing about them. In this plan we would use militia to direct people to designated bunkers at the last minute before green shirt raids. Unfortunately this plan required fuel. There was no way we had time to dig bunkers by hand. This meant we would have to use fuel guzzling backhoes in order to have the projects done quickly enough to keep them secret. We had to get fuel no matter what, and soon.

There was one bunker I remember in particular. It was super simple and quick to build. We chose a spot about two blocks off Main Street in an empty lot. We had two tractor trailer containers prepped to house a couple dozen people for several days. They had toilets, beds, and everything. We put up temporary fencing around the site and dug a big square hole with a backhoe. The containers got dumped down in the hole side by side and bolted together. We covered the site back over and spread out the leftover dirt to make it look like a big garden being prepped. There were rows and all. Right above the edge of the containers, we placed an empty electrical transformer box on a concrete pad. The transformer box covered the pad's hole where the ladder led down into the containers. Two men could push over the hinged transformer box and head down the ladder in seconds.

It took about 3 days of site work, and we were done from the outside without too many people even taking notice. We chose spots next to militia-member's houses where we could. That helped keep the work sites quiet. Some bunkers were out in the woods in the middle of nowhere, while others were converted basements with hidden entrances. One basement bunker was under a house that was burned during the Carver Street fight. The charred remains of the house served as great camouflage for the bunker's entrance. We felt like a bunch of burrowing rats there for a while as we built site after site. Some of these bunkers were crude, but when the time came, we would not mind some dust and dirt. The bunker sites best concealed were used as weapons caches. Since the green shirt raid on our town, we learned to hide as much of our equipment as possible so that we could pass surprise green shirt inspections.

Chapter 11
Back to the National Guard Depot

The Colonel came to my sniper team and gave us a new assignment. "Find me some diesel" he commanded.

Wow, I loved brevity from leadership. I started sending my teams out in all directions in search for what seemed like a search for Bigfoot. There for a while I would have rather been given the task of getting Bigfoot's fingerprints rather than finding spare diesel fuel. Other than a few gallons of gasoline for our ATVs and generators, we had almost no gas of any kind since the second week of the blackout.

The only places I knew to find diesel was green shirt motor pools or the National Guard Depot that we visited on our first mission. I preferred the depot because we knew the layout of the place and the gangs could be deceived with less risk than attacking the green shirts openly. A raid on a gang hangout might be easier to keep quiet if we could mask our presence somehow. I would have to come up with a plan when we got there.

The night of the raid I gathered the team and gave them the operations order. I had two guys from the transport section of the logistics group attached to my first squad of snipers. This was considered a heavy team and would be the largest group we had ever used on one mission. At dusk we headed towards the depot. The Kawasaki mule was fitted with a tank trailer that would allow us to transport fuel back to our waiting backhoes. The trick was how to get away with it. That detail was on my mind all the way as we drove through the empty fields.

We didn't' go right back to the same place on the hill as we did before. I directed the team to find a good staging spot off to the east of the Depot covered by thick woods. Night had fallen and the stars shone clearly as we approached our rally point overlooking the compound. The lights were on, but there were fewer lights actually working inside the fenced-in parking lot. I set up an overwatch position way up in the limbs of an old oak tree with my AR sniper rifle. As I looked through my scope, I saw that things had changed in the last couple of months. The buses and high-end cars were gone. The old HUMVEEs had been cannibalized down to almost empty frames. There were several tractor trailer containers with what seemed like a bunch of gangers rummaging around in them.

On the previous mission I could see the yard but nothing inside the Depot building itself. This time I could see through a couple of windows into the main building. The place looked like the inside of a real bar. Holy cow! There were pool tables, bottles on mirrored walls, leather sofas, and neon lights shining on the wall. My team held tight according to plan as we watched the comings and goings for about two hours. During that time I noticed how often trucks came in and out, and who inside the building let them in.

As I was about to get down and brief the team with my plan, I noticed something that made my heart jump. It was a glint of light reflecting off glass coming from the opposite side of the compound where I had set up the last time we were here. These guys had set up someone to watch over their compound. These gangers had learned at least that they needed sniper support. However, they most likely gave the job to someone that had no idea what he was doing. The gang sniper had made a mistake by not covering his scope lens properly. The light from the depot reflected back to me at the east side of the fence. The gang's sniper was watching the lit parking area to guard against what we were about to do.

I made my way back to the waiting team to make sure I was covered from the enemy sniper's vision. I pointed out the sniper to the team and laid out the plan. "Roll the tanker trailer quietly by hand close enough for the hose to reach the diesel fuel tank. Its sitting beside the depot building on that side," I pointed. One of my snipers would use his

Ghillie suit to covertly crawl through the fence, dragging the fuel hose behind. The logistics guys would operate the pump and fill our trailer. If everything worked according to plan, we would get out before anyone knew different. The rest of us would provide cover fire in case we were spotted. I told everyone to use break-contact drills falling back to our pre-assigned rally point.

The team knew this would be a challenge, but to a man they nodded in agreement. I left a sniper to provide overwatch from my oak tree but with orders to engage only of we were receiving fire from the compound. I led the team to the fence with my Glock 19 in hand and my sniper rifle slung over my back. I chose a spot that provided the best concealment on the opposite side of the depot from the gang sniper. I signaled my men to go ahead and make a discrete hole in the fence. Five minutes later my sniper crawled through with the hose in hand. The whole time he worked his way towards the tank, I thought about the darkness of that black hose against the pale grey gravel of the parking lot. I didn't want my man spotted because somebody noticed that hose stretched across the driveway. No plan is perfect though. Little did I know how much we would have to improvise in the next few minutes.

My sniper made it to the bushes lining the depot building without any trouble. But this level of creeping is incredibly slow. We were biting-our-nails anxious to get this done. The sniper was about 10 feet from the tank when the hose stopped dragging forward. Our hose was too short or the trailer was too far away. I saw the problem and directed the security team to move the trailer closer to the chain-link fence.

Just as we started, I heard a truck coming around the corner about 200 yards from the front entrance of the depot. I had everyone drop and find cover immediately. But I could do nothing about the hose across the driveway. The truck turned into the lot and was met by the gang members assigned to man the gate. I could hear the driver talking loudly to the passenger as he thumped over our hose thirty yards past the gate. Seconds later my heart started again and we continued the operation.

The sniper made it to the tank and connected the hose to a ball-valve outlet at the bottom. I signaled for the logistics guys to start pumping. I strained to hear our electric siphon pump over the noise from the depot, but nothing. It was looking good so far. Several minutes later our trailer was full. The logistics guys signaled that pumping was complete, so I had the sniper shut off the valve.

One of the logistics guys crawled to my position and whispered in my ear, "Huck, I think we just emptied their tank. The line went dry right before we shut it off." We shared looks of impending doom under our camouflaged faces. We knew the generator would stop in a few minutes, the lights would go out, and we would be knee deep in angry gang members looking for a fight. This is one of those "aw crap" moments where we had to make a new plan on the spot. I signaled our team to pull out as I headed inside the fence. My sniper watched as I quickly crawled to him on my knees. He gave a "what-the-hell" look because the plan as he knew it did not have me coming to his position.

I whispered, "We have to improvise, there is a problem. Get back to the hole in the fence and cover me as I come out."

I handed off my sniper rifle and pulled my Ghillie head cover to my back so I could use my peripheral vision to point shoot my Glock in case I was confronted.

I saw that only a few feet away was the first conex box which, knowing these thugs would be full of alcohol. I eased around and saw the conex box doors open with cases of liquor stacked to the ceiling. I slowly grabbed the nearest case as the enemy played pool some 20 feet away. The depot's rear bay door was wide open. I opened a couple bottles and poured them on the ground. The diesel fuel line ran from my position under the conex boxes out to the generator. My Seal Pup knife made a couple of small holes in the fuel line without problem. Back in WWII, saboteurs used smokes, or cigarettes, as timed fuses. I lit a cigarette and flayed the paper casing around the filter. Hopefully, it would flame up in what I figured to be a minute or so.

I retreated back around the building's side, looking toward the fence. The generator gave a weak sputter from a lack of fuel. I looked back at the cigarette smoking away and prayed the thing would flame up before the generator gave out completely. As I watched anxiously, a small flame issued from the cigarette. The flame ignited the alcohol on the ground. The alcohol fire immediately ignited what fuel was left in the fuel line just as the generator started to miss for real. Darkness shrouded the compound with the exception of the alcohol fueled flames. Fire engulfed the doorway of the depot. I took that opportunity to sprint across the driveway and duck through the fence where my sniper waited for me. We left behind a lot of screaming and yelling as we rolled the trailer back to the waiting Kawasaki mule. The important thing we did not hear was gunfire. I don't think those guys realized they had just been robbed. The trip home was in silence but all you could see was white toothy smiles among the green painted faces of my team.

The Colonel wanted to debrief us as we pulled up to our meeting area with a full trailer of diesel.

"How did it go? Did you get anything?" he asked.

"We took every drop of fuel those gangers had; right from their own tank," I said proudly.

"Did you lose anybody? They must have put up a fight," the Colonel asked as he looked at all my men, counting faces.

"No," I said. "We blamed it on them and they did not fuss with us at all."

The Colonel looked confused so I let him off the hook.

"I started a fire with their own liquor bottles so they would think one of their own guys had carelessly started it. I bet they didn't even notice that there was almost no fuel left in their fuel tank. Last we heard they were trying to put out the fire. We didn't have anyone follow us or shoot at us at all. I doubt they will get much sleep tonight. One thing we did learn was that they are starting to use snipers or at least designated marksmen. We may see more of them in the future," I warned him.

Chapter 12
Counter-Sniper Operation

There was a counter-sniper mission soon after our fuel raid. News of a green shirt sniper working only a mile or two from our community was picked up by our intelligence group. I chose to go since I was the team leader and nobody else had done counter-sniper operations yet. Not that I had experience either, but I was the leader so I volunteered myself to go. Gunny gave me some helpful tips and shook my hand sending me on my way. I remembered his advice the following day as I bellied down near a corn field where the sniper had been reported to operate.

"Scopes see better when you don't run them through nature's car wash."

Was that the phrase Gunny used? Gunny was always coming up with the one-liners straight from his hip pocket of wisdom. Somehow these words of wisdom did seem to stick though. Of course you do tend to remember these things only when you see your scope covers left open on your sniper rifle in a rain storm. I refrained from blowing on the lens. Doing so creates a foggy coating that leaves a nasty haze limiting the scope's effective range. A sniper lives by seeing others first. I corrected the mistake and slowly closed the Butler Creek caps over my Leupold MKIV tactical rifle scope.

The sun was somewhere behind those rain clouds, popping in and out of view, which could only mean that the clouds would sooner or later give up and move on out of the area. Meanwhile this also meant that the winds would stay a pleasant swirling 10+ miles an hour making any shots this afternoon that much more difficult. The fact that the clouds were passing intermittent shadows meant that longer shots would have to be corrected for elevation depending on whether the target was under sunshine or not. Funny how the light off a target can actually curve at 600 yards, forcing you to correct a come-up that was recorded in cloudy weather. At least in this time of year, spring, green grass was evenly spread over the corn field and the temperature was a balmy 65 degrees. I looked through his Ghillie head cover to once again scan the northern end of the field. Nothing….. yet.

If you intend to stay hidden, you must remain vigilant to move ever so slowly and never allow your head to snap to any sudden sight or sound. The human eye picks up rapid movements and signals the brain before the watcher knows what he is seeing. "A Sniper must always move like a three-toed sloth with sore feet." That must have been Gunny's favorite line by far due to the frequency he said it during training. Of course Gunny was right. We saw it several times during training. A recruit would stalk towards their target for two hours only to get frustrated with some grass or other some such weed and snap it off quickly. Gunny would pounce on these acts of sudden movement and make it a point to teach the recruit never to make the same mistake twice. Usually a not-so-nice punishment was issued, like sniper low crawling 50 yards with a tree trunk instead of a rifle. If that didn't teach a recruit, then there was no point his continuing the sniper course. Some people just don't have the right frame of mind for sniper/recon work. Yes, I remembered those training days with relish as I had chosen to go through the training like everyone else.

It was just as I panned around to my left that I saw what I had been looking for. There was just enough of a movement to look out of place; something had rapidly changed the color of some woods at an unnatural speed. Carefully I opened the scope caps on my AR sniper rifle and adjusted into position. I would not make the same mistake the other person just made. The rain was fairly light now, not much more than a drizzle. Rain patted lightly in the background off the brightly leafed trees. The scope lenses luckily had only a few rain drops which did little to obscure the objects across the field.

I scanned the area where I saw the movement and slowly made out the outline of a small bunker nestled in a patch of woods just off to the west of the field. "I knew I would find you guys sooner or later," I swallowed under my breath. The movement that I had seen was an occupant of the enemy observation post, or OP, fixing the cover of his shelter to keep out the rain. Bad mistake when you are supposed to be camouflaged from sight. It is human nature to seek comfort by keeping dry but you have to move in such a way that does not give away your position.

The enemy OP looked as though it was a temporary "blind" likely covering little more than a glorified foxhole. These were common crude little structures meant to keep people from view so they could observe open fields while allowing the watchers to move inside without fear of being seen. The sudden movement of the plastic roof cover had given away the location of the hide and allowed me to bear down on the OP's location.

The OP looked to be about 36 inches tall based off the surrounding shrub height and width of the small farm dirt road nearby. 36" is always good because it is easier to calculate distance through a Mil-dot scope like the Leupold MKIV. According to my estimate, it looked like the OP was just under 2 Mils in height. A quick calculation, $(1/2)*1000 = 500$ yards, revealed that this was well within the range of my AR15 sniper rifle. I reached up to the top target knob of the MKIV scope and dialed it up counter-clockwise 11 minutes to compensate for the 56 inch drop my 68 grain bullet would make over that distance. I normally kept my scope zeroed at 100 yards out of preference for street warfare which was more common than this long-range stalking business. I could just make out the dark slits of the OP where the occupants were able to see out over the field. These dark spots contrasted to the surrounding woods as being too perfectly dark to be natural. This was a common mistake in OPs because the inky blackness of the ports stood out against otherwise well camouflaged positions.

I checked the area to my left and right again to make sure I was aware of my immediate surroundings. Situational awareness keeps the sniper from getting tunnel vision on his prey and unwittingly becoming the hunted. You can let someone creep up on you if you get solely focused on your target. I saw the gentle rustling of rain drops falling from the spring green leaves over last fall's browning leaves. Nobody was on this side of the hill. There were no give away signs or sounds in my immediate area. All was quiet. The sun started to arc making the tree trunks cast shadows over the thin woods. I planted myself by an old fallen tree which had been blown over during a storm some two or three years ago. This allowed me to peer under the tree's large trunk and scan the entire field with a feeling of relative security.

Now came the fun part, waiting and watching perhaps for the rest of the day. Today's mission was not to shoot up the OP unless there were enemy snipers in the area. I was to find and observe all green shirts in this area until 22:00, then exfiltrate and report. I slowly slid my hand under my Ghillie suit and reached into my multi-cam TRU pocket. I pulled out my weather-proof notebook and began a S.A.L.U.T.E report.

S – Size of enemy unit – 2 green shirt troopers…so far

A – Action of enemy – observing field – visual recon.

L – Location – Map 12 grid Bravo 2

U – Unit – unknown at this time

T – Time – started observing 15:32 hours

E – Equipment – (Looks like M16s, no heavy weapons sighted.)

The occupants of the OP could now be seen moving around the OP as they passed by their own observation port. They evidently had no clue someone was watching them from the adjacent hill. "This OP must be manned by a couple of tenderfoot goofballs," I observed.

That is when I perceived things to be going just a little too well. Something smelled to the high heavens about this whole situation. It was too simple, too straight forward, too tempting. There must be a sniper running counter-sniper operation in the area and the OP was meant to be bait. A lot of "designated marksmen" would find the OP a tasty opportunity and would engage the occupants without scanning the area for other snipers. This would reveal their position and enable a counter-sniper to identify his position after the first shot. I started to scan the area for the most likely sniper hide. Perhaps he could be in the old garage or the old falling down tobacco curing barn. Upon examination, these positions did not have spaces between the boards which would enable a shooter to engage targets around the field. I looked further up the hill towards the old farmhouse. Most people would think that the second story windowless room would be a perfect hide offering a wide field of view covering the whole field and the surrounding hills. However, I saw a fatal flaw in that position.

The farmhouse was another 200 yards beyond the OP and stood in what used to be a nice open yard. According to a quick mil-dot calculation, the window looked to be slightly less than 700 yards from my current position. This was really pushing it for the ammo I had in my rifle. I wished I had heavier bullet, but that was all there was available.

"Hmm, I wonder if that sniper really thought this out," I breathed.

Through my scope, I saw just what I was looking for, something to smoke out a sniper from his hide and get him in the open. An old propane tank was still hanging under the rusting dilapidated grill on what used to be the front porch.

I slowly slid my trigger finger forward and pressed the magazine release of my sniper rifle. I loaded two red-tipped XM288 tracer rounds into the top of my Magpul magazine. With the magazine re-seated, I cycled the charging handle ejecting a round and loading one of the tracer rounds into the chamber. I picked up the loose round then slid closer under the fallen tree trunk in order to minimize the exposure of my body to the enemy sniper. Once in place, I reached up and added another 9 minutes of elevation to compensate for the additional distance to the farmhouse. The XM288 round was also 68 grain. This matched the ballistics of my standard sniper round. Intending to shoot a tracer is of course, INSANE; but also a calculated risk in this situation.

I was betting that the OP was not equipped for accurate long range shooting so it was unlikely they would be a threat right away. Once again I was looking through the scope at the upper window....looking for the slightest movement or color change in the background. After 40 minutes of closely watching the window, a sudden gust of wind delivered exactly what I expected. The wind blew through the cracked siding of the farmhouse making the sniper's veil flow in the breeze. It was not anchored at the bottom as it should have been. The veil, which shaded the sniper from view, now cast a different shade of gray ever so slightly as it swung closer to the bottom of the window. This was all I needed. This guy was mine if all went according to plan.

I pressed the Magpul UBR stock tighter into my shoulder and took up the slack of the Jewell two-stage trigger. The wind gusted off and on for another 3 minutes. Finally, there was a lull. I shot the first tracer at the propane tank. The round glanced the off the edge of the cylinder without penetrating. The second tracer followed a second later, with a slight correction for what little wind that had pushed the first round off target. The second round pierced the propane tank igniting the few ounces of flammable liquid left inside. Instead of the tank blowing up in spectacular fashion, the bullet hole acted like a small blow torch. Fire spewed as the tank writhed under the rusted grill. Even though the day had been rainy and damp, the old wood of the farmhouse porch began to burn in earnest. Years of dry leaves, trash, and general debris fanned the flames of the old farmhouse as the lower floor engulfed in flames.

I held tight onto the farmhouse position even though the O.P. was actively dumping rounds within 20 yards of my position. As I guessed, the O.P. was only equipped with standard iron sighted rifles which could not really send out accurate fire even though my tracer rounds pointed directly to my position.

Sure enough, the sniper now faced with burning to death or exposing himself to plain view, now realized his mistake in choosing the farmhouse. In order to make his escape, the sniper would have to jump out of the lower floor window some five feet off the ground and sprint 30 yards to the nearest cover of a well house. The sniper's rifle broke through a window of the flaming 1st floor followed by the sniper diving towards the ground. I had been waiting for this opportunity. As the enemy sniper hit the ground, I had taken aim and fired the 68 grain Hornady hollow-point for a spot about 12 inches off the ground. With only slight deviation from a mild gust of wind, the round penetrated the sniper's left side as he reached for his rifle from the ground. Instantly the man knew he was hit but could not yell out because the round had punctured his left lung as it passed through him at 1350 feet per second.

I now turned my attention back to the O.P. I quickly acquired the two men inside because they had their rifles on full auto trying to give their man some covering fire. This only served to give away their position as I panned right and started zeroing on their muzzle flashes. Since my scope was set for 700 yards I now had the choice of turning down the elevation or using Kentucky windage. I chose to end this as quickly as possible, so I aimed at the bottom of the bunker and lined up the windage line of the mil-dot reticle overlapping the muzzle flashes. Crack! One of the men in the bunker had clearly been hit because I saw the outer camouflage ripple as if it had been crashed into by a dead weight. There was silence. The silence contrasted strangely after the four sniper shots and several magazines worth of automatic fire from the O.P.

The only sounds now were from the farmhouse's walls crashing in. The green shirt sniper still lay on the ground smoldering from being too close to the flames without the energy to move.

I decided I had pushed my luck far enough for one engagement and had to go before green shirt reinforcements showed up. I gradually scanned my immediate surroundings and flicked the safety of my AR15 onto safe. Satisfied I was alone on the hill, I started crawling away using the fallen tree trunk as cover. Fire was no longer coming from the O.P. so I figured the second man in the O.P. must be more concerned with treating his wounded partner or had just given up blasting away at something he could not possibly hit.

I pocketed my spent cartridges and retreated around the low lying ditches of the hill feeling as though I had stolen something. It was truly amazing how the fortunes of war could change on someone like that sniper in the farmhouse. That guy had everything going for him; force of numbers, concealment, but his only crime had been not recognizing the inherent dangers of making his hide in the farmhouse with that wide open yard. If he had only remembered to leave himself a covered getaway, he would have survived the engagement.

Summer

"Rise of the Green Shirts"

Chapter 13
Summer without Electricity

We had a lot going on that summer. But times were getting harder for everyone. The power went off a month after the financial markets crashed. The nuclear attack on Washington back in the spring seemed too distant to be real. By summer, we realized what a heap of trouble we were in. Normally you think of summer as a great time of year since it is warm; but that warmth made for a new set of problems.

A lot of our elderly people were in dire need of medicine about now. Most people normally had a few weeks worth of medicine on hand. But we had been months without any sort of new supplies. Gangs kept us from using the roads, and the larger neighboring towns were under martial law. Drug stores had been closed or looted. Hospitals were so far away that sick people could not possibly consider traveling to them. Public hospitals had long ceased normal operations due to the rioting. We were convinced that we were on our own for our medical needs.

As the summer heat rose it made the infirmed that much sicker without their normal medications. Simple illnesses were abnormally severe since most people were not fed well enough to shrug off simple things like a cold. Colds became pneumonia before you knew it. There were no medications to fight something as severe as pneumonia. Bacteria in unpurified water gave people the runs, and those whose bodies could not overcome the dehydration, died. We lost a lot of our elderly people because we lacked simple medication. Unfortunately there was little we could do, but we tried every home remedy known to man.

However, the militia was getting stronger and more organized into effective fighting teams. Early in the summer I was spending loads of time running the sniper squad operations and sending teams out every other night. I sent two or three sniper/recon teams out with orders to find the much needed items to keep our town going. We just knew there had to be collection points for all the items confiscated.

When green shirts raided a town of its supplies, they had to store the stolen items somewhere. We wanted to raid one of those caches, but that was proving to be difficult. On a couple of occasions our teams spotted these collection points, but by the time we got a raiding party together, the goods were gone. We had to come up with a new plan, and we were in dire need of critical supplies. It became apparent that we needed to get really good at scrounging if we were going to make a real difference to the viability of our community. This gave me the idea of finding people I had known before the lights went out. It was my hope that we could strengthen the sniper teams to the point where we could operate as an offensive weapon someday. For that we needed some serious weapons.

Chapter 14
My Friend the .50 Caliber

The fifty caliber rifle dominated the battlefields of my time. You see, the fifty caliber round can peel through most thin armor plate and can bring down a world of hurt on people and equipment from extremely long ranges. It's one of those rifles that kill on both ends if you don't respect it. You really have to tuck that rifle into your shoulder and hold on if you want to keep shooting after the first shot. My goodness that thing can pack a punch at super long ranges. Of course that is why it was such a treasured weapon for the militia since we had no mortars or artillery. We used the .50 cal. to counter heavy weapon platforms like armored personnel carriers and make-shift tanks.

That is what led me to seek a friend of mine that I had known from my competition shooting days. My friend forgot more about 1000 yard shooting than most people would ever know. At the next militia meeting I talked with the Colonel to suggest we try to find my long range rifle expert friend and see if he could help supply some much needed weapons. He was last seen in a town about 15 miles to the north, near his home, but had not been seen since before the power went out. I knew the risks of finding him would be worth it if we could get his expertise working for us. My friend was a real master level shooter and had competed in 1000 yard matches for decades. It was my hope that he had evaded the green shirts and been able to retain some of his long range rifle gear.

Our ranks were growing so fast it was hard for our logistics guys to come up with enough rifles to outfit the sniper squads. During this time the logistics guys were more concerned with other tasks like finding food supplies and medical items, not searching for special weapons. That is not to say we weren't looking for weapons, we absolutely were. We also had to get some ammo soon, or we would be down to throwing rocks.

My sniper recon teams were busy on missions so I assigned myself the task of finding my friend. The Colonel gave my plan the okay, and authorized me the use of a motor-cross style motorcycle. This would get me there and back as quickly as possible. I appointed one of my sniper squad-leaders in charge of our unit and talked with Fred to get his opinion on the best covert route to take. Fred had been keeping track of all the gang movements and green shirt road blocks, so he was able to give me at least a plan for my trek north. Unfortunately we did not have much current information on Roxboro, so I would have make it up as I went along. Our recon searches had not been that far north due to early upheaval of the populous and the resulting green shirt crack down. My friend had lived in the outskirts of town in a quiet housing development covered in old growth hardwood trees. It was my hope that he had escaped the chaos and was keeping safe somewhere. As I made my way north, I imagined how I would greet my friend and try to explain how we were organizing the militia. It was my hope that he would be willing and able to help us with rifles and ammo for our fight against the green shirts.

I left on my quest at midday so I could travel through the fields and woods with as much speed as possible. Roads were out of the question due to gang activity and sporadic green shirt road blocks. About 3 miles outside of my town I crossed the damn of a dairy farm pond and continued through a series of fields keeping just out of site of the main road. My motorcycle had a longer exhaust pipe and a larger than usual muffler which was designed to make the bike as quiet as possible. I was never as glad of this, than when I reached a spot on my map where I intended to cross a major four-lane hard top road.

Just as I approached the road from the thick edge of the woods, I looked right. By goodness, I wasn't 70 yards from some sort of checkpoint where two green shirts and a squad car sat blocking the road. Lucky for me, it was customary to watch, wait, and listen, five minutes before a sniper crosses any open territory. That little adherence to detail saved me from capture or at least a nasty chase I could not afford. At least, I assumed they would chase a guy all decked out in camouflage with a Glock on his hip. The road I wanted to cross was four lanes wide with a grassy median between. Crossing meant more than 100 yards completely exposed. There was no way I was crossing here, so I shut the bike off and quietly backed off down the incline of the roadway keeping to the darkest of the woods.

With my heart thumping out of my chest I checked my map and made sure to mark this intersection and update Fred's map when I got back. My map indicated a small river a mile or so west that passed under the roadway. If I was lucky, I could cross under the roadway if the river was shallow enough and make my way across without being spotted. Once I felt myself far enough away from the checkpoint, I fired up the bike and headed out. I found the small river in the woods and turned towards the roadway. The bike easily followed the banks of the river and passed under the roadway without being observed. I kept to the deep woods now as much as I could. We had little information on this area and I was not willing to risk being spotted by gangs or green shirts this far out on my own. I was there to find a friend who most likely had been a target of the green shirts from day one. Careful was my middle name.

Some hours later I arrived near my target neighborhood and found a thicket with an old tobacco barn. The old barn offered a good shelter where I could hide out until dark before continuing my trip. Once I saw the stars pop out and the bright moonscape, I climbed aboard the bike and headed the last mile down the side of the road. As I approached his house I noticed a large break in the trees but no house. My friend's house had been burned down, his garage office was gone, and what looked like 2 acres of empty burned woods were all that were left. My heart sank.

All the houses on the street were dark. No lamps or sign of life were immediately visible. I got off the bike desperate to find some clue that might point me to some secret hiding place.

As I looked around I noticed a glimmer of light from a house window maybe 100 yards away. My friend knew the person that lived in that house I was sure, because I had seen him mowing the lawn once. With my Glock 19 in hand, I worked my way around to the darkest entrance of the house and quietly knocked on the door. I had no idea who I would find inside, but I hoped I could deal with whoever answered the door. But I needed information critical to the militia, so I was ready to stick my Glock in their face if I had to. The little old lady that answered the door with her broom in hand disarmed me in an instant. She had opened the door a crack and asked who was calling at such a late hour. He voice was squeaky and weak from age. I smiled and tried to think of a way to introduce myself while concealing the pistol in my hand.

"Ma'am, I apologize for this late call, but I am looking for a friend of mine that used to live next door. You see, his house is gone but I need to know if he is still alive." She looked at me with the most annoyed expression.

"Sonny, you didn't answer my question at all, who you are you?" I loved this lady immediately. She had spunk for someone that looked to be in her upper eighties as she stood there clutching her broom.

"Ma'am, some call me, Huck," I said evasively. She looked surprised and opened the door just a bit further.

"You are?" she asked. Now this made me down right shocked. Just how the hell did she know the code name Huck?

"Yes ma'am, I am. I need to know where my friend and his wife are that lived next door."

She said, "Oh they are gone but, they left you a message".

"They did?" I asked incredulously. Okay this was weird because I had not seen my friend since before the lights went out. How did he know I would show up, and how did he know the name Huck?

The little old lady told me to come in and close the door behind me. She made sure the dark curtain draped over the glass of the door and bade me to sit down at the table. That must have been a sight from across the room. Here I was all decked out in camouflage speckled with mud splotches from the motorcycle while sitting across from a little old lady in a house coat and fuzzy slippers. Two more different people never sat down to a candle-lit kitchen table I am sure.

She looked at me and said, "Your friend gave me the message a few days after their house was burned," He said, "Tell Huck, if he ever shows up at your door, to go hunt geese." Now ain't that the craziest thing you ever heard? I mean, what in the world was he talking about? Anyway, those green shirted no good rascals were all over here asking people all sorts of stuff. They tore the place apart and they were the ones that burned the house which almost got my whole garden. You see what they did out there? My goodness those boys were a bunch of knuckle heads playing with matches."

I looked at her as things became a lot clearer in my head. My friend knew that whatever message he left behind must make sense to only me or else it would lead back to his hiding place. Luckily, I knew right away what it meant. A few years back my buddy and I hunted geese on a piece of farmland some miles away. This farm had an old cabin that we considered buying to use as a hunting lodge. I was close enough to get there by road but it was going to be a challenge to get there before dawn with only the gas I had left in tank.

I asked the little old lady if she had any gas, and she told me to look in the shed. She might have some for the lawn mower, but she was not going to mow any more at her age. I thanked her profusely and politely excused myself before she made me wash my hands or something.

I walked back up to the bike and rolled it down to the shed. As I was emptying the contents of an old plastic gas can into the tank of my bike, I saw lights coming down the road. Oh crap, trouble, that's a squad car. I quickly replaced the gas cap and threw the can aside as I fired up the bike. I wheeled around and sped off towards the woods as the squad car's spotlight shone across the burnt remains of the house. Shots rang out as I serpentined around trees, as I sped away at full throttle. The squad car followed as best they could, but my bike was able to go places a car could never follow. After a couple of miles without seeing the squad car, I slowed enough to get my bearing and plan the rest of my trip.

It was early dawn before I drove onto the long driveway of the farm. I kept to the side of the gravel drive so I would not leave tire tracks for anyone to follow. The morning was hazy and cool but burning off quickly in the rising sun. I pulled up to the cabin which looked empty and a complete wreck. As I got closer, I realized what looked like interior darkness was really painted windows meant to give a passerby the impression of an abandoned building. I walked to the door and knocked ever so lightly hoping to find a warm greeting and not a green shirt gun barrel. The door clicked open and out poked a shotgun barrel. I recognized the barrel immediately as my friend's Waterfowl Benelli 12 gauge.

"Hello....Huck", came from inside. "We have been expecting you; it's about time you got here. Want some breakfast?"

I was among friends now and was relieved; I wanted rest and food rather than playing moving target for some green shirt. It was an early summer day with few clouds and moderately warm temperatures. The leaves on the trees were deep green and grass was knee high everywhere you looked. No fuel means, no more mowing grass, which I never liked anyway. If it had not been for the craziness of the times, this may have gone down in memory as a great getaway trip spent with friends. However these were not normal times, and we had to do some serious talking.

I spent the day sharing my adventures to date and learning what was going on way up here in the northern part of the state. Roxboro had been on the green shirt list early on and was pretty closed down. I learned that only green shirt vehicles were allowed on the four lane roads, and most connecting roads were monitored or blocked. This was news to me, but I was not surprised. My friend was not surprised when I explained that I was part of the NC 3rd militia and had started their sniper program.

My friend smiled broadly when he said, "I knew it was you when I heard stories of a militia sniper named Huck operating down in your area. You sure made a bunch of these criminals piss their pants when you guys resisted the gangs. Stories are floating around how you guys ambushed one of the raiding parties in your town and then got spanked pretty good for it by the green shirts. The green shirts have been collecting guns all over. Word has it that you guys are in pretty bad shape down there." My friend was putting it out there knowing that I could not really say much without giving out compromising information. He knew my response would be telling enough.

"Good, that is just what we wanted people to think," I told him. "We have been working hard to keep it secret that we are operating the 3rd militia from our town, and we want to keep it that way. We have been using their appointed preacher to spread the word that we are unarmed and demoralized so the green shirts will think we are pacified. However, we are getting stronger and are pretty well organized. Have you organized fighters around here?"

"Not really, we have people that can fight but there is no organized effort up here yet. We are just too spread out to keep in touch with all the farmers scattered all over. But we are starting to meet here at the farm every couple of weeks to keep in touch and pass along information. Most everybody is on board with resisting, but all the big city politics seems far away when it's all people can do to get enough food for their kids. But hey we are going to make a big push up here to get people to join because I know you are going to need help when things get really rolling."

As the day went on I shared as much information as I could with my friends to help them organize their volunteers into a fighting force as part of the 3rd Militia structure. I relayed how we had broken up into specialized teams in order to help equip the units. Then we followed up on training techniques for recruits and ideas on how to call up forces on a moment's notice like the minutemen of the old Revolutionary War days of 1776. We worked out a code system for radio messages and a plan for some of our sniper teams to keep information flowing in case the radios were compromised. I wanted my friend to use his little farm hideout as a northern base for 3rd militia efforts because I knew the value of not having all your eggs in one basket. At that time I could not offer a formal rank, but I told my friend that he should be considered a team leader in our organization. I just needed to clear it with my Colonel.

But the best was yet to come. As dusk fell, right before I was to head back, my friend presented me with a gift. The gift was a .50 caliber Barrett M107A1 sniper rifle with a NightForce scope, along with a case of match ammo and a couple of spare magazines. I was like a kid on my birthday. He had saved this rifle and precious few other firearms from his house. The green shirts had nearly killed him before he was able to escape their raid. The .50 cal was one of the few rifles he managed to save. After his escape, the green shirts set his house on fire consuming his remaining shooting gear.

I rode with that giant .50 strapped to my back trying to keep my balance as I steered out of his driveway waving goodbye. The motorcycle puttered along with the heavy case of ammo secured to the rear cargo rack and the 30 lb.

rifle added to my weight. It was a miracle I did not break my neck as I snaked my way back home.

I made my way back as stealthily as I could, so it took me until midday with a gas tank almost dry, before I returned to the militia cache point. I stowed the monster .50 cal. rifle for safe keeping in a waterproof case. Boy, that rifle made an impression on the guys at our next meeting. Almost none of our volunteers had ever seen a .50 cal. up close; let alone shoot one. Gunny had experience with the Barrett M107, so he gave us a plethora of knowledge on how to employ it in battle. I could hardly imagine how the green shirts would react to the .50 for the first time, and I was anxious to introduce them.

Chapter 15
Our New Green Shirt Office

I think it was right in the middle of summer when the green shirts came into town with just a couple of squad cars, a school bus, and a panel truck. All the vehicles were painted green along with the PPR logos and what not. We got word they were coming from our lookout post, but leadership chose not to hit the panic button and blow the bridge. We were pretty sure we had the green shirt goons fooled into thinking our town was made up of simple farmers that had been disarmed and demoralized. We were happy to continue our deception until it was necessary to teach them otherwise.

Anyway, they rolled into the fire station parking lot and started looking around for a place to set up. There had been a couple of businesses in single story buildings right beside the fire station, but they were now closed. The gentleman that owned the building came in as word spread through town that the green shirts were back and wanted to see him. When he apprehensively approached the green shirt official he was handed a few papers that transferred ownership of the property to the "public". The "public" meant it wasn't yours anymore, go pound sand.

The lead green shirt got up and spoke to the gathering crowd. He informed them that all former post offices, schools, libraries, fire stations, jails, prisons, army bases, depots, and all other like properties, were now under direct PPR control. Nobody was allowed inside these building unless directed by the proper "authorities". Our little hospital with all the critical medicines set up in the fire station was confiscated. It was all we could do to keep the firemen from going to jail or wherever they were taking people nowadays.

Of course there were some people asking questions about loved ones, when we were getting relief, fuel, or electricity. We must have medicines and quickly if we were going to save people. The response was simple. The new PPR information office in town would handle all complaints once it was up and running so the faster we dispersed, the faster they could get things going. By now most people in town realized that too much argument would result in additional arrests. Complaining never got too heated. We watched as the green shirts went through town and looked over everything.

Luckily we finished our bunkers earlier that very week. We watched to make sure the green shirts did not find anything of value. The militia intelligence guys shadowed the green shirts and volunteered to help in any way they could. It is easier to keep your eye on your enemy by getting in his back pocket.

One of our guys watching the proceedings muttered the appropriate words, "It looks like there is a sheriff in town boys."

Chapter 16
Scavenger Missions

You see our priorities changed sometimes on a daily basis. We always had a few items on our always-get list. Of those things you would find food, fuel, any medicine, parts for water purifications systems, and heavy weapons. Our sniper recon teams had been searching high and low as far away as we could travel on foot in order to find the items we desperately needed. We found very little for quite some time. That is, until we hit the jackpot.

One of the sniper recon teams out on a mission reported that a green shirt container truck sat on the side of a road only a few miles away. It seems this truck had broken down and was waiting for a repair crew or tow. Since fuel was such a commodity, that meant whatever the truck contained was worth a LOT to the green shirts. The snipers reported they could take out the driver and the security passenger if needed, but we chose to keep this quiet if at all possible.

The Colonel needed a quick reaction raiding force, so I volunteered. Most of my guys were already out on missions so it made sense for me to go. It was afternoon as the four of us who were in the bunker, raced towards the truck. We took the Kawasaki mule to just in case we could salvage something from the truck. As fate would have it, one of the people that came along was a local gal that had been working in intelligence department. Her code name was, "Seven." You see some of us in leadership were sci-fi nuts and she kind of looked like Seven of Nine from the old Star Trek series Voyager. She hated her code name at first. But these things were more like nicknames and somehow, once they stick, it's yours for good. She was a knockout blond that typically wore her hair in a pony tail. Stories of here spread like wildfire when she joined. Seven brought her own pistol to her first meeting and demonstrated that she knew how to use it better than half the men. Secondly, she was the type that was aware of her surroundings at all times. From what I heard, the Captain of intelligence was truly impressed with her work and considered her more than just a pretty face. In my opinion, I was worried about morale of the teams. I didn't want my guys to get distracted by a cute girl and get killed by the green shirts because they were not paying attention.

I didn't really know Seven too well before the war. We saw each other as teenagers a few times because my folks knew her folks kind of thing. We lived in a small town and you know everybody at least a little.

As we drove through the back country we hashed out a plan. We would set up a raiding team as near to the truck as possible. When ready, Seven and our best runner would walk towards the truck along the edge of the road. The idea was to make it look like the girl and guy were fighting about something. We hoped the driver and security guy would be distracted and try to get involved. We planned on our guy running off and being chased by the green shirt security guy. Seven would knock out the driver while the raiding team plundered the truck. We didn't know if the driver was really a green shirt, so we wanted to preserve him if at all possible. We radioed the sniper team as we approached the area. They met us as we parked the mule.

We quickly briefed the sniper team of our plan, and approached the roadway to set up our people in position. Once we were settled in we sent our "quarreling couple" down the road and waited to see the reaction from the truck's occupants. Sure enough, the security guy heads right to our man and starts a foot race. The driver took Seven by the hand to console her. In an instant, Seven tazed the driver unconscious before he could blink twice. The team and I raced down the embankment and approached the back of the truck. We were on the edge of an open roadway in moments. This was way too exposed for my taste. I wanted to grab whatever was inside and GO. We had been lucky so far and I did not want to be here any longer than I had to. The lock was cut off and the container doors were swung wide open.

HOLY COW! It was like Christmas, New Years, and every birthday you have ever had inside. It was a gold mine of guns, pistols, reloading equipment, and ammo. There were big 55 gallon plastic barrels full of every long gun you could imagine. Other barrels had pistols, there were cases of ammunition, knives, backpacks, and everything you could imagine or ever want to start your own army. Holy cow these guys must have raided a week to get all this. It was phenomenal the sheer volume of stuff.

"DAMN!" I shouted. "It's too much."

We would never be able to haul all this stuff. If we tried to take the truck back to town, the green shirts would find it for sure. If they didn't find it here, they would not stop to their search for it. With a great lump in my throat, I instructed the raiding team, "Take the AR15s and higher quality pistols like the Glocks, M&Ps, and XDs. Find all the magazines you can. We will take as much ammo as the mule will carry. We destroy the rest."

The guys gave an audible, "AWW really?" as they continued to shove guns in every pocket.

My sniper came dragging back from his chase. He had a bloody nose and some scrapes on his face where he had been ruffed up. Smiling with a bloody lip, my man said the security guy caught him down by the creek.

"It was all he could do to beat the guy off and knock him out with a rock."

We exceeded the Mule's hauling capacity and loaded the rest into backpacks for us to carry on our backs.

That's when I heard a sound that made my heart sink. As I heard the engines top the hill, there was no mistaking the growl of two Harley Davison's as they topped the hill and pulled off to the side of the road behind the truck. My team had sprinted back into the wood-line undetected. Meanwhile, I stood looking out the back of the truck with my hand in the cookie jar. The gangers got off their bikes and pulled out revolvers which they pointed in my direction. Both were grinning from ear to ear. These guys thought they had just caught me with my pants down. They didn't know that my right hand held my Glock 19 pointed down into the barrel. I watched them approach the truck cautiously. Just as the biggest ganger opened his mouth to speak, Seven stepped from the woods and said "Hi" with a little wave. They both turned instinctively to see the unexpected female voice. That was all the distraction I needed.

You see, I was a pretty good pistol shooter back then in my competition days. I double tapped the first guy before the other one even saw me move. The second biker turned halfway toward me, but I stitched him with two rounds before he could get his pistol pointed in my direction. As the second biker fell, he managed to squeeze off a single shot that ricocheted off the truck's door. A bullet fragment struck Seven in the arm as she leaped sideways trying to get out of the line of fire. As the rest of the team scrambled from the woods, I jumped from the container truck and ran to Seven's side. With leaves and grass all over, she sat upright holding her bleeding arm. Her wound was a simple flesh wound on her upper forearm that bled modestly.

As I bandaged her wound, I said, "You did great today. Thanks for the distraction."

She stared at the two gangers lying at the back of the truck, "He was really going to shoot me." Her tone was one of disbelief with a distinct loathing. Seven looked at me as I finished her bandage, "You saved me, Huck. Thanks." Her eyes were too much for me to handle and keep my head about me.

I looked around trying to get my mind back in the operation, "Can you walk? We need to get moving." Seven got to her feet and walked over to the truck and helped with the last load of cargo.

I called out to the team, "This is the last load! Get back into the woods." I took a final look around to make sure there was nothing left to do. There wasn't.

We had to get out now while the getting was good. I told the team to pack the last few handfuls of guns and get back to the mule. The gunfire was bound to attract attention and we did not know how far away the green shirts were. I threw down a crappy 9mm pistol out of the truck to make it look like someone had left it behind after the ganger shooting. After searching the truck for a second, I found a one-pound can of reloading powder that I used to spread over the oddball ammunition we could not take.

Like Rambo in the sporting goods store, I lit the powder as we hoofed it away from the truck. The other team members drug the second biker over to the driver just to confuse the situation. We hoped the fire in the truck would melt the guns enough to make them unusable and perhaps mask the fact that we stole a bunch of them. The bodies of the bikers would make the scene look like a gang raid on the green shirt truck if we were lucky. The truck smoked for a while as we jogged through the woods. After a long minute, the truck erupted in pops and blasts as the powder and bullets cooked off. The explosions motivated us to get back to our bunkers to stow our new treasures.

It was going to be a long trip since we would not travel back to town directly. We had to make it as hard as possible for people trying to track us. It was imperative not to underestimate whoever was investigating the incident at the container truck. You never know whether there might be some real slick detectives working for the green shirts.

Along the way, a couple of the team expressed surprise that I was able to get both bikers with my pistol so quickly. One of my snipers guessed that I had pulled a machine gun on the bikers and did not believe I had used my Glock 19. Everyone seemed to associate me with being a rifle shooter. My ability to use a pistol affectively was a bit of a surprise to them.

I apologized to Seven because l had not shot her ganger first. She was nursing a bandaged and sore arm as we walked. I told her it would make a scar worthy of stories for her grandkids. She smiled red faced for several minutes. I have to admit that I did not mind the way she looked at me for saving her though. Yep, I was happy to be her hero for a day. Her smile could melt a man.

The mule was packed with ammo and guns to the point where we had to help it through creeks. We had that thing so overloaded I wondered if we could get it back without breaking an axle. Our arms ached under the weight of the rifles. But it would be worth it when we got back. I think my arms were 2 inches longer as we arrived at the nearest secret militia bunker. That was one of the hardest hikes we ever did because we were so overloaded.

After stowing the captured weapons, I reported into the Colonel. I told him it would take a whole squad to go through the weapons and distribute them to the different bunkers. I was right too. We ended up with Bushmasters, Rock River carbines, Colts, DoubleStars, DPMS', and a host of other guns along with some 15,000 rounds of ammo. I don't know how many pistols we captured, but it was more than you could fit in an A.L.I.C.E. backpack. I regretted that I could not get more of the guns from the truck. But there was no way to steal the whole truck and get away with it clean. The last thing I wanted was a green shirt to find that truck in our town.

Chapter 17
New Missions and New Recruits

The summer was a recruiter's dream, because we got people interested in volunteering left and right. But for those of us in charge of getting people trained, it was nightmare time. Our teams had only been working for a month or two as an organized force, so it was not like we had seasoned veterans or anything. We were getting handfuls of new volunteers every meeting though. Some guys traveled from the surrounding farm lands while others were coming in from nearby towns. The problem was equipment. Most of the new guys came with little or nothing in the way of real fighting gear because the green shirts or gangs had raided their town. Some guys had their dad's double barrel shotgun with one box of shells. One gun and a box of shells can start a fight, but not finish one. We proved that to the gang on Carver Street.

We had a bunch of rifles and pistols, but we were short on magazines, ammo, food, and ammo carrying equipment. I gave wish lists to the logistics teams and they flipped me the bird. Well, maybe not the bird, but they were never happy to see me.

Early on in the militia formation we made up cover stories for men coming in and out of town. We used farm work as an excuse for men to come in for a few days, work, and then return home. My buddy Fred instructed new militia volunteers to come into specific farms under this cover story, work during the day, and train with us at night. These designated farms were usually militia bases where we had covert bunkers. After a couple weeks, our ranks swelled to over 100 volunteers, but only half were actually equipped and trained. We had a lot to teach these guys in ways to covertly travel, work in fighting teams, learn basic land navigation skills, and so on.

We started a "basic training" course where recruits learned all the skills of operating in the militia. Of course, we also had to watch who was coming in as new recruits. In history, every fighting force had used spies to infiltrate the enemy's infrastructure. For quite some time we would only allow people we knew or could easily identify as coming from the local surrounding farms. We were pretty sure most of them. But we were watching everybody. Some people trained with us for several weeks before they were told much of anything. All they knew were the basics of how to operate and how we did things. Only after our intelligence group okayed someone's background would they be trusted with the first level of information. For instance, the recruit might only know one level of password or perhaps the location of one or two bunker positions. We liked to keep things simple as possible just in case someone was turned or was playing both sides. Lucky for us we had very few green shirt supporters that tried to infiltrate our ranks.

We did have green shirt sympathizers in town funny enough. Oh yes, there were a few people out there that didn't mind the church registration office because they didn't go to church anyway. These green shirt sympathizers didn't like us fighting the gang on Carver Street either. They didn't like much of anything without their Oprah playing on TV every day. Most of these green shirt sympathizers were just desperate to have their creature comforts back and were willing to do anything to have their old life-style returned to them. We tolerated these people and pitied their attitude.

A few hot headed militia members wanted to mark these sympathizers and get rid of them quietly. However the leadership and I disagreed with that approach. We would avoid these people and ignore their views as long as they did not actively hurt our ranks. If someone started pointing out militia members to the green shirts or actively joined the green shirt ranks, we would take action. But those actions would not be without restraint. We planned a whole process to put restrictions on hasty actions that could result in someone being shot. In fact, we formed a whole code of conduct for our militia forces to ensure an individual would be held responsible for his actions if they violated our rules. We wanted to make sure our people understood that we were acting more like legitimate police forces than the roving gangs we were fighting.

Something that kept coming up was concern over the freedom of the gangs to operate so openly in our area. It looked like the green shirts were not too interested in occupying individual small towns, but the gangs were having field days in some of our neighboring communities. These gangs followed closely behind the green shirt gun-confiscation raids. Townspeople were left completely vulnerable. It was becoming clear that the 3rd militia would need to organize some teams to help protect the towns in our immediate area.

Chapter 18
Fight to Save Our Neighbors

Now that we had a green shirt office in town, it was more important than ever to keep our militia a secret. Stories of the 1st militia making a stand proved the green shirts would pull out all stops crushing any resistance. There was no way we were going to lay down and take it though. We had to get serious and start doing something about the gangs.

The Colonel came up with a plan to create some squad sized teams to go out and do gang interdiction. These squads consisted of 6 riflemen, 2 snipers, with maybe an explosives expert or someone from the intelligence group. Our victory at Carver Street inspired us to resist these gangs before they could inflict so much damage on our neighbors. For now, we would stay away from engaging the green shirts if at all possible. We also wanted the gangs to fear us like we were the boogey man, always lurking in the shadows.

On one occasion we were able to ambush a gang as they pillaged our neighboring town some three miles west of us. This town is where I used to play golf way back before the lights went out. I knew the place well. They had just had their guns confiscated by the green shirts the day before. According to what we had seen in the past, we expected a gang raid any time now.

We formed up an advance squad and positioned them near town as the last green shirts left. I had been itching to use the Barrett .50 cal., so, I volunteered to lead the second squad. The day of our team's arrival, we coordinated with the 3rd militia members stationed nearby. One of the explosives guys set up a command detonated device under the street in the underlying drain system. We had hopes of taking out any vehicle short of a tank, if the need arose. The local militia team was only about 6 people strong so we had them located in a key building along the main street to act as a blocking force. This was much the same way we had used the three story brick garage back in the Carver Street battle a couple of months ago.

The plan was for the local militia to command detonate the mine under the gang's lead truck while our team swept in from a hide location off to east. Since I had the .50 caliber I choose a vantage point where I could see most of area where we expected the battle to unfold. We found a small rise or hill and set up our overwatch position. I chose one of my sniper team members to spot for me and help direct the teams in the street by radio since we could see the majority of town from our position. He was carrying a classic M1A rifle setup with a Springfield scope and 168 grain match ammo. I would set up the Barrett to take out priority targets while he worked the radio and give the teams directions. I adjusted my scope for the proper elevation based on the distance and waited.

24 brutally long hours later, it started just like we expected. The gang showed up on the edge of town and began their smash and grab routine. They were a bit more organized than they were during our fight in Carver Street though. These guys had some make-shift armored personnel carriers built from a couple of 5-ton dump trucks with plate steel covering most of the windshield and windows. It looked like these trucks had gang security guards in the dump beds so as to project the convoy from any armed resistance. Little did they know how much resistance they were about to receive.

We watched the gang's progress. They were tensing up as house after house were devoid of townspeople. We moved the people out of town yesterday and gave them directions not to come back until all the shooting was over. Those gang jerks were still doing their usual smashing and grabbing routine though.

The lead dump truck crossed the manhole cover which was the mine's marker. KABOOM! There was smoke, fire, and bikers flying through the air as the device cratered the small city street. I don't know what was in that bomb, but it made a freaking giant hole. I trained the Barrett on the truck in the rear of the convoy and squeezed the trigger. BLAM! That .50 is one loud gun! I ranged the distance to the street the day before and mapped out key locations for exact range distancing. The truck was just over 800 yards from our location, well within range. The 643 grain armor piercing incendiary round dropped 140 inches as is raced to the target. Even at that distance, it was still traveling at 1930 feet per second as it reached the truck. That bullet tore through the fender of the truck and drilled through the block of the big turbo diesel engine. The truck ground to a halt and immediately caught fire. Three pickup trucks full of scrambling gangers were stranded between two burning dump trucks and utter chaos. The blocking force and our team were hammering the exposed gang from two directions in a classic "L" ambush.

Sounds from the street that far away were quite different from our Carver Street battle. Back there, I was about deaf after the firefight because we unleashed so much 5.56 fire onto the gangs. Here, the crackling sounds of gunfire from my position were heard a full second after I saw the weapon shoot. It was weird, almost as if you really weren't there or not really part of the action. I heard my spotter point out target after target as we engaged the remaining gang members running for hard cover. The bed of the dump truck provided false hope for one guy that tried to use it. No luck for him though. The next API round tore a hole through the truck's bed and his left side before it ricocheted around the inside. One ganger jumped into a concrete building on the side of the street and started popping up in the window spraying bullets between magazine changes. That was no help either. I trained the rifle on a spot about 12 inches below the window and sent a round through the wall. No more fire came from the window.

Overall the mission plan was going right on track. Our teams were maneuvering on the remaining gang members who seemed to be leaderless and disoriented. There must have been fifty of these guys at the beginning and we had already killed maybe half.

Ten minutes into the fight, I was changing my magazine and heard a sound I had rarely heard in the last 4 months. It was the unmistakable thumping sound of helicopter rotors coming from the south somewhere, maybe less than a mile away. My sniper/spotter was on the radio trying to notify the teams because we realized that they could not hear it coming with the firefight right in front of them. We managed to get a hold of our team right before the first rockets streaked down the middle of the street. The helicopter was a Huey UH1 fitted with 2.75" rockets and at least 1 door gunner. He had followed the road right down the main street and unleashed a series of rockets that impacted from the dump trucks all the way up to the point where the local militia guys had set up shop.

I saw this and was determined to do something about it. However shooting a slow moving truck is one thing. Shooting a flying helicopter is something else at 800+ yards. The UH1 circled around and made two passes while I waited for an opportunity. After a couple of runs I realized that he would never slow down enough for me to get a clean shot. In deer hunting you train on the running deer and you whistle for him to stop. When the deer turns to see what is whistling, you shoot. I decided to try it. I would have the M1A be my whistle. I told the sniper/spotter to unload on the helicopter with a full magazine as soon as I was ready. He looked at me in a "What in hell are you talking about?" kind of way.

"Trust me!" I said over the distant din of gunfire.

"Get ready....now!" I ordered as I watched the Huey through my scope.

My spotter started cranking off rounds at the helicopter which had the exact affect I wanted. The UH1 stopped its run and banked toward our position. Because it was now heading our way, it had eliminated the need to lead the helicopter giving me a straight upward angle shot. Given the high angle and closeness of the helicopter, I had to raise the 30 pound Barrett off the bipod and got into a hasty sitting position. I knew I had only one chance at this or else we would be eating the next rockets fired. I took careful aim and squeezed off two rounds in rapid succession at the Huey's center mass.

Let me just say, double tapping a Barrett is a lot like playing tag with a freight train. You lose. The recoil of that thing tumbled me head over heels out of my sitting position and backwards down the embankment. As quickly as I could, I recovered my hat and searched around for the rifle. With the rifle back in hand, I looked around to see if I had made my shots. My spotter sat grinning at me. I must have done some damage to the Huey, because smoke rolled from the port side engine cowling. There was a grapefruit sized hole in the co-pilot windshield. The door gunner wasn't firing anymore. The chopper veered off and disappeared over the trees. Clear blue sky shown behind the streaks of smoke left behind the green shirt's air cover.

My sniper/spotter said something profound about the pilot's mother and we saw no more of that chopper. I remember how the clear sky contrasted so drastically to the town's smoking main street Black smoke rose from burning truck tires obscuring the street and surrounding buildings. Sporadic pops of distant rifle fire could be heard but otherwise the battle had died down.

My sniper and I realized that we needed to get everyone out of there immediately. If the green shirts had prepared a helicopter to be on standby, they would not be far behind with lots of troops to wipe out all remaining resistance. In fact, I was betting that the green shirts would even engage the remaining gang members just to cover up the evidence of their involvement in the raids. We packed up our gear and hoofed it into the edge of town. Cautiously, we made contact with our team. The remaining gang had pulled back down the road they came from. Everything they could not immediately carry was left in the street. The street itself was a smoking ruined mess. Bodies lay among broken bricks. Green leaves fell from splintered trees that lined the once quiet thoroughfare. Burning truck tires clouded the clear day with thick acrid smelling smoke. Bullet impacts marked stone walls. All this destruction occurred in roughly ten minutes of fighting.

Our ambush team had been caught right on the edge of the rocket attack area. They lost two people. Almost everyone else was injured in some way but still able to walk. As our team medic tended to the wounded, I went searching for the local six-man team. This local team had been the blocking force for the ambush.

What I found was terrible. The local team had been using an old cinderblock 2-story hardware store as cover. I approached the remains of the building which was little more than a debris pile now. The Huey had targeted the building on each attack run and scored at least six rocket hits from what I could see. There was rebar sticking out of broken block walls, body parts, hunks of flesh, and blood splatters strewn all over the place. None of the team had survived. I called my ambush team over and we picked through the gear lying around to make it a little less obvious that these were the remains of a well-armed militia team. I hoped there would be no significant evidence under the rubble that would point to our involvement, but there was no time to do anything about it now.

We had to leave town before the green shirts got there. We carried our own dead in some makeshift litters and headed north out of town. Along the way we ran into some curious townspeople that came to see what had happened. We strongly warned them to tell everyone they knew to leave the area immediately because we suspected a brutally harsh green shirt retaliation for anyone foolish enough to be caught in town. No one would be safe until the green shirts had cleared out. I apologized for the men they lost, but said they had died like true heroes for which no medal can adequately reward.

Our team quickly headed out of town and kept to the deepest thickest woods possible. As we traveled, we heard some heavy road traffic off in the distance along with some sporadic gunfire. One distinctive sound was a full auto .50 cal. letting loose. It was looking like my guess about the heavy duty weaponry had come true. I only hoped the people had kept out of town and the gunfire had been for the remaining gangers.

We traveled radio silent just in case the green shirt vehicles were equipped with radio direction equipment. Even though we had wounded people, I chose to take us the long way home. We must have walked 12 miles before crashing into one of the secure bunkers outside of our town almost 16 hours after the ambush. We wanted to make sure we had not been followed or tracked in any way even if police dogs were used. There was no way I was going to lead those green shirts back to my home town after this firefight.

Luckily, the Colonel posted some of our people on guard in every bunker waiting on our return. They fed us and took care of our wounded so the rest of us could sneak our way back home before we were missed. Our dead were buried with as much dignity as we could manage. They deserved a full 21 gun salute in my opinion, but we had to keep things quiet. We settled for a reverent grave side service.

I reported to the Colonel, and dragged myself home to sleep in my own bed. Green shirt convoys passed through our town all night, but they did not stop. It looked as though they considered our town a quiet community that had been pacified.

Chapter 19
Gangs and the Broken Prison System

Some days later the Colonel came to the sniper leadership meeting which consisted of me, Fred, and a couple of squad leaders I had appointed. We were working on some Intel maps that we kept updated from recon reports generated by my sniper team missions. We then used the maps to plan out new operations and allow other teams to get a picture of what was going on in our area. The same maps were then used by our raiding parties to plan routes in and out of town as well as planning the most likely targets for the much needed supplies.

The Colonel said, "Gentlemen I need to find out the status of the federal prison complex. I know this is not a small task but we have to get an idea on these gangs and where they are coming from. I need to know if the prisons have been compromised or of they are simply empty. I need to know so we can plan for our next move because it is becoming apparent that the green shirts are either directing the gangs or allowing them to operate out in the open. Your team is on the hook for this so get it done. Our logistics guys have two special vehicles for this mission, so follow me."

We all crawled from our bunker and came up into the barn. We immediately saw two Harley Davidson motorcycles, a 2006 Wide Glide and an older Road King parked in the straw.

"You mean these are our new toys?" Fred grinned as he ran his fingers on the seat.

Then it dawned on me.

"Now wait a minute, you want us to dress like a couple of gang members and sneak our way to the PRISON COMPLEX, don't you?"

The Colonel said calmly, "Yes I do. You guys are the only ones that can pull this off. My Intel people are tied up on some other important projects right now, and you guys can pass for bikers better than any of my people anyway. We tried to think of any other way to get this done, but we are coming up dry. The prison is over 15 miles away and there are no other options right now. This Road King is my personal bike and the other was donated for this mission. Please bring them back in one piece. Logistics has been lucky on gas procurement lately; so they have given you two full tanks to get there and back. Plan your mission and go on your own timetable. Report back when you are done." He left us looking around at each other not quite believing what we were hearing.

Holy crap, this is a nutty scheme. Could we get away with simply riding all the way there without getting stopped, hide out, observe the prison, and then somehow get back? Hmmm. Yeah sure if we were real lucky, I mean draw an inside straight kind of lucky. Let's do it today, why not?

First things first, these bikes are too clean because they have been sitting in garages for months. I told my guys to go out and dirty the bikes a bit, because bikers during that time rarely washed their rides. We needed the bikes to look the part as much as us. While they were off playing mud turtle with the Harleys, I worked with Fred to find a route that would get us to the prison with as few checkpoints as possible. We also had to scrounge some proper clothing for two of us to pass as hell-raising gang members. Our guys came up with some leather jackets and some chaps that made me worry we might look more like village people than thugs. The team came through in true scrounger fashion though, and in a couple of hours we were ready. The bikes were dirty and I looked like a leather-bound fruit cake as I asked who was going with me.

Everybody looked at me and said, "Huck, maybe you shouldn't go. You are the leader of the entire sniper unit and maybe you should stay here."

I was taken aback. "Guys, I cannot ask any one of you to do something as dangerous as this without me going."

So, who is going with me? To my surprise Fred volunteered by trying on the spare set of leather chaps and muttered something about this might be his last chance to ride a Harley. I told the sniper teams to go get a spotting scope, my field notebook, and a couple of camo nets. Another teammate handed us a couple of Smith and Wesson model 66s in .357 along with a few trinkets like pocket knives, lighters, and speed loaders with ammo. You never know when these might come in handy.

We stowed the gear on the bikes and headed out. We were far enough from town to navigate freely on the roads until an expected checkpoint lay ahead. Before we reached the checkpoint, we headed off road and skirted around through the trees in a roundabout way towards the main road. Harleys are not exactly off road vehicles and we had to pull each other out of muddy spots several times before we got to the big four lane road. Before long we edged our way onto the road and headed towards the prison. The first couple of miles were the worst. It seemed like every curve might hide some pending danger that would get us caught or get us shot. We stayed to the back roads, hoping to avoid any other traffic like green shirt cop cars or bikers that might be passing through. There was no way we could bluff our way through a checkpoint or even pass the slightest scrutiny just because we were wearing a full Harley store front. Our only hope was to stay hidden right out in the open without being questioned.

We cruised through back roads as fast as we dared; we knew our luck would only go so far. We saw only a few scattered people standing in their yards as we passed. The sight of us made people run into their houses and slam doors. By the time we reached the prison system I was enjoying the sunshine on my face and thrilled to be on such a nice motorcycle. This was almost like a pleasant drive in the country on a Sunday afternoon if we weren't in the middle of a communist takeover.

As we got about two miles from the prison complex, we blasted past our first green shirt checkpoint. The green shirts were blocking the road that dumped onto the one we were riding along but had not closed this portion of the road. They watched us pass by but we took notice that they gave us the "what the hell" stare as they watched us disappear down the road. Fred yelled out over the roar of the bikes and said he was pretty sure we would have company any minute. I agreed and pointed to a road that turned off to the left. We slowed and headed down the road at a slow pace looking for a place to hide the bikes. I had been down this road several times and knew there was a nursery off on the right which would be good for us since the prison was about a mile through the woods. When we turned into the nursery we saw a police cruiser pass by on the road we had just come from. It was too much coincidence for us, so we decided to hide the bikes here.

The nursery still had a bunch of trees and bushes growing in the beds but, the owner's house seemed to be vacant for quite some time. Fred went back to the driveway with a tree branch and covered our tire tracks. I started searching around the house and found the place to be empty. In fact it looked like it had not been lived in for some time, maybe months.

As Fred and I watched and waited, the cruiser came back and turned down our road. Oh crap these guys were looking for us. The cruiser passed the nursery slowly and continued down the road out of sight. Fred and I busted the back door open and stashed the bikes inside the kitchen. We watched the road with the spotting scope to make sure the green shirts were not lingering around and saw nothing. As we watched we did notice something unusual. We saw nobody, not a single person in their yard or in their garden. Nobody was in sight. You see, you normally see people outside doing laundry, hoeing the garden, gathering water, all that in this post-electricity era. In fact it is strange not to see at least one person on any given street.

Only a little freaked out, Fred and I prepared for the next phase of our mission. We wrapped up in the camo nets so we could pass through the woods undetected. Fred pulled out his compass and map then pointed the way for us. The trek was uneventful but we were also being careful to keep our movements slow and deliberate. After 45 minutes of stalking through the woods the trees began to clear. Dense hardwoods became thinner pines with very little underbrush for cover.

We found a place where we could lay halfway in a ditch and see the perimeter fencing of the prison. I set up my spotting scope, putting a bird's nest into the lens so as to keep the glass from reflecting sunlight. Fred was using his binos and mapping the area while quietly taking notes. From our vantage point I could see the fences were not damaged in any way. There were two fences covered in concertina wire, separated by a small vehicle roadway between. The complex was a series of huge white X-shaped buildings inside the perimeter fences. One square building seemed to be the warehouse/entrance to the whole place, because the fencing worked right up to either side of the building. There were cinderblock guard towers every 150 yards or so, and the place was crawling with guards.

In fact, the only strange thing we saw at first was the masses of blue tarps inside the fencing. Were they housing prisoners outside of the building in the open yard? It looked like a makeshift tent city of some sort. We watched as container trucks came in and out and the green shirts patrolled the perimeter. I cranked up the power of the spotting scope and looked at the people inside the wire. Fred snapped pictures through the scope as I scanned the area. I did not see what I was expecting.

Normally when you see a prison at recreation time, you see uniforms or T-shirts all the same color on all the inmates. I was not seeing that. I was seeing all different clothing and not just men in their twenties to thirties as I expected. I noticed women and men together as well as people a lot older than I expected to see in a prison. Just what the hell is going on here? Could this be a relief camp where they are housing people? As trucks came in I noticed a few people at the fence talking towards the green shirt guards passing by. The green shirt guard raised his hand, but I was so far away I could not see what he did. It was my guess that he pepper sprayed the people inside the fence based on the way they backed away.

We had not been there long as we noticed there was a patrol walking towards us in the wood-line not some 200 yards away. As I spotted the guards, Fred whispered Rin Tin Tin which meant they had a dog. We pulled back hating ourselves for not getting more info but we could not keep concealed from a dog. We crept back to the heaviest woods and took off towards the bikes. I was afraid the dog would pick up our scent and get us in real trouble. The further we got away the faster we ran. In the distance, I heard the dog bark and knew he was on our trail. We had to move and quickly! Fred and I dropped our camo netting and raced back to the nursery.

With sweat pouring out, I crashed through the kitchen door and pulled my bike out onto the back porch. Fred complained of a stitch in his side as he labored the second bike outside. Together we fired up the bikes, stowed our gear, and drove out of the driveway. We headed out of the area as fast as we could as we realized that we risked either the roadside checkpoint or the guards catching up to us at the nursery.

Fred and I gunned it passed the checkpoint, but the green shirts had evidently been on high alert for us. They took a few pot shots at us as we sped by. Their pistols scored a freak hit on Fred's engine. Smoke and oil were flying everywhere as his bike lost power and came to a grinding stop. I immediately spun around and blocked Fred from the green shirts running in our direction. I blasted six shots from my S&W in quick succession, not worrying about aiming but rather point shooting in their general direction. I must have made at least some impression on those boys, because it gave Fred enough time to hop onto the back of my bike. We spun the tires and threw gravel as we sped off towards home. I am pretty sure our hearts did not beat regularly again for an hour. Lucky for us it was getting dusk as we made our way home. Twice we avoided increased green shirt squad car patrols. They raced up and down the otherwise deserted highway looking for us. However, we were able to keep clear of them.

We made it home in the dark after leaving the remaining bike deserted in a dark part of the woods about a mile outside of town. Our gas tank was empty from all the extra riding it took to evade capture. We ended up walking the last part of the journey.

"Fred, you are going to tell the Colonel how you got his bike all shot up."

Fred looked at me grinning, "It was the green shirts that done it, Huck."

Upon arrival of the bunker we reported to the Colonel and passed along our information. Lucky for us Fred had snapped some photos through the spotting scope and we were able to hand them in for further analysis. We had limited computer ability to analyze pictures because we were using generators only when gas was available. So, it might be another few days before the Intel team could get anything from the digital camera. I was afraid that our report would be so incomplete that it would not be of much use. We found out otherwise.

I noticed Seven was in the operations bunker on some errand for the Intel group.

"How's the arm Seven?" I asked with a grin.

"It's not bad, Huck," she smiled then looked up from the table. She noticed my biker outfit and began to snicker, "Where's the policeman and the construction worker? Oh, oh, and the Indian?"

The whole bunker was dying in laughter. Fred overheard her comments and was lying on the floor laughing uncontrollably. I was giddy from the day's stress and said quickly, "They're at the Y.M.C.A." I framed the letters doing my best imitation of the old 1970s song. The place melted down for a full five minutes. We were all wiping tears after that one. Afterwards, I noticed Seven was smiling a lot around me. Hmm.

Chapter 20
Intelligence Group Makes a Discovery

We were finding it more and more difficult to operate our growing militia with the green shirt office right there in the middle of town. You see, we had to walk wherever we needed to go. If the green shirts saw you doing more than normal work in the fields, it got their attention. We were using the excuse of local migrant workers to hide the people coming from outside town, but we were worried the green shirts would get wise before long.

During militia meetings there were rumblings that we should take them out and rid our town of their nuisance. Our people knew our overall strength was well beyond what the green shirts could resist if we attacked. Our intelligence group saw things differently. Intel reported that they had successfully planted two people as temporary workers in the green shirt office over the last couple of weeks. The Intel group leader said it was proving very informative and to please give them more time to gather information. It turns out that our militia people were seeing reports of a sensitive nature and they needed more time to decipher what was going on. We agreed to hold back if we were getting vital information. Plus we were all aware that a full-out assault on the green shirt office would earn us some serious reprisals. The 1st militia last stand was still on our minds. We did not want to provoke what was sure to be a losing scenario.

The night of this meeting the Colonel called a leadership meeting in one of the remote bunker locations after everyone else had gone home for the night. Intrigued, all the department heads showed up in the bunker and lit the lamps. We sat around the table and poured some coffee, which was so rare that I knew we were in for a serious meeting. Our Colonel got up and thanked everyone for attending and said we had been gathered for a special information session that had to be kept secret for the time being. This was unusual for the militia, because our normal practice was to inform everyone of as much information as possible. We risked information leaking out sometimes, but we valued our team's opinions because it was their butt on the line as much as ours. We had to garner trust, and you cannot do that by keeping secrets from your people.

The Intel team leader got up with a grim look on his face and spoke.

"This meeting is classified for now. I realize we will have to tell our teams at some point, but not yet. As we mentioned in the meeting earlier, our Intel organization has infiltrated the local green shirt office, and I have some information to pass along. Our operatives have read some reports that the green shirts have been compiling since they showed up in town about two weeks ago. Please keep in mind that the green shirts did not have this information sitting on their desks and that should let you know how far our people are going to get this information."

"The first report was pretty much what we expected. The green shirts have maps of town as well as the surrounding farmlands. They have identified the buildings that would serve "the people's purposes" which means they plan on seizing these places for their offices or whatever. This is not new since they closed the school buildings, took over the fire station, library, and so on."

"However, we did discover that there are calculations on the farming capacity of this area, what is planted, and the expected dates of each crop's harvest. The farms are highlighted as people's property as well."

That really got our attention. We all exchanged nervous looks at one another. The green shirts were planning on seizing our harvest. They were just waiting for us to grow the crops and work the fields so they would swoop in and claim the fields as public property.

The Intel leader continued. "Gentlemen you have not heard the worst yet. Another report was a detailed census of the population that included information on the number of farm workers available, the expected work capacity of the community, as well as the resulting "SURPLUS POPULATION". It turns out that they estimate 50-60 people are not physically able to contribute in any meaningful way to the production of our crops. It seems the green shirts are making a list of people from our make-shift hospital records in order to find those people with major illnesses. Everyone that was being treated by our EMTs is on the surplus population list."

You could hear a pin drop in that bunker. The only sound was the wick of the oil lamp as it hissed slightly under the burning flame. After several long moments of incredulous looks, we tried to get a handle on what it all meant.

The Colonel spoke to us in such a way that it made us all pay close attention.

"Gentlemen those of you who have studied history will know that this is nothing new. Every communist takeover in history has followed the path that we are on now. The communists take public office and use the authority of those offices to control the machine of government. They now control what is left of the US Military and Police forces which we have respected all our lives. The green shirts knew the leadership of the police departments would follow the direction of civilian government as long as it looked like laws, no matter how absurd, were coming from legitimate governmental sources. They also knew the public's willingness to take orders from the police when supplemented with dire need of food supplies and medicines, would ensure the people's ultimate submission to communism."

"That is why we had a complete news blackout before the power went out back in the spring. The green shirts knew that information had to be controlled and if there is no way to control it, you must shut it down. The power had to be shut off and the only way to do it was through the oil embargo. If the oil starts flowing again and the power comes back on, we will have nothing but Peoples Party Revolution TV and radio from then on. They will want to control every resource like water and food stores so that the people are directly dependent on the green shirts for their survival."

"I will bet the gangs we have seen are released prisoners that have been contracted to redistribute the wealth and we will see these stolen items being handed out like rewards to good and faithful servants of the state. That is why we saw the National Guard Depot full of truck containers with high-end stolen goods. This is often how communists work. The ruling classes don't want to get their hands dirty working in the fields or seen to be outright stealing. That would undermine their authority. They sponsor other groups covertly to get the nasty business done. The green shirts have most likely used ex-prisoners and drug lords to steal and plunder from town to town so as to give the green shirts as much plausible deniability as possible. However, I will bet that once the gangs do their jobs, they will no longer be necessary. The green shirts themselves will purge the gangs. We have already seen the beginning of this process."

"Our worst fears have now been realized, as we have discovered their intention to reduce the population. Population reduction has happened every time communists take over. Stalin in the Soviet Union killed about 65 million and Pol Pot of Cambodia killed about two million of their own people last century. After Huck's recon, we got an idea of what is going on and where. The pictures Fred took reveal that everyday citizens are being housed in the former federal prison system. The photos also show something none of us dared dream. These are bulldozers digging giant trench systems behind the prisons. We cannot see any use for these trenches other than mass graves."

"The green shirts are here for real and we have to stop them. Ultimately we have to reverse our state government at such a time when we can mass our forces with the other militias and throw out all these green shirts. Maybe we can coordinate the timing with other militias in other states and see if we can reverse what is happening to our country."

The Colonel continued as we listened intently. "We have to get a lot of our teams trained as soon as possible. We must also get some supplies, so we have to step up our scrounging. We need to have more gear than we can handle because we are bound to have some stuff discovered at some point. We have to be able to maintain a fighting force even if some of our gear is discovered. And if we can, I want to blame as much of our mayhem on the gangs themselves. If we can get the green shirts to mistrust the gangs, then we may have an opportunity to get them fighting earlier than we expect. We will let our people know all this when we have a solid plan of action. I want them to keep focused and not get themselves killed trying to exact revenge before we are ready. Remember the 1st militia."

"Now let's get started making this militia into a real army. We need new recruits, and we need to start coordinating with other militias as much as possible."

That speech was why he was Colonel. I didn't think I could ever do his job.

Chapter 21
Coordination with other Militias

New Recruits were needed from our whole area of influence. Who can you trust? I mean how do you know if someone is really dedicated to your cause or just a spy trying to sell you out to the green shirts? There were food rewards for any information on illegal gatherings or other organizations not authorized by the state. Militias were absolutely on the top of the list of undesirables. Luckily we were diligent to identify traitors through a series of investigations and references from people we could trust. We had a few traitors and a few loose tongues, but for the most part the militias themselves did a pretty good job of weeding out the potentially dangerous people.

We also weeded out the psychos. Anyone that had a serious screw loose like neo-Nazi types or anarchist groups was not allowed to be part of the militia. Those groups did not have the best interest of all the people in mind and we were not about to be associated with hate groups of any kind. You cannot trust people like that, and we operated solely on each other's trust to keep safe in the field. I would rather have those psycho groups join the green shirts and let us openly fight them. I wanted no part of their ilk. There were a few of those guys in our area, but for the most part it was rare to mess with them. Those types usually got themselves killed by the green shirts early on anyway. They were few and far between nowadays. We wanted people who were dedicated to freedom and liberty unique to the American experience. No nut-jobs, thanks.

We were careful with our local Ham radio operators now that the green shirts had the equipment to track radio transmitters. There was no way to code the messages or use a crypto cipher the feds could not break. So we had to assign meanings to otherwise common phrases. We used a simple hard copy book to share between groups that detailed the meanings of each message. I am reminded of the old WWII messages like "*John had a long mustache.*" Each message had a meaning to someone listening as well as some gibberish thrown in just to make it confusing for the people trying to decipher our code method.

By the end of the summer we had established communication with the 2nd and 4th militias, as well as the newly formed 5th group. Usually a sniper or Intel person would make contact with their militia and pass along a code book after we established a working relationship with their leadership. This was the only way to set up a dialog without phones or internet in the post-electricity era. The Ham radio operators would broadcast messages on a regular cycle during a rotating schedule. We could get several massages received and sent at each designated broadcast time without too much trouble. The trick was to keep it real brief in order to keep the radio direction equipment from locating your position. Even then the radios needed to be mobile and never broadcast from the same place twice.

Some of the first stories shared by groups concerned the 1st militia and their defeat in Pittsboro. 1st militia had been so badly mauled that they were no longer large enough to operate more than a single squad. We kept their insignia and number off the books and used them as a reminder. Never take on more than you could chew. "Remember the 1st" became a popular motto.

Once we got through to the trusted leadership of each militia, we passed on the information we discovered about the surplus population efforts and the diabolical uses of the prison system. Everyone took notice of the astonishing information. A few of the other militia leadership were skeptical of our findings. Still more admitted that the information they had collected, pointed to a mass detention effort underway, but there were few details. Now things were making sense as everyone had suspected the gangs were either ex-prisoners or drug cartel affiliated.

The 2nd militia shared a bit of information that we expected but had not been able to confirm. It looked like the green shirts were using the mental health facilities as re-education camps. The actual mentally-ill patients were transferred to the prisons. The 2nd militia also confirmed that the arrested ministers and preachers had been sent to the re-education facilities. If someone did not respond to re-education, then it meant expulsion to the prisons. We knew there had to be re-education camps, but we did not know where. The Dorothea Dix mental health campus was on the other side of Raleigh, so it was really far for us to investigate personally. But we trusted the information, because it made sense based on everything we had seen from the green shirts to date. This kind of news did not brighten our day, but it did confirm that others were experiencing the same problems we were, and we were not alone.

It also seemed that the Muslims were somehow immune to this persecution. The Mosques all seemed to be open, and none of their Imams seemed to be rounded up. We guessed that the green shirts were upholding some agreement with the oil barons in the Middle East by giving their brethren in the U.S. a free pass.

After some meeting among militia leadership we split up militia coverage into territories. 3rd Militia was responsible for the North Central piedmont region above I-40 and west of Raleigh. 2nd militia was everything east of Raleigh. 1st militia had been responsible for the south and west of Raleigh below I-40 so after their downfall, the 5th militia was assigned their territory. The 4th was everything west of and including Winston-Salem down to Charlotte. Of course that was a monstrously huge territory, but they would just have to make do until more people came forward to help or other resources became available.

Charlotte did not have a resistance as far as we knew. A lot of the bigger cities simply were in so much chaos after the initial power outages that we feared the mass populations were displaced or otherwise eradicated. Think about it, once the power goes out and the food stops coming in, the people have to leave the cities just to survive. When the gas in your car ran out, you had better be in a place that can shelter, feed, and provide you with fresh water, otherwise you are toast. Those big city types were in real trouble. We figured that is why we did not hear from those areas much. As far as territory goes, that left the Western part of the state, past Winston-Salem and West, a relatively free area. The green shirts had a few offices, but they were definitely not there in force.

As new militia groups came online, we would give them their own territory but at this time there were no specific efforts for us to start new groups outside our own zones. We simply could not travel in force without fuel. All recruiting had to be local within our region until such a time when either the power came back on or fuel started flowing again. In the mean time we worked on our lines of communication and waited until our numbers and resources got to the point where we could mount a counter-revolution.

Chapter 22
Search for Our Missing Townspeople

That whole issue of missing people was more than a little difficult for us to cope with as we grew stronger over the summer. You see, when we realized the extent of the re-education camps for ministers and the sheer number of prisons spread throughout the state, the problem was too big for us. Even if we had the strength of arms to free everyone, we had no way to hide or feed the thousands of people. And by no means did we have the volunteers trained or armed well enough to start freeing an entire prison full of people. Heck, even if the doors flew open by themselves, we had no transportation to get all the people back to our town. Even if we did have food and rooms for them all, there was no way to hide everyone. That meant if we were to get our people back, we must focus only on our own folks and nobody else. We decided to make a go of it and see if we could somehow find our people and bring them home.

After a couple of secret meetings with the Colonel, he instructed me to form a new covert team of people with the purpose of carrying out clandestine missions. Even among the militia this would be a secret group of people comprised of specialists from the sniper squads and the intelligence operators. This team would be dedicated to our most difficult covert tasks which called for complete secrecy and sheer nerve. I called the team "Batjack" for one of the greatest film heroes of all time, John Wayne. You see, John Wayne was a devout anti-communist, and he co-founded the Batjack Production Film Company. It seemed a cool name to me, and very few would associate the team names even if they heard it in plain conversation.

I choose my three best snipers with a knack for gathering intelligence for the team. These guys always came back with loads of information that was both useful and pertinent. When you mixed the sniper's ability to sneak and peek, then blend in like you were born in that town, it took special people to make it work. I interviewed each person individually and told them I was forming a new team that would be covert in nature and was high-risk at best. To their credit, each one of them volunteered before I could ask.

The Colonel sent me three Intel gurus that were his best. And boy, let me tell you, they were good. Our 3rd militia Intel people could have been CIA or OSS or some other alphabet soup, because they were slick as eel snot. I mean, they could lay false trails, think unconventionally, and dig for information like nobody else. Two of these were the ones working in our local green shirt office already. They were brave as all get-out, and I hated pulling them from our regular units because they were so good. But we needed the best if we were to succeed. I was secretly looking for Seven, but she was not chosen.

I even snuck procurement requests through the sniper squads just to make sure our efforts were masked even from within other parts of the militia. I wanted a team so good that we could infiltrate the ranks of the green shirts and do some real spy versus spy crap. It would take it to get our people back. Once we got the team assembled, we started planning and training for our first mission.

On the first meeting of Batjack, I chose a new meeting hide that none of us had ever used before. In fact it was such a new hide, it was not even known by the regular units as a militia bunker. We had no signal code to meet like other teams did. Our only signal to meet would be from others in our team by word of mouth or through a set code word, "lustrum". Lustrum in the olden days meant five years. I knew it from a John Wayne movie, "True Grit." In fact, the six people in Batjack were code named from that movie to keep their identity a mystery, Rooster, Mattie, Le' Beef turned into just "Beef", Cheney, Pepper, and Moon. The team reported to me, but the Colonel forbade me to go operational with them. He wanted me to command the team, assign their missions and provide support, but absolutely forbade me to go on missions. I said okay, but I didn't like it much. I was used to going along and getting dirty like everyone else.

More volunteers were recruited every day. This meant a larger effort for those of us in leadership roles. As men came into our ranks, the more they needed support in training and direction. I was more of an operations person at this time and had maybe 25 active sniper/recon people with another 10-12 in training. We were growing pretty fast, and they needed me to serve as the sniper team leader for quite some time to come. No matter how you cut it, I was not going to be allowed to lead Batjack.

At Batjack's first meeting I gave the team the information we discovered. I told them about the prisons, the gangs, and the newly discovered plan to label people "surplus population". Most of the people had already guessed at bits of what I told them, but not all of it together. Some were shocked and others took it in stride. I had to make sure they realized that Batjack would be completely covert and all of our information had to stay inside our team until we released it to the rest of the militia. I laid out our mission to find and rescue our minister as well as the others that had been arrested. That woke them up.

"Wow, how are we going to do that?" came the first question from one of my snipers.

"That is what you are going to figure out, Rooster. I named you Rooster after the John Wayne character for a reason. You are in charge of the team."

Rooster looked petrified, but only briefly.

"This team's first mission is to come up with a plan to find our people and bring them back. You get mean, you get dirty, and you stay so sneaky that those damn green shirts don't even know you were there. Tell me what you need and we will see if we can get it for you. Questions?"

The team knew they had a green light to do whatever it took, and I liked to give my teams as much leeway as possible. Give people direction and mission and let them figure out how to accomplish the job. It is their neck on the line and I wanted to foster some leadership qualities in the team leader, Rooster. He was a good man in the sniper teams and I knew he would lead this team back to safety if at all possible.

It was about two weeks before Batjack came to me with an operational plan. We met to hash out the details and got going on the items they needed for the mission. First things first, the green shirts were not big on records so that made finding the location of our people more of an educated guess. Most of the reports pointed toward the prison Fred and I visited as the most likely place our security people and townspeople had been sent. Our minister was most likely sent to a mental hospital somewhere east of Raleigh for re-education. There seemed to be no way to find out exactly where. Without knowing his location, the only remaining option was to go for the people in our area. Our minister was not forgotten, but we would have to wait until we had enough information to mount his rescue.

The team decided that the only way to gain access to the prison was to sneak in as green shirts and try to bluff their way through. However that wasn't the scariest part. Rooster suggested that one person from the team get himself arrested to see if we could find our people from the inside. We knew the prison housed hundreds, if not thousands, so it was the only way we could stack the deck in our favor. With someone on the inside we could have the best chance of finding our people and getting them ready to move. This was tricky, but it seemed like the best plan for getting our mission accomplished.

Here was the plan. Batjack would use three green shirt uniforms and a squad car "borrowed" from our lovely green shirt office in town. Rooster, in true leader fashion, volunteered himself to be the prisoner, while Mattie, Cheney, and Moon posed as the green shirt goon squad. On the first night, Rooster would be ruffed up and transported to the prison by Mattie, Cheney, and Moon. 3rd militia would provide some cover in the way of a town emergency for the local green shirt office and buy the team some time. Once Rooster was delivered, the others would return the squad car back to town and make everything look like nothing was ever out of place. Rooster was to have 72 hours to find everyone and get them ready for transport. Our list of names was 23 strong, which meant we needed a bus or something to get everyone out.

Transportation was a serious problem for that many people. Our solution was simple enough though. We had the 3rd logistics guys grab a school bus, paint it green and print PPR logo and insignia on the side. Mattie, Cheney, and Moon would drop off Pepper and Beef as sniper overwatch outside the perimeter in case there was trouble. The bus would continue to the prison arriving right at 72 hours after drop-off to request the list of people to be handed over for transfer to the Dorothea Dix complex. We even had a letterhead with some official looking seal ready to serve as an official document with the name of some official we were sure was green shirt affiliated. Once out of the prison, the bus would pick up the sniper team and take back roads towards my friend's cabin way up north of us. Batjack would get rid of the bus, and we would have time to disperse everyone and get them home as safely as possible. That was the plan anyway.

You see we had learned a lot over the last few months, but this was a high risk operation, and there were any number of ways it could go wrong; and it did. Horribly wrong. The first part of the operation worked very well. Our local Intel guys worked out an elaborate hoax for the local green shirt office to "handle" as an emergency in town. I don't know all the details, but it lasted so long that the green shirt office was empty most of the night.

The team picked up the cruiser and was gone for maybe two hours. I watched the cruiser return with Mattie, Cheney, and Moon right on schedule. Their looks told me that they had successfully dropped off Rooster and had everything in motion.

For the next three days we waited for the opportunity to hatch the second phase of our plan. We had been so lucky in the past that it was difficult to imagine things not going our way. Our plans were good; our people were cunning and brave. But sometimes the fortunes of war do not shine upon you.

It was about 9 p.m. when Batjack headed out to the hiding place where the logistics team had stored the freshly painted school bus. I watched the bus leave out of town from my house and waited anxiously. After about three hours, I worked my way to the communications bunker where we listened to radio reports. We did not transmit from there because the green shirts could track radio transmissions. This place was just a listening post. My friend up north was scheduled to radio us at this time and I wanted to hear how the operation went. The Colonel was there with one of our radio guys, but nobody else. This was still a covert mission and was classified.

The radio came to life with the familiar voice of my friend's wife, but the message was not what we hoped for. I don't remember the actual phrase we used, but the meaning was simple. "No news from the team to report." That happens in warfare though. I didn't sweat it too much. You always have to expect the unexpected. There are almost always delays. The next scheduled broadcast would be in six hours; we would find out then.

I lay in bed, wondering what had happened to the team. I had been late several times as I made my way back from missions. I knew I had scared my teammates to death when I didn't come back on schedule. But this time was different; I sent that team out. I was in charge of them. I was responsible for them. Six long, sleepless, agonizing hours passed. Again, I returned to the bunker waiting to hear the news. However it was the same message as before. No news. CRAP! Where were they? They did not need to be driving that school bus in daylight. The checkpoints might have gotten them or maybe gang raids blocked their escape routes. Everything scenario went through my mind.

Twenty four hours past due, there was still no word. Forty eight hours passed due, nothing. Seventy two hours past due we started to plan sniper recon teams to head in that direction and see what we could find. We knew a 15 mile trek all the way to the prison was unrealistic. The Colonel approved outbound teams to see what they could find anyway. I just forgot to mention that I had planned to go on this mission and was planning on riding the Harley again dressed like a biker. I grabbed an S&W model 66, a GMRS walkie-talkie, my biker outfit, some gas in a plastic can, and then headed for the Harley.

I reached the Harley at nightfall and fired up the bike in search of my team. There was no intelligence information to go from, and it had been three days since anyone had heard from Batjack. I throttled up and pressed the Harley for speed. Lucky for me the bike had been left in an area past the green shirt checkpoint near the four-lane road. This meant I did not have to try to get around the checkpoint through the woods in the dark. That would have been nearly impossible. The road was clear for the most part, and I passed only a couple of vehicles off in the distance. I guessed these were most likely gang bikes, so I steered clear of them. As I approached the prison area, this as near the checkpoint where Fred almost got his ticket punched. I rounded the corner cautiously; thank God I did.

The whole road was blocked by the green shirt security forces. There was no way to get through without passing about a half dozen armed men. I braked hard and spun the tires to get out of range as the green shirts popped off round after round at me. They were serious about keeping everyone out of there. I could see lights from police cruisers which that meant I was in for a chase. I pushed the bike hard and jammed the throttle wide open. The night air was cool for summer, and I was sure I ate about three bugs while zooming down the road. The squad cars were quickly closing the distance between us, so I had to come up with something quick. Bikes can go places cars can't, so I used that to my advantage. The trick is to find that place and make the best use of it without wrecking. I knew not to head towards my town. I could not lead them back to my home no matter what. Instead, I headed north so that I could be within a few miles of my friend's farm if I had to end up walking.

About three miles from the farm, I went off-road towards the train tracks I knew to be about a half mile through the woods. To the squad car's credit, he followed me pretty close as we zoomed down deserted dirt roads. As we neared the tracks, a large ditch kept the car from pursuing me further. After several shots in frustration, the squad car gave up and left. I sat on the bike's seat to watch the car head back towards the main road. They most likely thought I was a renegade biker, and warranted no more effort.

I decided to wait until dawn then try to make it to my friend's farm. Hopefully the back roads would be open by then. In the meantime, I made myself a little nest under some evergreens and rested until the next morning. Let's just say, it was not a restful night. My walkie-talkie crackled me awake sometime near dawn. The voice was instantly recognizable. It was the Colonel calling me. I responded and waited for him to start a string of curses, but they did not come. He used the code words I had been waiting for. There was news from Batjack. I had to make it to the northern command as soon as possible.

"Roger that!" I responded in plain English. There was no time for coding.

Chapter 23
Batjack Report

My friend's farm, where I got the Barrett, was close, so I made it there quickly. I radioed to let them know I was coming and what to expect with me on a Harley in biker outfit. I was betting that my friend would give me all sorts of ribbing over this one. But my mind was preoccupied on the team, and my questions on the mission ripped at my insides. At the farm and was greeted by a militia member with a long-rifle on security duty. He cleared me and directed me to the cabin along the old logging road. As I stepped off the bike, another camo dressed militia man took the bike and directed me inside. There had been some raids nearby and the place was dangerous to be standing around in the open. He said he would hide the Harley in the barn and see what he could do about gas. I left him to it and went inside. The house had a dozen or so people inside working on various things like maps and radios, and everything else in a typical operations hut.

One guy pointed me to the upstairs and said, "They're up there; go on up."

As I got to the top of the stairs my friend greeted me and ushered me to a couple of cots in the old bedroom area. There on the bed lay Rooster and Pepper being attended to by a half dozen militia EMTs.

"They just got here forty five minutes ago. Our medics are working on them now," Bullet told me.

Rooster looked like he had been fighting a Grizzly bear, and Pepper looked like he had just finished the Boston marathon for the second time, but not injured outwardly. After several minutes, the medics granted me a few seconds to talk with Pepper. Rooster was unconscious, but he looked stable for the time being.

"Pepper, what happened?" I asked with more than a little concern.

"They got us good this time, sir. Everyone else is gone. Dead, I mean. "

"How Pepper? What happened?"

Pepper looked up at me with pain visible in his face. To his credit, he took a few seconds trying hard to not blurt out his first thoughts, "Well, Beef and I dropped off right on plan. We went from the nursery through the woods just like Fred laid told us. Then we set up the overwatch position where we could see the prison entrance doors, gates and so forth. Our bus was already parked in the parking lot. It looked like everyone was inside already. We saw Rooster come out under the lights escorted by Moon as they loaded onto the bus. That's when it all went bad. Muffled sounds of gunfire came from inside the main building while the whole parking lot erupted in machine gun fire. We saw Rooster came scooting out of the rear emergency door and headed towards the woods. But that bus was hammered by the guard tower. They must have had a M240 or heavy weapon, because they tore the bus apart. You could see light shining through form the other side as the gun blasted it to bits. It was terrible. Moon provided cover fire for Rooster, but he was likely cut down right away. Mattie and Cheney never came out; they must have got it inside. Rooster ran our way as we started nailing the tower guards. The whole place was coming alive with goons. There was no way we could handle them all. Rooster made it to our position, but we could see that he had been hit by a lot of shrapnel from the bus. He was not what you would call in good shape to begin with either. He must have had it pretty rough inside sir."

"What happened to Beef?" I asked.

"We got Rooster back to the nursery knowing we were going to have to get out quickly then hike our way to the rendezvous point. Once we got him patched up a little, we started to move out. A green shirt squad car came down the road and caught us crossing the hard top right out in the open. Beef let them have with his M-4, but one of them must have gotten off a lucky last shot which hit him right in the head. There was nothing I could do for Beef with Rooster torn up so bad. I grabbed the carbine and we started our way back. It took us three whole days and nights to get here. Rooster was out of it most of the time due to blood loss, so I was not able to get much out of him. It was all we could do to keep one step ahead of them, sir. We pulled every trick in the book to sneak past those green shirt devils until we ended up at this farm."

I told Pepper that he had done a great job and would create a medal for him if one did not exist already. He smiled, but I knew he would trade any medal for the team back.

Rooster was alive, but it would be some time before he could talk. I took that time to update my friend on what was going on around the militia movement. He also gave me some news about how their numbers were growing and how the information I provided him was a great help getting all the new people organized. I could see that things were really shaping up for this northern arm of 3rd militia. I promoted my friend to team leader directly reporting to my Colonel. We took the rest of the day resting and passing along information. I contacted the Colonel and told him I would come back in a day or two. He didn't even scold me or anything.

Rooster slept the rest of that day, and by the next morning, showed signs of recovery. The medics said it was a miracle he did not bleed out during the 12 mile escape and evasion from the prison complex. They credited his survival to Pepper who kept him alert and patched up throughout the ordeal. Pepper's diligence made all the difference.

I sat next to Rooster and asked if he felt ready to talk. He looked at me with even more emotion than Pepper. He said he could talk, but I could see it was a strain on him.

"Sir, things are worse than we imagined," he started. His face was distorted with emotion.

"Start from the beginning," I told him quietly with as much clam as I could muster. Inside, I could hardly wait to hear what happened in the prison.

"The team dropped me off at the prison just as we planned. Mattie was great. She had those guys believing she was some heavy hitter from Raleigh working for one of the green shirt offices. She even prepped them to know she would be picking up people in a few days for transport to another location. This seemed to surprise them a little, but what could she do at the time? She had to keep her story consistent, or else run the risk of tipping her hand. The green shirts put me inside one of the prison's wings and just let me walk around without putting me in a cell. I expected some sort of processing or paperwork, but there was none. They just threw me in one wing of the place and that was it. I had never seen the inside of a prison before, other than TV shows, but I was pretty sure this was different. The cells were open to the whole block of the complex. The central building was closed off. You could not pass from wing to wing."

"My first thought was to find our people and set up our escape right away. I went from cell to cell looking for anyone on the list, but all I could find were people from other towns. Nobody knew our folks at all. And sir, these folks are not criminals or anything like it. These were business owners, newspaper writers, and teachers, common everyday folks. Sometimes there would be whole families in cells, but I could not find our people anywhere."

"On the second day, I asked the others how things worked around there, and if anyone from our town was nearby. The problem was that nobody knew anything about the place. Everyone in my wing had just arrived the day before. The outside yards, with the blue tarps, are the first stop for all inmates coming in on busses. On the second day, the guards send you to one of the four wings in the complex where you are housed. You cannot see into the other wings for the most part; other than people passing from one block to the next. There was a limited water supply in the building, and the power was on just enough to shine a few lights at night. Otherwise, the place looked more like a warehouse than a jail. Forty eight hours in, I recruited some other inmates to study the prison guards to find out how they operated on a daily basis. We watched and noted their movements, but none of it made sense. During the day, busses loaded with prisoners came in every few hours, filling the yard. The night of the second day, we heard a series of doors open and we looked through the cracks. The wing, across from ours, emptied prisoners into the adjacent building."

"The connecting building is the only structure that connects the prison to the support buildings. It looked like every single person and their luggage was being herded out towards the rear buildings where we suspected food services to be. Not that they served much food. I only saw soup served twice during my three day stay. Anyway, the prisoners were taking suitcases, and what looked like everything they owned with them. Evidently, they had lots of stuff with them in the prison. We watched for quite some time as they were all marched down the corridor towards the rear of the complex. I noticed a little girl that looked about 10 years old with her yellow fuzzy boots that kids wear nowadays."

Rooster broke down sobbing like no man I had ever seen before.

"Son, what is it?" I asked. "What did you see?"

When he was able, he continued.

"We watched them for maybe a half an hour, but it was really hard for us to see things clearly from our detention wing. You see, we were closer to the loading dock buildings where the container trucks were located. The food services were further back on the other side. That's when I noticed it. One of the container trucks had backed up, but not all the way, leaving a gap between the building and truck. There were green shirts loading those big cardboard boxes on pallet jacks and one of them tipped sideways as it was being loaded. I saw those yellow boots stacked on a massive pile of shoes and luggage. It was then that I realized the truck was labeled, "RECYCLING".

"That was not the first place I saw it either. Mattie and Cheney brought me in through the main office entrance. On the counter, I saw a sign that said Department of Resource Management "RECYCLING CENTER." Then it all dawned on me all at once, sir. The weird numbers on the detention wings, nobody having been there for any amount of time and people coming in every hour, never any busses leaving with prisoners, everything became clear in an instant. The numbers on the detention wings were dates. Each wing was a different day about 5 days in advance from the arrival of the occupants. They were moving people from the yard and marking the wing with a date. On the wing's date they shipped the people out back for recycling of their possessions. I saw all of it loaded on the truck out back. The busses left EMPTY EVERY DAY! THE PRISONERS DON'T COME BACK AND THEIR WING IS FILLED THE NEXT DAY!"

Rooster was on the verge of passing out from his wounded and weak condition. "I don't know how they are doing it, sir, but those people are gone, they're dead. They go out back and they don't come back. The bulldozers can be heard running all day, every day. There's no construction going on, no materials for buildings. The green shirt guards don't even patrol out back while the prisoners are ushered through the door. That's why all the houses are empty for a mile from the prison. They don't want anyone to see what's going on behind the prison!"

"It's a modern day Auschwitz!"

I sat there stunned as Rooster passed out from exhaustion. He was only able to recover long enough to give a brief encounter how the green shirts had called our team's bluff on the attempted pickup. It seemed that the Department of Resource's chief of staff was visiting from

Raleigh that very day. Word of Rooster's unusual arrival alerted the green shirts that we were trying to pull a fast one and they suspected militia activity. Secondly, no prisoner ever left the facility, and that is something we just had not anticipated in our wildest dreams. When our team arrived, they were outgunned and outnumbered. It was likely that the green shirt guards let Rooster out the front door just to see how far they could play our people for information. I imagined that they intended to shoot them all as they boarded our stolen school bus. We don't know what happened to Mattie and Cheney inside that office, but I bet they took out a bunch of green shirts before they were killed. It was the accurate covering fire of Beef and Pepper that made Rooster's escape possible. The rest we knew from Pepper.

We sat stunned in disbelief, not knowing what to say. We knew the green shirts were in with the gangs. We knew they were serious about a communist form of government, but all that seemed light and airy when you compare it to mass executions. Never fail to realize that every communist takeover results in a reduction of the surplus population. What do you say when it is happening to you in your sleepy little town in America? We sat for the longest time struggling to find words appropriate for the situation. There were none.

Chapter 24
Things Got Worse

Late in the day, after Rooster gave us his story, we tried to make contact with 3rd militia leadership and speak to the Colonel. Unfortunately we were not able to raise him on the radio. That made us all even more apprehensive. I decided to head back to town and take Pepper home when night fell. I knew I had to get back and share this new information with our group as well as with the other militias. This had to happen as soon as possible. Rooster would have to stay with the Northern Command, as I liked to call them, until his wounds healed a bit more. The Harley was loaded while we told everyone to keep themselves safe. I codenamed my friend "Bullet" after Steve McQueen's famous movie and his fondness for firearms. I told Bullet to get his people ready to fight and to train as many as he could. We would need all the people we could get in order to fight these green shirts.

I was determined to stay hidden on our return trip, but in the back of my mind I wanted to start hunting green shirts a soon as possible. Lucky for us, I was able to avoid most everybody during our trip home. There was more traffic on the main roads than I had seen since the power went out. Someone was getting more fuel into the country or things were getting better in the distribution of remaining gas. Either way we actually had to avoid squad cars and green shirt scooters on the road three times during our ride. It took hours to get back, but we arrived safely just outside the farm where the main sniper bunker was located. We parked the Harley in an old tobacco barn to camouflage it in hopes we could use it again in the future. We walked the last half mile feeling like we were in our own backyards in the cool summer night. We felt at ease so close to home as we strolled casually down the logging road.

Just as I walked down the last bend before the field's entrance, a bush said, "Huck?"

It was Gunny's voice coming from what looked like a small squat evergreen bush. Pepper and I both stopped dead in our tracks. We scanned the area, personally hating ourselves for not seeing the clump of leaves on the other side of the bush before now. Gunny was decked out in his ghillie suit watching the field in the darkness. Even 10 feet from where he lay, we could barely make out the silhouette of his rifle and his body. Pepper and I stood frozen knowing only that we were in trouble.

We heard Gunny speak ever so slowly, "You better rethink going down there unless you intend to sign up as a green shirt."

Still standing in place I looked up the field towards the barn where our bunker was hidden. Oh crap! There must be 20 green shirts with flashlights not 200 yards away, going over the field and barn with a fine toothed comb. These guys were well armed and definitely looking for something. Here I was standing like a biker totem pole with Pepper frozen beside me in awe of what we almost walked into. We slowly leaned over, bent down onto our knees, and then onto our bellies trying NOT to make any sudden movements. I asked Gunny what the hell was going on in a hushed voice.

"It looks to me like the green shirts have come into town in force", Gunny whispered. "I barely made it out with my gear before they arrived."

"Did they blow the bridge?" I asked.

"Nope, must have been a dud or else somebody didn't blow it for some reason. I don't know which. Most of us were not on duty tonight, so I hope the others got the warning to bug out. Glad you're back, I am not sure if the Colonel got away."

I asked Gunny if the trigger had been set on our bunker.

"If they open the door, the place will go up in their face and we will be picking elbows and toenails out of our hair," Gunny assured me.

"Gunny, we need to pull back and see what was going on in town." We all slid back away from the field and slowly made our way to deep cover and a stash of weapons that we kept tucked away from the bunker.

Armed with an M-4 and an assault vest full of ammo, Pepper and I followed Gunny towards town. We found town under total green shirt control as lights from squad cars and vans littered the street. People were standing in front of the fire station as if in a concert looking at a small stage. This gathering had to be mandatory because EVERYONE in town was there. Some were half dressed or in bed clothes as they must have been pulled from their houses at this late hour. A green shirt was checking ID cards against what looked to be a sheaf of papers that had to be a town roster.

After several minutes of observation from a safe distance, we noticed a few things. There were no busses. They were not here for arrests. Second, these new green shirts were not the normal goofy 20-somethings with long hair and too much college education. These guys were serious and they were in town for business. The local green shirts seemed to look upon these new guys with a mixture of fear or reverence, but I could not tell which from my scope in the darkness. What I saw from these new green shirts was a body language that suggested authority with unmistakable aggression.

Gunny, Pepper, and I had set up about 200 yards from the fire station around an empty house. The surrounding bushes provided several discrete observation points allowing us to stay concealed. Gunny and I watched the crowd as Pepper watched our rear. We didn't want green shirt units to catch us by surprise. As I watched this "town meeting" I could just make out a few words every now and again, but it was not necessary to hear the words. The town was being told what to do and how to do it. I looked for Seven, but I didn't see her anywhere. I think it was right then and there that I decided to ask her for a date when I got the chance. After all we had learned over the last few days, I was scared to death I might not find her safe. But I had no idea where she was. The idea of a date seemed strange. Movies were out, dinner in a restaurant was out, what do you do? Goodness, the weird things you think of when under so much stress.

Just as I wondered how long the green shirts would continue this nonsense, the green shirt speaker got louder and louder as he shouted to the crowd. The townspeople were deathly silent until the Colonel was dragged on stage with his hands tied behind his back. From my scope I could see that he had been beaten severely. The crowd showed signs of displeasure and there were sounds of people crying for his release. The reason our Colonel was so popular in town was due to the fact that he had been our Mayor for the last 15 years. He had been elected by a unanimous vote as our militia Colonel due to his unique ability to motivate people and provide clear concise thinking during times of crisis.

I knew what was coming, but knowing it did me no good in this situation. There was no way I could stop the green shirts without getting half the town killed tonight.

Gunny could easily take out the green shirts on the stage and I could take several guys with my carbine easy enough. But the remaining 20+ armed green shirts would just start wasting the crowd without mercy if we started shooting. We dared not engage these guys openly, and it frustrated us to no end. As I watched through the scope, I saw the green shirt in charge pull out his pistol and shoot the Mayor, my Colonel, squarely in the head. The crowd screamed and cried out in protest as they were being taught the depth of resolution the green shirts would undergo to demonstrate control over the people.

This was a typical communist demonstration of state power that everyone who has ever studied history knew all too well. Communist power is absolute in nature. Personal feelings, personal property, personal accumulation of wealth, must be sacrificed at the altar of the state. If they say jump you had better be in the air as you asked how high. That is why churches are so persecuted in Communist movements. Belief in God, belief in the rule of law, personal liberty, cannot be allowed by the state. In Communism, the state must replace all those things we hold dear as Americans. Our town was being taught to obey the state, or else.

We watched as the crowd was subdued into silence once again. After what seemed like an eternity, the green shirts sent everyone home, and we pulled back to the safety of the woods. We didn't dare head to our homes yet in case the green shirts were searching for those of us not attending the demonstration. We also hoped that our bunkers remained secret or else we would have nothing to fight with by morning. Gunny, Pepper, and I spoke briefly about when and where we would meet to call the next militia meeting.

It was now vital that we share as much information with all the other militias as soon as possible, but the green shirts had to leave first. We had to get the word out about the prison systems to the other militias just in case 3rd militia was about to experience the same fate as the 1st militia in Pittsboro. We had to find out what was left of 3rd militia and see if there were any arrests. We all wanted to find our families and make sure they were all right, but we dared not move until things settled down. During the night more and more green shirt units left town feeling confident of their strangle hold over our community.

After stashing my gear in the cache near the sniper bunker, I dressed in my farmer outfit and headed for home in the early morning sun. I was drained from lack of sleep over the last couple of nights as I shuffled my way towards home. All the emotions of the Batjack operation and their horrific discovery weighed me down to the point of almost collapse. I walked through town that now seemed devoid of people and green shirts, at least until I passed main street.

As I walked down the road, three green shirts stopped me and demanded my ID card. I gave them my card which I was darn lucky to even have on my person. For security reasons I didn't carry the card on operations. I just happened to have it in my farmer outfit. The green shirts went through my pockets and gave me a proper once over that would make a street cop proud. I was ready for that and had stowed everything of any value in the weapons cache. I didn't even have my Glock 19 which almost never left my side for the last five months.

These guys were checking my name against a list and found my name on it. The questioning began in earnest as they tried to find out where I had been last night when the town meeting had been called. I told them I was there and that someone just marked my name wrong or something. They were not buying it until I pointed out to them where each one of them stood during the speeches. I just failed to mention that I saw them from my rifle scope and was not actually standing in the crowd. Luckily, they let me go after a few minutes of my detailed accounts of the speeches and how we knew that they were in charge. I was just glad to see the regular green shirt knuckle heads and not the hard core nut jobs from last night. These guys were easily persuaded by using their own code words like "public duty" and "for the public good."

I rolled up into my house and sacked out. Only after I lay down did I realize just how worn out I was. I must have slept for 24 hours in my own bed, in my own house, with the war waiting for me to get back to it.

When I was able, I got out of bed and stretched the soreness out of my legs. The sun was peeking through the windows as it rose over the few trees across the street. If you didn't know any better, you would have thought it was a typical Saturday morning. Kids were playing baseball in a neighbor's yard. The smell of summer grass flowing through open windows reminded me that I had not eaten in almost two days. I went to the kitchen and fixed myself something to eat. Boy, I would have liked a full breakfast of eggs, bacon, and biscuits, but those days seemed far distant memories. Cold oatmeal was my feast for today. I sat trying to work out the soreness of my body as I ate. All this late night sneaking, hiking, and stress was taking its toll on my body.

I left the house in my farm clothes and made sure I had my ID card. It was all I could do to not chuck that darn ID card in the ditch just because I was now "REQUIRED" to carry it at all times. I went through town and saw fewer people hanging out as we usually did when not working in the fields. After the assembly last night, it was no surprise to see everyone with fear etched on their faces. I made my way to church and looked around in the kitchen. We were doing another lunch service and I spent a couple hours lending a hand. This was also an opportunity to get information on what was going on throughout town and see how everyone was doing. The mayor's funeral was set for this afternoon and everyone had been "officially" instructed to stay away. It was an outrage, but not too surprising since the green shirts wanted our allegiance and did not want the people to view the mayor as a martyr.

During lunch I made contact with several militia members and told them to spread the word that we had to meet soon. I also found out that only two of our secret bunkers had been found, but luckily there was nothing incriminating other than some food and water reserves. The weapons had been removed by a quick thinking Seven. She had seen the green shirts coming and realized that it was likely those bunkers would be discovered. Seven had risked everything to make sure that we would still have the means in order to resist our new masters. Seven had missed the assembly because she had single handedly carried eight weapons, plus ammo, a mile through dense dark woods just to keep them from green shirt hands. I would have to create a medal for sheer grit if nothing else. But most importantly I learned that our mobile radio was still intact. I was absolutely dedicated to making everyone aware of the information we had paid so dearly to discover.

At the next militia meeting, I relayed our findings to the team leaders. They in turn were directed to pass along the information about the prisons and the dark secrets they held. I wanted everyone to know the sacrifices of Batjack and it was definitely time to let everyone in all the militias know the secrets we discovered. It was important for us to have some heroes to look up to. Sooner or later we were going to fight for real, and I wanted us to have a strong backbone and a willing spirit.

But before we got too far along, the team leaders spoke out and said we needed a new Colonel. They looked at me and stared silently.

"What me? Oh heck no! I am a shooter and I don't want to be an administrator. Let me stay in the sniper teams where I can do some good," I told them.

They listened to me and elected a local business owner that had some former military experience. I was glad because I wanted payback. I wanted to see that green shirt officer that shot our Colonel in my scope someday. I wanted to be the one behind the trigger when his time came. I remembered every detail of that man's face, and I knew if I ever saw him again, we would have a reckoning.

The new Colonel met with our militia leadership where we updated everyone on Batjack's operation and the intelligence team's discovery. Our people were more than a little disturbed, but not as surprised as you might expect. Since our previous Colonel had been killed in the town square just two nights prior, our people's expectations had changed. A few hours later the other militias were informed of our findings and warned to keep under the radar for now. If we were to have a fighting chance, we had to gather strength and train until we could fight the green shirts man for man. We had to pass along the information to as many people as possible just in case some of us were wiped out.

We could not let the knowledge of the green shirt "recycling" effort die with us.

For the time being we were safe, but certainly not out of danger with the harvest coming in a few weeks. The green shirts were watching our every move, and their presence was nothing less than oppressive. Our town was for all intent and purposes under military law and expecting more trouble at any moment. Any resistance to green shirt authority would result in garnering you the label of "surplus population." We knew that to mean liquidation.

Fall

"Harvest"

Chapter 25
Anticipation of Fall

Fall is my favorite time of year. The leaves change color and the heat of summer relents to crisp cool evenings. Leaves gradually change their normal dull greens to shades of brilliant reds, yellows, and oranges. Ah, I love fall. The Bradford Pear trees go from rounded dark green leaves to the most pronounced apple-red colors you ever see. The Bradford Pears are always my first indicator that summer is gone and autumn is here.

As a sniper, any time of year when there are fewer bugs getting under your cammies and biting your tender parts, I'm happier. Man, you don't know what it is like lying off the edge of a field unable to move for fear of the enemy seeing you, while a beetle crawls up your leg. Gee-whiz, I don't miss those days. I do miss all the men I knew back then. I wish they were still around.

We anticipated fall to be a time of expected interference from our local green shirts. But, there was something else lingering in the back of our thinking. We dreaded the promise of winter. There was no fuel for chain saws, there was no fuel-oil for houses, and the power was still out. A lot of homes in those days were not equipped with a fireplace. In fact, most people were forced to cook on open fires in their yards. How in the world would we be able to cut enough wood to heat our homes this winter?

Chapter 26
Green Shirt Puppets

The tone of our operations changed as autumn's winds blew. We were getting better organized all the time. We took every mission seriously. Not that we didn't in the past, but now we realized that our livelihood was directly threatened by the green shirts. They had an unsettling hold on our town. Since our previous Colonel's death, the teams worked exceedingly hard maintaining a heightened state of alert.

I sat in the sniper bunker making our operation schedules for the following week and poured over maps. The processed sniper reports from the last few recon missions were still on my desk awaiting distribution. Our recon reports were copied to the new Colonel and his Intel group, any relevant information was passed to Logistics, and finally maps were updated with my buddy Fred. He was in the maps and codes department. Boy, this paperwork crap was for the birds. However, it would not do for our men to risk their lives getting the information just to sit on it. It was up to me to pass along the information they collected and get it to the relevant departments. I reminded myself of this as I went through yet another stack of papers. My thoughts drifted to all the changes we had made in organization since the beginning.

Gunny was in charge of sniper training now and had the rank of Squad Leader. He refused any title that made him sound like an officer. Our previous Colonel gave us directions and support on everything from tying our shoes to gathering intelligence. He gave us a lot before the green shirts killed him to demonstrate their authority. The new Colonel definitely had a mind for militia operations, but he was new at it. It takes time and shared experiences to garner trust.

We had some new titles nowadays too. You had the regular militia called Volunteers or Fighters. Squad leaders or Team leaders were in charge of six-man units. Captains were department heads with a bunch of squad leaders reporting to them. The Colonel was in charge of the whole 3rd militia. We felt these few levels of rank provided just enough structure to keep people motivated. There was nobody above the Colonel because we did not have a hierarchy across the independent militias. This brevity of leadership kept human nature from popping up too much. You don't want people to start social cliques where friends are socially promoted. We could not afford leaders without the skills to lead men into combat. We had enough trouble; we did not want bickering to foul things up.

We did have squabbles from time to time. Some people left our ranks because they didn't like the way a Captain did things or thought they could do better. For the most part we tried to keep the lines of communication open with those groups. I tried to step in and keep quarrels from becoming too much of a problem. The last thing I wanted was divisions that would keep us from working together. We needed everyone we could get.

And by the way, a recruit from the sniper teams did make a play on my name and said I was "Captain Huck." He curled his forefinger like Captain Hook from Peter Pan. I got him back smiling as I called Gunny over to explain the chain of command concept to the young sniper candidate. Gunny took the recruit in hand and assured me that the sniper would be fully motivated to respect his elders. However, from that day on the hand signal for me was the crooked forefinger. Whenever I was called to the front of a patrol, that gesture was used down the line. It is amazing what sticks. Seven agrees.

It was time for me to assign missions for the next few days. So, I sat pencil in hand looking at the maps on the wall of the bunker. The lanterns hissed while their flames flickered on the table. Strange shadows projected on the map covered wall. As I watched and waited for an idea to come to mind, a shadow flicked across the old National

Guard Depot. I quickly looked at my board and assigned two of my trainees just coming out of our boot camp to hop over there and take a peek. We knew this place to be a gang collection or staging point, but we had not been there for quite some time. Looking at the roster I noticed the code name "Pan" who just so happened to be the young man that gave me the hand-signal nickname. It was funny how he got that hyper-macho code name, "Pan." Yep strange, a downright coincidence if you ask me. I sent him and another young graduate code named "Coffee" to recon the Depot the following night.

When it came time to hand out assignments, sometimes it took several hours or perhaps a day or two to notify the people involved. You see, we were doing these missions in our spare time away from home and away from our regular day job. A guy might not get his "GO" code until one of the other team members passes him the code. The code's meaning told the operator to report to a certain bunker on a certain night for a mission. Or perhaps a Volunteer would check in regularly to a certain bunker and await orders until called out on an assignment.

Most of the time the time the Volunteers would only know one or two bunker positions just in case our ranks were compromised. No one person could spill the beans on the entire infrastructure. Those of us in leadership knew almost all the bunkers by location, but we stuck to our own areas for the most part. I mean, I was welcome in the Logistics warehouse bunker. But if I were to pull out my notebook and start working at their table, they would look at me funny.

When it came time for the mission prep of the National Guard recon mission, I showed up at the bunker and waited for the snipers to arrive. I met the squad leader assigned to this group and told him that I would be delivering the mission brief since I conducted the last two missions to that facility and knew the place well. To his credit, he did not bat an eye at my request. He was the very sniper with me on the mission to steal the diesel fuel from that Depot back in the summer.

When the Volunteers arrived, they looked apprehensive as I handed out their mission brief containing their orders, maps, and details from the last two missions. Here is what I told them.

"Gentlemen, we need you to go to the old National Guard depot marked on your map and give us an updated report on the operations of the facility. As you know, we have been there a couple of times and know that the place has been used by a local biker gang since the start of the blackout. Be careful, there have been as many as 40 guys there with shotguns. They have been known to use a sniper in an overwatch position outside the compound as well. Here is where he was last time, I pointed to the map. Don't assume them to be in the same place though. Keep an eye out for security. I want you to travel there tonight using this route. Observe the operations of the facility for 24 hours, then report back here.

Build your hide carefully because you need cover for the daylight observation. This is a stand-off mission only; do not engage unless you have to. In fact, I want you to go with one precision rifle and one covering rifle, along with your standard load of goodies. Collect a full report and return by this route unless you make contact. If you make contact, use our escape and evasion procedures and report back when you can. Questions?"

Both guys looked a bit sheepish because this was their first mission on their own. We mentored new recruits throughout training, but this one was their first by themselves.

I looked at Pan and told him he better do it right because he was, "On-the-hook." He looked at me and grinned, knowing that I didn't hold a grudge. Instead of giving me the thumbs up, he gave me the crooked finger and said, "Aye Aye Captain." I liked that guy.

Pan's team headed out along with four other teams that night. I watched them retreat into the darkening woods heading out to their objectives. I went home after a while but stayed long enough to listen to radio chatter. There wasn't too much going on that night; most of the teams were able to travel to their destinations without much trouble. There were a few extra reports of road traffic, which we noted, but otherwise a quiet night.

The next day I imagined the team set up in their cozy little hide under some camo netting and underbrush all covered in bugs. Meanwhile, I worked in the corn fields. I sent a lot of teams out over the last few months. But after the Batjack debacle, I worried for my teams a bit more. My understanding of the burden of leadership was more developed after sending men into combat. I could send men to their death, but I wouldn't do it lightly. That day passed slowly waiting for the team to return.

As evening grew into night, I made my way to the bunker where Pan and Coffee would report back if everything went according to plan. I was two hours early sitting at the table trying to busy myself with reports and paperwork listening to radio chatter. The clock must have been slow in that bunker or something because it seemed like it didn't move at all. I waited and waited before I heard the familiar voice of Pan signaling the all clear code as he entered our perimeter. Pan and Coffee made their way into the bunker and plopped down their muddy gear.

"Okay Pan, we are all dying to hear what you guys saw, spit it out," I told him.

Pan looked back at me and wiped the outer three layers of filth off his forehead smiling a contrasting toothy white smile across his smudged green face. "Sir, that place is under new management."

"Oh, really? The gangs are gone?" I asked visibly surprised.

"Yes Sir, the green shirts have the depot now, and they have changed the place significantly. The Humvees are gone, and the building is painted green with their logos on the walls."

I was not expecting this move just yet from the green shirts, but I knew immediately I had to have the full report now. "Go ahead and give me the mission report now guys. This sounds like something we expected sooner or later." I grabbed a piece of paper for notes and told them to "go ahead."

Pan and Coffee sat down and gave me the following brief.

"Sir, last night we followed the trail just like you laid out on the map. About midnight we got there, scanned all over in the dark for a good spot to build our hide, and got settled. We searched and searched but could not find any sign of a sniper operating in the area. The lights were on in the compound, so we had a good vantage point for seeing the back of the facility. From our first observation that night, we counted six police cruisers, ten conex containers on the ground, and two flatbed trucks for hauling the containers. There were also two busses marked "Community Service" on the side. During the night there were three guards on a rotating shift watching the yard. But they don't come out of the fenced in area. There were some wrecks it looked like against the back wall of the compounds that we could not make out until it got light that morning."

"The junk piles we saw were stacks of motorcycles and pickup trucks that had been shot all to pieces or burned out. Sir, it looks like the green shirts have been cleaning up the gangs. I could tell by the looks of the trucks through the spotting scope that these were the same type and configuration you guys saw the gangs use in the past. The way they have steel plate around the driver window and what-not was just like the training photos we saw."

Coffee added in, "Yeah."

I looked at Coffee and waited, but that was all he had to say.

Pan continued, "The Depot really didn't come alive until about 10 a.m. when all the townspeople showed up. There must have been around fifty people all lined up at the gate when the place opened. They all went through a check-in process and boarded the busses which left at 10:30 a.m. It looked to me like it was all a routine. The people have done it for quite some time. That's not to say that they wanted to get on the bus though. The guards made sure everyone got onboard. Their body language suggested that there were to be no questions about it." Pan took a gulp of water while we sat and listened.

"There wasn't much going on until around lunch time when a truck brought in another container. Otherwise it was quiet until about 14:00 hours when another group of people showed up. They came around to the side of the building and signed-in. Then, they went to work in the containers out back. They carried boxes and moved stuff around, then set up some tables."

"Pan, could you see what was on the side of the containers?" I asked.

"I saw 'Dept. of Recycling' on the side, but nothing else," he replied. Pan went on, "About 14:30 hours a whole mess of people started showing up across the street from the Depot and hung around by the gate. At 15:00 on the nose, the gates opened and the people were marshaled around to the waiting tables. We couldn't tell what exactly was going on, but it seemed like the people were there getting some sort of hand-out. The people left with arms full of stuff like clothes, shoes, and regular household items. It was really weird to watch. This went on for about two solid hours before the green shirts abruptly stopped the giveaways and sent everyone home."

"The people working the tables left about 20 minutes later. Then about dark, the busses came back and parked where they had been in the morning and everyone got off. We made note that these were the same people that got on the bus too. After that, there were only a couple of green shirt guards changing duty. I noted it on the log, but otherwise it was really quiet until we headed out."

I sat there with my mind racing. This was just the information we needed from our teams. If all our teams were as thorough as these guys, our command would be in great shape. I sent the pair of snipers home with my thanks. I headed to the operations bunker where I hoped to find the Colonel.

When I arrived at the bunker, I found the Colonel and got him off to the side when things freed up.

"Sir, the time we have been waiting for may have started," I told him.

"What do you mean, Huck?" he asked as he sat down to hear my report.

"Sir, it looks like the green shirts may have started to get rid of their gang puppets. I have a report of a known gang collection point that is now a green shirt "Community Center." They are giving away household items from trucks labeled Dept. of Recycling. They are displaying trashed gang motorcycles and pickup trucks stacked like cordwood for everyone to see. It is just like we expected; they are claiming credit for reducing the violence by getting rid of the very people working for them."

"Huck, let's get confirmation by sending more teams to known gang warehouses and see what's there. I will check in with the other militias, and see what they are hearing as well."

I looked at the Colonel's determination and told him, "Sir, I have four teams out tonight, I will send another five out tomorrow. I will give you an update tomorrow night."

I left the meeting knowing that we were doing some good. That night I slept better than I had in weeks. We were able to track the green shirts and anticipate their moves better than ever before.

Over the next couple of days, we got reports from all over the state that the green shirts were actively destroying gangs. Reports told us that green shirt officers were not even attempt to capture their gang brethren. Rather, they wiped out gangs in force whenever the opportunity arose. It was an awesome thing to see. We knew the death and destruction caused by the gangs was horrific, but the terrifying thing was how efficiently the green shirts were wiping out all trace of their alliance with the gangs.

Other militia groups reported witnessing the same type of events in their areas. 2nd militia reported that bikers were openly hunted down in the streets in some cases. The 4th and 5th militias reported that gang collection points were being turned into Community Centers like we had seen. The once powerful thugs were quickly becoming extinct.

I know that in the back of our minds, we wanted to defeat the green shirts before they got too powerful to overthrow. Their effectiveness in dealing with the gangs scared us a bit.

Chapter 27
Reformation of the Church

Over the next week, things got a bit busy in our small farming community as harvest time approached. The harvest was only a few weeks away, so we busied ourselves getting ready for really long hours in the field without normal farming equipment. The seemingly impossible objective was to save our crops. We wanted our people to eat through the winter. People were already going hungry; we needed the foods from our fields to survive the winter.

Then a distraction came that none of us saw. Two PPR Community Service busses pulled up to my church accompanied by a couple of squad cars. Anytime you see that combination of vehicles, it made you worry. However this time, the busses offloaded people. Several of us had come to the church that day for a special lunch prepared for the community farm workers. We were sitting under the beautiful Bradford Pear trees that separated the church parking lot from the main road as the busses pulled in. Fred and I watched as the squad cars opened their doors and green shirts got out. The green shirt preacher that had been assigned to us was evidently expecting the workers and began giving directions.

The people from the busses were directed to start working on the church and get their tools. The people from the busses blindly gathered their tools and started their work as if they had done this 100 times already. I could not imagine people so demoralized as these people seemed to be. They did not speak, they did not look around, and seeing them was like watching zombies from a movie.

We sat there and watched as Fred and I reminisced in the sunshine how this was the very place where we were motivated to join the militia. We didn't say militia out loud, we referred to it as the "the club." That is where Fred and I got our first beat-down by the green shirts. Fred still swears they dislocated his pride that day.

We sat and watched and wondered for some time until the ladders went up out front. The letters on the outside of the church now read "Community Services Center." Another ladder went up and I saw the cross being taken down off the outer brick wall of the sanctuary.

I saw red. The next thing I knew, I had arms grabbing me from behind pulling back toward the ground. My coworkers pulled me away from the two green shirt officers standing in front of us. Our commotion got their attention as I fought to get at the green shirts. The officers approached, seeing that our group was not at all happy, but not willing to fight them openly.

The green shirts sneered, "Looks like you might need some re-education in the new era. Looks like you are hung up in the past. This is a new time, a new beginning, and we are taking down those symbols from a broken society. You workers get out of here and get back to your public duties," he said with relish in his voice.

The guys got me out of there and calmed me down. I still could not imagine I was actually seeing our church turned into some sort of public office. Fred caught up as we stopped halfway back to the corn field.

Fred said, "The work crew is taking every reference to God out of the church. The hymnals, Bibles, Ten Commandments, and the cross, are all being removed. I talked with one of those laborers, and he said that they have been doing this for a few weeks already. The crews are pressed into service, and anyone who refuses public works projects is arrested."

I immediately responded, "We are stealing back as much as we can. Trust me, when these guys are done, there won't be a Bible left in town. We must pass the word and get our people scrounging right away. Again, remember to leave a few things behind so the green shirts won't get a hint of what we are up to. GO!" I commanded them.

I grabbed one last man by the arm, "Go back to the church and see where they stash all the stuff they take. Report back to me tonight."

My guys fanned out in search of other militia volunteers working nearby. I watched the men leave, and tried to get my mind wrapped around what was happening. Admittedly, I was a little weirded-out by sending men to go steal Bibles from churches; but it was the only way I could think of to save them.

Afternoon turned into evening, but instead of going home, I went right to the sniper operations bunker. I had a report in my box from the man I sent to find the stash of stolen church items. The green shirts had used a small barn on the edge of town to store all the items stolen that day. The report also included a list of the churches that had been raided and stripped. It turned out that every church in the area had been visited by the work crews. By the end of the day, every church was either boarded up or converted to a Community Center. Lucky for us, about eight of our guys had been pretty successful squirreling away the heirlooms from at least five different churches. The report finished by saying that the logistics group was busy stashing Bibles. They would be done by morning.

I assigned two sniper teams to go liberate our cross from the barn and told them to store it in the roof of the sniper operations bunker when they got back. My guys did a good job and got back within just a couple hours. That night we sat in the lamp light listening to radio chatter looking up at the ceiling with the cross staring back at us.

Take that green shirts.

Chapter 28
Return of Electricity

The work crews came every day and worked on the green shirt designated public offices. I don't know where they got the paint, but they painted damn near every public office that same emerald-green color as all their busses and uniforms. We watched the crews spruce up the high school, fire department, the local green shirt office, and our church turned community center. The remaining "public offices" like the library, the local grocery store, gas stations, churches, and the volunteer fire station were boarded up and posted no-trespassing or risk arrest.

The final project taken on by the work crews took us by surprise. Just like every other day, a work crew of tired looking people got off the busses and began their assigned tasks. However, this time they went to work on our water pipe project. This was our town's only water supply since the power blackout. The militia laid the pipe to bring water closer to where the people lived because the river was so far away.

I was out working in the field when one of my guys came running up out of breath telling me how the green shirts were tearing down our water system. When I got to Main Street, I saw a crowd gathering to protest the dismantling of the water system. The green shirts had known there would be resistance because they had several extra green shirt police standing by. I found the new Colonel standing at the back of the group and stood beside him.

I nudged his arm and whispered, "We have to calm this group down because we cannot give them an excuse to start arresting people. They have twice the police as normal and they have busses nearby."

The Colonel looked left and right as he whispered back, "You're right. Fan out and get our people to help out."

I found several of our people and gave them some covert hand gestures that communicated the idea that we should calm everyone down. Gradually we were able to get people to stop yelling and start getting on board with peaceably protesting. It must have worked because the green shirts let us vent for a while before dispersing the crowd. Nobody got pepper sprayed or arrested, so I considered our effort a success. The green shirt work crew left later that day and the wives of the militia volunteers made the men fetch water that night.

After about a week of public works, it was apparent that something was coming. We just did not know what until a green shirt squad car came rolling down Main Street calling everyone into the Community Services Center at 7 p.m. that night. The language of request suggested that the meeting was mandatory and there was going to be a special announcement that involved the entire community.

Needless to say, everyone by now was curious as to the nature of the town hall meeting. Those of us in the militia were especially sensitive to the security concerns by having everyone in the same room at the same time. Several hours before the town hall meeting, I instructed a squad of volunteers to stay out of the town hall and position themselves nearby. They would serve as a rapid response team in case we needed a quick rescue. I put the squad's names on the list of workers needed in a nearby community farm. We were required to give these reports to green shirts every day, so they could track each worker's productivity. These reports were a real pain for the militia. Our teams had to adhere to a pretty tight schedule sometimes in order to report for work on time. Luckily, the green shirts did not check our reports too often, and we were able to make them look any way we wanted. Either way, my men now had an excuse for missing the meeting.

As it came time for the meeting, the townspeople strolled in by family groups and ones and twos. We were all dressed up according to orders. The town's street lamps were burning brightly, marking the road in the dusk. If this had been a regular night before the chaos of the last couple of months, you might think this was a big town event like a 4th of July picnic or something. It was a picture perfect clear and cloudless sunset with a slight nip in the air.

I followed the crowd down the street towards the church. Along the way, I spotted Seven with her parents and slid over to walk with them the rest of the way. Seven and I greeted one another as old friends because we had known each other before the militia. Our parents had been friends for years. I was not sure how much her parents knew of her involvement in the militia, so I called her by name and not her code name. It was difficult to think straight with her so close and looking so nice. Tonight might just turn out all right considering the beautiful evening and the girl I was walking beside. Seven was wearing a blue dress and had her blond hair put up in her usual ponytail. She gave me a sly grin and took my arm.

We filed into the sanctuary and once again saw green shirts taking down names of all the attendees. I was glad I had a team on standby just in case we needed them. Every green shirt in town was at this meeting. No green shirts from out of town, thank God, but every single one of the locals was there in an official looking capacity. As we chose a seat in one of the wooden pews, I sat beside Seven and brushed her side. I felt the concealed pistol holster on her waist as her eyes briefly glanced in my direction. She knew I had discovered her secret. Without blinking, she casually one-arm hugged me around my waist feeling for the Glock she correctly guessed I had on my side.

We both sat rigid eyes-forward in the pew for a full minute trying hard not to break a smile or laugh out loud.

Seven whispered in my ear softly, "Shoot the one nearest me this time. I don't want any more scars." That was a reference from an incident where a couple of ganger on motorcycles almost killed us. Seven came away with a small scar on her arm. Man, I was going to marry that girl if I survived these damn green shirts.

The church was rather dimly lit even for this modern day of oil lanterns. Night was upon us and the windows had been opened to let the lamp smoke escape from the enclosed room. Even so, the haze collected in the roof of the sanctuary because it was not designed to have actual flaming torches in the aisles. I am surprised we did not have more fires than we did back then.

The local green shirt in charge got up to speak as the last few townspeople crammed into the room. It was all we could do to get that many people in one area like this. We were jammed in there like sardines. The lead green shirt was a young man looking like he was about my age of perhaps 30 years old. But he had the distinct air of a person that never left college. It was my bet that this guy had never held a job in his life and had spent his years getting a doctorate in modern hippie studies. As we listened to the opening remarks, I glanced from side to side to take a mental note of who was where and how many guns were in the room. I did not trust green shirts after all I knew about them.

Fred sat off to my right, across the aisle with his wife doing the same as me, looking around. Just about every militia member was there. That by itself made me nervous for our resistance. What did the green shirts have in mind? What was so important that they wanted us all here? What do they intend to do with us? I know those questions were on everyone's mind as we sat quietly listening to the speaker.

"Ladies and gentlemen we are gathered tonight on an historic occasion. As you know, our country has had its toughest trial in its history. We are witnesses to the transformational change that we have all been eagerly awaiting as we usher in a new era of cooperation working together as one body...blah...blah...blah," as he read from his prepared speech.

"What the hell is this guy talking about?" I sat and wondered with my arms folded.

"Blah..blah..blah....and as such, your generous government is sending food, medical supplies, and fuel for the people's tractors, so we can harvest the people's crops and make our contribution to feeding the workers of this state union. "Blah...blah...blah," he continued.

I sat there thinking, "Hey, I'm a glorious worker that has been busting my butt trying to keep the farms going and you are telling me you are sending fuel now? And what do you mean that I will be donating my crops? What are we supposed to eat this winter?" I sat there fuming, turning these thoughts over in my head.

"Blah...blah...blah, We have seen the fall of a greed-based system of capitalism. Now, we are entering the new era of cooperation based on the needs of everyone according to the benefit they provide to the community. There is no more rich class demanding its share of the poor man's sweat and toil. The worker will contribute his skills to the community...blah...blah...blah."

My God this man has been talking for an hour and a half non-stop. I looked over at Fred who was mocking like he was going to slit his wrists. This would be funny if I wasn't considering pulling out my Glock and shooting myself instead of hearing any more of this crap.

"Blah...blah...blah...and I am proud to announce the new leader of the People's Republic of America, Robert Jones."

We sat in silence blinking at each other. My brain was trying to process what I was hearing. We had a new name for the country? Who the heck is this Jones fella anyway? Did he just say we had a new president or secretary of the republic? What? It was all too much to process. We sat there dumbfounded.

The green shirt in charge continued, "As a demonstration of the efficiency of our new leader's ability, I am asking my colleagues to now extinguish the lamps and help us usher in a new era of collective cooperation." The men came down the aisles, and one by one they ceremoniously doused the lamps.

There we sat in darkness and silence. Then it happened; the church lights flickered and came on. The power was ON!

The people gasped audibly and some even jumped to their feet in complete shock. Some of the people cheered and others applauded, while the rest of us sat blinking at the strange lights. We hadn't had seen electricity in months. I cannot tell you the mental affect the promise of electricity had on each one of us. Power meant clean water. Power meant heating in the winter. Power meant the country was recovering, and the events of the last few months might have the chance of fading away into history.

Once the crowd settled down the speaker continued, "Your government is seeing to it that unemployment will be a thing of the past. Everyone will have a job in the new republic. Starting this Sunday at 10 a.m., everyone will attend a weekly community information session like the one we are having tonight. During these sessions you will get information on the public work projects underway, and you will fill out these questionnaires that detail your skill sets. Once we get you classified, you will begin your new careers."

The meeting ended sometime after that, and the people were released to go home. Most of us did not know what to say or think as we exited the building under the glow of electric lights.

I heard a crotchety old woman with a permanent frown commenting in the background, "I told those guys that the government was going to get things back on track. All we had to do was be patient, and they will take care of everything. I am going home to watch TV and get my refrigerator ready for the groceries to come in."

I could not believe what I was hearing. She had just been told that her country sucked from the beginning of time, her house was owned by the government, we had a new name for the country, and we had an un-elected leader. Now she had been commanded to work for the government with no promise of payment. And the woman was happy about it?! I could not comprehend that mindset; there was no amount of bribery that would make me accept total dependence on the government.

Seven, along with her folks, walked down Main Street with me as we headed home. The further we walked, a realization struck us. The power was not on everywhere. Only the Community Services Center, the fire department, and the green shirt office had electricity. Nobody was going home to watch Oprah tonight, sorry lady. I wish I could be a fly on her wall when she got home and realized that the promises of the green shirts was only worth the thin coat of paint on their newly painted offices.

After kissing Seven good night, I went home and walked through the door. I could not help myself as I flicked the light switch a couple of times just to make sure my power was still off. Dang, I hated being right.

Chapter 29
Militia Review

Our town hall meeting had been on a Wednesday night, so it was Thursday morning the next day when I headed down to the corn fields. Several of the militia leadership had dropped by the underground operations bunker when I got there. We knew there would be a lot of discussion about everything we had heard the previous night. As I entered the bunker, the Colonel was posting a memo calling the meeting for all department heads and squad leaders for 10 p.m. tonight. He looked around and told those of us standing around to get out and pass the word so that we would have everyone at the meeting.

That day was a long painful one. My mind was not on my work because of all the green shirt promises from the night before. I thought about the lady going home to find that her house was still without power. I wondered how many of the townspeople thought like this woman and if all these promises of food and electricity would affect their attitude towards resisting the green shirts. Dating Seven crept in my thinking from time to time as well. It's hard to work that way.

As night fell, I made my way to the meeting place selected for this leadership council. I thought it was fairly ironic that tonight's meeting was taking place inside one of the church's that had been recently boarded up and closed down. This particular church was on the outskirts of town off a single lane dirt road we could easily monitor for green shirt activity. With this much of 3rd militia's leadership in one place, we had a security squad positioned down the road to act as a buffer in case the green shirts decided to break up our party.

From the outside, it looked as if the church was completely boarded and empty. However, if you walked around to the left side you found that the wizards of smart had missed the crawl space underneath the sanctuary. We used that crawlspace as a doorway to conceal our entry and exit to the building while maintaining the look of abandonment. Inside, the church windows were covered with cloth and the interior sanctuary was lit with oil lamps.

Nobody was late for this meeting. We all wanted to get together and share ideas and get the Colonel's take on the situation. I plopped down on the second left side pew and sat my AR15 sniper rifle next to me. It was an amazing sight to see 20 guys sitting in pews with their camouflage outfits in their load bearing equipment. M-4 rifles sat propped up on seats beside their owners in the flickering lamp light. I almost expected a preacher to get up and start preaching on ballistics. That would have been too funny. However, we were there for more serious issues.

The Colonel started the meeting by saying, "Welcome gentlemen. We are gathered tonight for an update on the green shirt situation. I want each department to give us all a brief on what is going on and where we stand today." The Colonel then asked the Minutemen Captain to start.

The Captain of Minutemen spoke, "Sir, I have 140 volunteers trained and ready to fight. Some of these men are pretty spread out in the surrounding farms, but with a 24 hour notice we can have our entire force mustered. We have almost enough rifles for everyone, but we are pretty short on magazines. Ammunition is always a concern because we have so little. I estimate that we could sustain a six-hour direct action, but it would deplete our resources to the point where we would have to pull back. We also have two other commands near Reidsville and Oxford who could not be here tonight. They total another 125 or so fighters each.

The Logistics Captain followed, "Sir, I have 25 people spread throughout our town and three surrounding farms. We have enough bunkers to hide the entire town if the need arises. Between the bunkers and other secret hides, like this church, we can briefly hide another 50 people in a pinch. Our teams have scavenged every round of ammunition in the area and we have exhausted all the reloading supplies. We have 20 gallons of fuel and enough lamp oil for another month at current usage rates. Food stores are almost depleted. We have enough stores to feed the militia in hiding for three days but no more. We have a manufacturing department for all the specialty items we need, but resources are getting scarce.

When Logistics finished, the Colonel pointed at me. "Sir, I have 30 trained sniper recon specialists, with another 10 in training. We patrol almost every night and have been collecting recon reports with a range of 5-8 miles away. We have enough rifles for 25 snipers and the rest are using hunting rifles for the time being. We have enough ammunition for supporting recon missions, but if we went to an offensive footing our ammo would run out in about a day.

Our northern command outside of Roxboro, headed by Captain Bullet, has 125 Minutemen with another 15 dedicated snipers. They are about the same situation as us with ammunition. They have enough ammo to start a fight, but they cannot sustain a running gun battle.

When I was finished, the Explosives Captain started, "Sir, I have six people trained in demolition work, and we have a small construction effort underway for booby trap devices. We have enough demolition equipment to take out maybe three large bridges or perhaps a large building or two. However, we are very limited on military grade detonators, and wire is almost as short. We can support specific projects, but we have very few resources.

The codes department continued the review. "Sir, we have six people taking in all the operational information from the minutemen and sniper groups, so we all have the same updated information. We have three radio transmitters locally that we keep mobile because we are seeing an increase crack-down on rogue radio broadcasts by the green shirts. Our group also handles all the codes and monitors communications with other militias. So far so good, our messages are going through and the system is up and running. We have not seen intrusion or other indication that our codes have been broken, yet.

And finally, the Intel group gave their position. "Sir, we have about a dozen people working to gather information on a daily basis both from inside and outside the green shirt office. We have operatives passing out disinformation all the time through channels we discussed earlier. As for the other militias, here is what we know.

"2nd Militia has the largest territory, but most of it is rural and sparsely populated. They have three commands within 50 miles of Raleigh, with as many as 500 Volunteers total. They report that East of Wilson has no official militia coverage and without fuel they are not likely going to be much good."

"4th Militia reports Winston-Salem and Charlotte as almost a complete loss. 4th has several commands in the rural outlying areas with as many as half a dozen commands. They estimate they can have as many as 2,000 men available, but their small arms standards are not as strict as ours. A lot of their people are carrying hunting rifles."

"5th Militia has been operational south of Raleigh all the way down to Laurinburg. They estimate 500 volunteers are trained and ready with another 100 ready within the month. They report Fayetteville almost a compete loss, but they have a better weapon's stance than most. It seems their scroungers were able to raid some Army supply points early in their formation. They may even have a few heavy weapons."

Intel then continued, "From all commands we are getting similar intelligence reports. The green shirts are actively seeking out their former gang partners and are wiping them out. There are not arresting the gangs, they raid their hideouts and shoot everyone in sight. All civilians are kept away. The gangs have been all but wiped out in under two weeks."

"Secondly, all militias report that the green shirt conversion of churches is underway throughout their area of control. They are using a conscript labor force like we have seen in our community. All items related to God are removed and replaced with state propaganda. There seems to be a ban on religious gatherings of any sort under the premise that some people might be offended. Green shirts are bussing workers from one location into towns miles away. This seems to help keep worker's focus on the task at hand when it is not their own community. Nobody would destroy their own church, but the same people are more likely to strip someone else's church in some far off community."

"The only exception seems to be mosques. They seem to be immune from this persecution. An unconfirmed theory says that the P.P.R. has made a deal with the major oil-producing nations in the Middle East to protect their Islamic brothers in the U.S. in exchange for the oil embargo. This embargo seems to be coming to an end, because we are seeing more and more fuel being delivered to green shirt controlled motor pools. Civilian use of fuel is restricted due to environmental reasons."

"And finally, we are getting reports that most large cities and several smaller areas are starting to see the return of electricity on a limited basis. Electricity is only connected to green shirt controlled offices and government buildings. They are also controlling water supplies through government offices directly; so we can expect to see our town's water supply be re-directed to one of the Community Centers."

The Colonel stood before us as all the department heads took their seats.

He spoke in such a way that frightened us all, when he said, "Gentlemen I don't think we can win an open fight against the green shirts. I chose to meet here with all you because I respect you and know what determination you have shown thus far in the resistance. You know as I do that if we continue down this path we are going to have to get tough and I mean mad-dog mean. Our people are going to die, our families are at risk, and the people we are trying to save are at risk. We must make a decision tonight on the future of the militia."

You could hear a pin drop in that deserted church.

The Colonel continued, "We have the option right now of walking away and forgetting everything we know. The green shirts have the people by the throat and every day that grip gets tighter. They control the water, they control the electricity, and on Sunday morning we will be herded in front of review boards to determine our job skills for our new careers. Our volunteers are so spread out across the state that it is likely we will never have enough forces to mount a coupe that has a realistic chance of succeeding. All the green shirts have to do is continue on their course for a few more months, and they will have the full strength of the state behind their movement. They will then be invincible. Or, we can choose right this very minute to hunker down and start preparing to overthrow these green shirt bastards!"

Every man in the room cheered without care of giving away our secret gathering. We would have gladly taken on the entire green shirt army right then.

The Colonel continued, "Gentlemen, I don't plan on retiring in some green uniform eating oatmeal out of a government bowl, wearing government shoes, in some mental hospital just because I want to worship God, own my own house, and keep the money I earn. I don't want my kids or your kids, working as slaves to the People's Republic of America. "TO HELL WITH THAT!"

Again we cheered with every man raising his rifle in the air.

The Colonel ended the exuberant meeting with a prayer promising how we would try to deliver God's people from bondage and return the United States back into a free nation, under God, indivisible, with liberty and justice for all. Then he ended by asking the Lord to prepare eternity for a whole bunch of green shirt souls. He would let God decide on heaven or hell.

Amen.

Chapter 30
New Green Jobs and a Green Education

The following Sunday morning, the townspeople gathered at the church, or Community Services Center, I should say. We filed through the doors the same way we had the previous Wednesday night but were directed to the fellowship hall this time. Tables had been prepared and sat ready for our arrival. Sitting at the tables were a new group of green shirt workers that seemed to be more office management types. Heck, these people were more like temporary office workers than conscript labor. It was my guess that these were former government employees from a department like motor vehicles or something.

We were directed through a series of turnstiles where we waited our turn to be processed. As I came to the end of the line, I saw Seven standing directly across from me. I quickly skipped under the rope and stood next to her as she turned to face me. I simply smiled and looked into her eyes as if nothing else in the world mattered. And for that brief time nothing did other than her gaze back at me. Soon it was our turn to approach the tables and I made sure we were right next to each other.

As we stood in line and waited, a familiar voice echoed from the foyer.

"The power is not on at my house. When is someone going to come and hook it up? When do I get a heater? My house doesn't have one, and I don't know what I am going to do this winter."

It was the voice of the woman from the other night who expected the government to provide her electricity. I was betting that she never got too far in her requests.

The gruff woman behind the table checked my name off the list, and without looking at me, started to ask me a series of check-list questions. When she discovered that I had been a telephone engineer, she looked up and took notice. It then dawned on me to make up a story that Seven had been a co-worker of mine, and was also trained in the telecommunications field. I knew there would be a demand for skilled people, because our infrastructure was in need of reconstruction. I told the lady that we both had a variety of experience, and we would be happy to devote our skills to repairing the people's property. Hey, if you are making crap up, make it sound good.

The gruff lady processed our paperwork and gave us directions to an orientation event scheduled for later that day at the high school. We left the Community Center by lunch time and headed out to the parking lot. Once we reached the relative security of the Bradford Pear trees, Seven asked me why I had made up the crazy story that she was a telecom guru. I explained that if the power was coming back on, that meant a couple of engineers would be in a unique position to spy on the green shirt movement.

I told her, "I can train you in enough technical jargon to get you by. Most people don't know enough to weed out a lie on technical equipment anyway. And besides, we can work together where I can keep an eye on you and make sure you are safe."

She shook her head and just smiled as we left. Later that day, the townspeople gathered in three locations in town. Those of like tradesmen and engineers types went to the high school, the laborers and farmers stayed at the Community Center. What few remained, were directed to report to the fire station or the green shirt office, I am not sure which.

In the high school, we were escorted to classrooms where our IDs were matched to attendance records and verified of our work status. They sat us in desks with chewing gum clinging to the bottoms. There we received our schedule of training that was to last the next two weeks for 12 hours a day. The list of classes included things like "environmental awareness" where you were taught the dangers of fossil fuels. "Public Duty" classes were where you learned that being a good worker meant giving all your effort to the community with all your heart, mind, and soul. "Economics" was a class on how capitalism just about ruined the world before the great transformational change we were privileged enough to live through.

The list of nonsense classes continued on and on until you thought your head would explode. Then they served a weak soup for your supper break and you had to give thanks to our benevolent leader for the meal. I was ready to stick my government supplied pencil in my eye rather than listen to more of this stuff. I was already planning in my head for the next time I would get to sneak out to the sniper bunker. I used those daydreams to keep my sanity until orientation was called for the day.

Of course, the next day arrived way too early and I headed to my worker orientation class along with Seven. We had never gone to school together, because she was a couple of years younger than me. It was like we were two high school sweethearts walking to class every day. I joked about throwing spitballs at the teacher. She joked that this was the first time she had ever considered carrying a gun to school. As it turned out, I was able to have a little fun with our "teacher" when it came time for the history lesson.

Afterwards, I got the distinct impression that they do not tolerate anyone correcting the dates or places of the government approved lessons; no matter how many errors there were. I was lucky I was not arrested. Gee, it was like high school all over again.

I could not believe anyone was falling for this garbage, but we did have a few people that really got into the whole re-education thing. As everyone else in the militia, I made note of who we needed to watch. We had to keep our "club" a secret from those people willing to drink the cool-aid. Funny enough, there was a rumor that suggested the green shirts were putting stuff in the food to pacify us. We never found out for sure, but a few people seemed to be more passive than others after meals.

After the two weeks of indoctrination, the classes ended in a ceremony that issued us new identity cards that read we were now state-approved workers. Some of our classmates would go on to be highly prized government workers, while more of us in the skilled trades, would go straight to our work assignments. The unskilled workers would be formed into labor groups like the ones that remodeled our church.

Seven and I were assigned to a communications team just like we had hoped. This new work assignment would be an inconvenience for my leading the sniper teams because I would no longer be close to the sniper bunkers. I estimated that I would have to give up my Captain status. But it was my bet that I could give our Intelligence group a unique ability to access green shirt communications. The larger problem was how spread-out our teams were getting. Our militia was just getting used to working together as a team. Now we were lucky to get half our people on call at any one time.

Chapter 31
Fight for the Crops

We had always imagined there would be a big fight for the crops we had been tending by hand since the spring planting. Many in 3rd militia thought the pending confiscation of the crops would be the breaking point where we started fighting the green shirts out in the open. I must admit that I was already imagining how to purge those green shirts out of our town. Yet, I feared the dreaded reprisal. However, the time of harvest was not at all what we imagined.

The night after I graduated from the worker orientation, I was in the sniper bunker as the Colonel came in. He was quickly going from bunker to bunker trying to get an idea of how many volunteers we had available at a moment's notice. I gave him a report on the sniper squads which estimated we were nearly at 50% strength. Everyone was spread out with training and green shirt work assignments.

"What is it Colonel?" I asked.

The Colonel sat down and looked through his pieces of paper and then he said, "We are too spread out and we simply don't have the numbers."

"What do you mean; the numbers for what?" I asked.

The Colonel was outwardly stressed as he told me, "Huck, I just got a message from 5th militia on the radio. They saw a convoy heading our way with farm equipment of harvesters and a sizable security element. They estimate the convoy to be here by morning. The other teams are reporting about the same as yours; we have only 50% of our teams available. The green shirts are coming in force by morning. Even if we blow the bridge and cut off their main access, we don't have enough people to mount a real defense. We are about to lose the crops and there is not a damn thing we can do about it."

He leaned back in the chair and wiped his hand through his hair. I was glad I refused his job about now. He knew what the crops meant to our people. The effort they put into the crops was our only hope for food. Morale was the backbone of keeping our movement going and losing the crops would be a big blow.

"Sir, if we can't fight, we are going to take a hit in morale," I told him.

We sat there in the sniper bunker and hashed out plan after plan to see if there was any way to save our crops. How could we feed our town through winter without the harvest? But in the end, we agreed that any action we took right now would only result in a lot of us dying. If we resisted, what would be left of our town, would be under that much more control. The decision broke our hearts.

When dawn broke, the Colonel and I watched the convoy ramble into town. The green shirts had everything marked on maps and directed the harvesters to their work. What was more amazing was the reaction of some of our townspeople. Some actually cheered as the trucks rolled in. They saw it as help and perhaps did not realize that their food was being confiscated in front of their faces. It was disturbing to see how a few months of hardship warped some people's common sense. We could not afford to lose the backing of the people.

The Colonel leaned over and whispered to me, "If we are going to make a move to overthrow these green shirts, we had better do so as soon as possible."

Losing the crops to the green shirts was the blow we expected. Morale was low among the volunteers. We had to keep our people energized because they were not bound by anything other than their willingness to resist. This was about that time we started getting radio messages from other militias. Every militia was experiencing the same problems. The green shirts were consolidating power and had the people literally eating out of their hands. Every town, including ours, was having their food and water distributed through green shirt community centers. Only government buildings had electricity. The people were becoming dependent on the green shirts.

While the harvesters worked our fields, the Colonel called for another leadership meeting. The night of the meeting was cool as we converged on one of the radio bunkers. It was about 10:30 p.m. as we sat around the candlelit tables.

The Colonel started, "Gentlemen, we are faced with a problem. The green shirts are taking control of every aspect of our lives. They hand out a little food from time to time, they now control the water flow, and they are promising employment. Green shirts are harvesting our fields, and the people are cheering in the streets. We need to keep our volunteers focused. We need to keep growing our numbers until it is time to strike."

"We have to start planning for a combined militia action. This action must defeat the green shirts in one swift blow before it's too late. We are coordinating with the other militias as soon as we can call a leadership meeting."

The Captain of Logistics spoke up when there was a pause, "Sir, we don't have the resources to run a full combat action right now. When is this action going to take place?"

The Colonel looked at him and said, "I don't know yet. I will know after the conference."

We were all thinking the same thing. We were in no shape for a real fight. We would have to do some real scrounging to get ready. The Colonel excused himself as the radio crackled to life in the background. While the rest of us talked about our options, the Colonel and Captain of the code department copied the list of messages on a scratch piece of paper. After the messages, they came back to our group.

"The other militias have responded. We will meet in one week somewhere in our area. 3rd militia will be host to the conference," the Colonel announced.

One of the Captains of Volunteers spoke up, "How can we consider a fight when we cannot even defend our own crops? Our people are spread out all over the place."

The Colonel responded hotly, "We will fight with everything we have when the time comes. For now we will host the conference and hash out a plan to overthrow these green shirts once and for all. While I am gone, the Intelligence Captain will be in charge. Huck has made a request to transfer over to Intelligence and I ask him now to name his replacement as Captain of the sniper teams."

I got a lot of looks of shock as they turned to me.

I got up and named Rooster as my replacement. He had just gotten back from the northern command a few days prior. His wounds were healing well and he was operational again. Since the failed Batjack operation, I knew Rooster was a capable leader and would be fine. Pepper, the only other remaining Batjack member, would most likely lead one of the squads.

I then surprised the group once again by telling the Colonel I knew a remote location for the conference and I would be his guide for the journey.

The Colonel ended the meeting with orders for all teams to identify key facilities for us to raid in the coming weeks. We needed more bullets, more weapons, more magazines, and more components for explosives. Our scrounging would be our only hope.

After everyone dispersed the Colonel and I were left in the bunker alone.

"Huck, thanks for the support in the meeting," the Colonel said.

"Sir, I'm not sure we can make a real stand right now. I agree with logistics. We are not equipped for this. I don't trust the other militias yet, because we have never worked with them," I told him. I could think of no other way to say it.

He looked to me honestly and said, "Huck, you're right of course. But, we have to start somewhere. We have to start somewhere."

I looked back to the Colonel, "Colonel, how optimistic are you that we can unseat the green shirts, even with the full support of the other militias? Their hold is local. It's not dependent on a central structure for the most part. We may cut off the head, but find the tentacles still attached."

The Colonel looked at me and said, "It's the risk we have to take." Now, where is this place you mentioned for the conference?"

We looked at the maps to see the location of the old tobacco plantation located outside the town of Hillsborough. Its name was "Moorefield's," built in the 1780s. I had been there as a Boy Scout many years ago, and I knew the layout of the place quite well. It was also strategically located so that all militias would have an equal opportunity to attend the meeting in person. It was secluded and had a lot of cover. The Eno River ran nearby and that is always good for navigation.

The Colonel liked my idea and made notes for the information to go out on our next scheduled radio broadcasts. Within a day or two, the other militias confirmed our GPS coordinates for the meeting. I was sure glad the GPS system did not rely on the power grid.

Chapter 32
Counter-Revolution Conference

I checked in with my green shirt work assignment officer with my hair a mess and a runny nose. My chili-peppered bloodshot eyes and puffy face made it look like I had the flu. My fake flu convinced the assignment desk to postpone my work assignment for the time being. The woman ushered me out of the services center while holding her breath. Mission accomplished. However, I was not looking forward to my next task.

Convincing Seven that I would be okay sneaking all the way to Hillsborough, with just the Colonel for backup, was another thing altogether. I made my way to her house and knocked on the door. Seven answered and announced my arrival to her folks as we sat on the couch.

She looked at me and said, "You are going to the conference, aren't you?"

How did she know?

Seven smiled and said, "Some guys just say they want their space; you have to invent a whole planning a revolution excuse. I must say, it is original."

I knew she was kidding; she had such a nutty since of humor sometimes.

"Well, maybe we ought to get married when I get back I told her. You know Christmas is coming….," and I never got to finish.

She was kissing me heartily when her dad walked in.

"Whoa Nelly!" He exclaimed. "Come up for air you two," he said grinning as he plopped down in his chair.

"Dad, He is going on a trip and it might take a while. I was just saying goodbye for now," Seven told him.

"Oh, is it "club" business?" he asked knowingly.

She simply replied, "Yeah."

I didn't know how much her folks knew about her involvement, until now. They knew she was in the militia, but she was careful not to give them any details. Smart;

their ignorance of her involvement might protect them. Seven's father was ex-military and had been wounded in combat. He understood the risks we faced.

Her dad got up out of the chair and said, "Well carry on then." He walked out of the room with the same grin pressed across his face.

We said a few more goodbyes on the couch, and she sent me on my way without ever trying to talk me out of the trip. I reported into the sniper bunker that night for the final briefing and our departure. Several of the snipers were present along with a couple of guys from Intel.

Here was our plan. A sniper team from a small community between us and the objective would provide us a mid-way rally point. If we ran into trouble, they would give us a safe area to hide until things settled down. We would travel by Mule and the dirt bike according to a fairly complicated route devised by Fred. Once we reached our objective and searched the area, we I would radio the code word "Irene". Yes, it was cheesy because it was straight out of Blackhawk Down, but it was something recognizable by all those involved. Anyway, if the code went out, the conference would start six hours later. If there was need to abort, then all anyone could call out "Nancy". Once the conference was over, we would take an alternate route back. Again a sniper team would provide a midway rally point where we could get gas or whatever we needed. Simple, right?

Of course, things never go exactly to plan. But, if you plan well enough, you can avoid all sorts of problems. Everything was packed on the Mule. I choose a red dot M-4 with four extra magazines, my trusty Glock 19 with three spare magazines, and a whole host of pocket items. We might be gone a week, so I carried a multi-tool, black tape, matches, 550 parachute cord, binoculars, poncho with liner, flashlight/batteries, and compass. I knew we could not afford ANY gunfights along the way so I understood not carrying too much ammo. I just didn't like it. The Colonel took about the same as me, but his sidearm was a Kimber .45 auto.

All that was left was the gear for the meeting itself. We planned on using some old tobacco barns as our actual meeting room. So in order to host the meeting, we needed lighting, drawing materials, blackout curtains and maps. Our Logistics Captain and Colonel even configured an inverter for the Mule. The inverter allowed us to run a PC or charge batteries as needed. All our precious intelligence was copied on a few flash drives. These drives were further protected by a nasty computer virus just in case they were to fall into the wrong hands. The Colonel knew the code to disable the virus and the plan was to share it with the other militias. With all this gear packed onto the Mule, we made our final arrangements.

As darkness fell, I got onto the dirt bike and fired it up. Amazing how quiet it was. I had to keep checking the tachometer just to make sure it was running. The Colonel started the Mule which was almost as quiet, and we headed out through the edge of the empty corn field. Darkness was stretching its long fingers through the woods as we made our way past town. We were using a familiar, but seldom used trail, that bypassed the outskirts of town. Our route snaked us around fields and through streams. Sometime we were on well-defined trails, but more often we stuck to the thickest stuff on the planet. I stayed ahead of the Colonel a good 100 yards to scout out a passable route for the Mule. If I made contact, that would give the Colonel a chance to turn around.

We made our way at a pretty brisk pace for the first two hours. Once we reached a turn on our maps, I signaled to the Colonel that I was stopping. He pulled up beside me and we shut down our rides. After a minute of silence, I pulled out my map and used a small LED light to see it.

"How are we doing?" the Colonel asked.

"We are pretty close to schedule," I told him as I pondered the map.

"Well let's get going then" he prodded.

I was glad it was dark as I smirked and held back the first two things that popped into my smart-mouth brain.

"In the sniper teams, we take these breaks for a couple reasons. By looking at the map we don't get lost in the dark as easy. Second, we are getting into territory that has a lot of houses. I need to make sure we don't end up crossing a road right in the middle of Main Street somewhere. And sometimes you just have to stop and pee."

I could just see the Colonel's teeth shine as he smiled at my return. During the break, we secured loose gear on the Mule and drank some water. I adjusted the sling on my M-4 because the red dot site was rubbing my back raw. We took a compass bearing and started again. Mile after mile of creeks and fields turned into thinner hardwoods. I stopped us close to our rendezvous point as we approached one of the last few obstacles. There was a quiet roadway to our front, 150 yards away.

After five minutes of quiet, I edged forward. But just as I started to pull out, a squad car zipped by on the road. My eyes popped and my heart stopped as I pulled my M-4 to my shoulder. We watched as several trucks passed. Another ten minutes passed as we once again approached the road. This time I my M-4 pointed the way as I idled up to the road. It was clear. I signaled the Colonel to cross and we continued on our way. In silence, we finally reached the coordinates and stopped under a large cedar tree. We dismounted with rifles at the ready and waited. No sounds.

"How do we find the sniper team?" the Colonel asked after two minutes.

"They are working their way to us; let's give them some time," I replied.

It then dawned on me that this man had likely not gone out on missions before. He knew the training topics, but he had never been on a patrol. I was so used to working in my teams. I never considered our Colonel to be so inexperienced.

About 20 minutes later, the sniper team showed up and directed us to a temporary blind set up for us. We parked and shook hands with the team. I introduced the Colonel to the guys because they were not local to us, but had trained with our people earlier in the summer.

One of the snipers spoke up and said, "We weren't sure if you were going to cross in front of that green shirt convoy or not. They almost tagged you, Captain Huck."

"Yeah, they surprised us alright. How much activity are you seeing southwest of here?" I asked.

"Well, those green shirt convoys don't come through here too often, but there has been some activity lately. Looks like they are moving fuel through here late at night," the sniper informed me.

"Let's get in some cover and talk." Under the cover of the blind we updated our maps and got the latest Intel from the snipers. We planned this route because it would allow us to cover the open country in daylight and the more populated areas in darkness. If all went well, we would be at our destination the following night. We ate and rested with plans of starting up right before dawn. From the snipers, I got a good read on where to cross the Eno River. Crossing the river had been a concern of mine and I was glad for the information. As dawn neared, we packed our gear and headed out.

We covered the ground rather quickly and only had one encounter that we did not see coming. As we approached the Eno, I was running ahead of the Mule as usual. Since we were still a quarter mile from our crossing, we chose to run the river's edge. It was there that I stumbled across two unwary fishermen. I almost ran over one of the guys before he heard me coming. I swerved the bike and ran up the embankment nearly killing myself in the process. As the bike collapsed in the mud, I staggered upright and held the two men at bay with my M-4. After making my point that they had better get face-down, I signaled for the Colonel to veer off the path. I did not want them to see the Mule. It would be easier if they saw just me.

I wanted to scare the life out of these two men in the hopes they would not dare mention my presence to anyone. Goat herding kids have killed more special forces guys than anyone on clandestine missions. Civilians can give you away in a heartbeat and we were too close to our objective now to allow bystanders to give us away. The last thing I wanted as to start a run-and-gun with the green shirts alerted to our presence. I made up a B.S. story how I had been watching the guys for hours and knew where they lived. They begged not to be shot. By the end of the encounter, I was confident they would keep quiet for a while. I left in the opposite direction of my objective and circled around to find the Colonel waiting for me.

I told him that we better get moving and pointed a new direction. We crossed the river and ran under the interstate as we planned. The Eno is not a large river, but the Mule is not a boat either. We followed along the banks until we reached under I-85. There we listened intently to the traffic above us on the roadway. It was our hope that we would quietly pass 30 feet below without anyone the wiser. I slowly ran along the river's edge and signaled the Colonel to come through.

About half way through, the Mule's right side tires slipped in the mud and nearly plunged into the deep water. I raced back and un-clipped the Mule's winch before it slipped further. I ran the cable to a bridge support and we pulled the Mule out. We were incredibly exposed for almost five minutes before we reached cover. I don't think I needed heart medication back then, but I was pretty sure I wanted some. The last mile was old-growth forest which provided lots of cover. We approached the plantation looking at a setting sun.

Chapter 33
Negotiations

The Colonel and I stashed the vehicles, and then headed out on foot. I knew the place well, and walked right to the old tobacco barn. I was glad to see the old place still intact after all these years. The plantation house itself had been saved from looting as far as we could tell. We circled around for a couple of hours seeing if there were any signs of recent disturbance. But there were none. We made our way back to our vehicles and moved them over by the old Moore family cemetery. The thick underbrush was great cover. Once satisfied we were alone, we broke out our gear. While the Colonel set up for the meeting, I walked the perimeter with my M-4 keeping an eye out for locals. The crunching leaves on the ground made me feel like I was out hunting in some bygone time when I was younger.

After making sure of our privacy, I reported that we were ready to send the message. At the pre-arranged time, I turned on my GMRS walkie-talkie and sent out the go code for the conference. "Irene." If all went well, the conference would start in six hours.

The time passed slowly as we finished the preparations. I was on guard outside as the first sign of outsiders came from the river. I watched carefully to make sure they were militia. As they approached, I whistled lightly and motioned for them to come ahead. They were as anxious as me, until we traded passwords. There were three men all decked out in camo carrying a mixture of rifles. They identified themselves as 5th militia, so I directed them to the barn. After only a few minutes, another three-person group came in from the south. They approached cautiously and I made my way to them. Again we traded passwords. They identified themselves as 2nd militia. Just as I directed them towards the barn, we heard the unmistakable sound of a car on the nearby gravel road.

Instinctively we crouched down and raised our weapons. Then we saw what we feared most; a squad car coming our way. There had been no sign of a car in anywhere; why now? Had we drawn attention to ourselves somehow? Our apprehension turned into fear in a nano-second. The car pulled down the driveway and slowly made it way toward our area. I signaled the others for a hasty ambush. I motioned to the others to take cover. As one of their guys looked at me, I made the hand motion of putting on a suppressor. I was asking if he had one. He looked at me and understood, but shook his head no.

We watched as the car pulled up and stopped, not 40 yards away. Three uniformed green shirts opened the doors and stood beside the car putting their hands on the hood. The driver looked to the woods and said to no one, "Irene". I took a deep breath and could barely contain the smile. We approached the car knowing this must be 4th militia. We knew they must come a long way, but to show up in green shirt uniforms was nothing short of astonishing. Sure enough, they identified themselves as 4th militia and explained that they had no idea where to hide the car. We directed them to a spot where we covered the car in brush. We also made sure the guys in the barn were warned before we let the 4th go in.

That night, we started our discussions. Since we were host, our Colonel set the stage for our meeting.

"Gentlemen, thank you for coming. I know that we all risk life and limb every day. Just getting to this meeting has been a challenge for us all. We would like to thank the gentlemen from the 4th who absolutely scared us to death by showing up in the squad car, thank you."

A light round of humored applause went around.

My Colonel continued, "But as you know, we are gathered here for some serious business. The green shirts have taken control of our lives and we have made some shocking discoveries in the last few months. It is my goal to walk away from this meeting with a clear plan for us to defeat these green shirts once and for all."

That night's discussions were meant to be introductory and have everyone set up an agenda. We talked for hours into the coolness of the night, sharing stories in the lamplight.

About an hour of talking among the group, I was talking to someone from 4th about sniper tactics.

One of the 5th guys asked, "Hey, you in the 3rd militia have that sniper they call Huck, right?"

I looked over at him and responded that he was referring to me.

"Really? We hear Huck was killed about three times already. You know the green shirts seem to think he is a Sasquatch with a big rifle up there."

"You know what? They're just about right" I told him smiling. I shared some of my stories and gave them advice for organizing their own units into better scouts and snipers. From the looks of it, their sniper programs were not as advanced as 3rd's. The only exception was the 4th. Their mountain men knew a thing or two about shooting long distances.

We rotated our guards all night and kept watch, but there was nobody lurking in the area. The next day we had breakfast and started the heart of our organized talks.

I gave a brief on our prison system discovery. I showed some that were skeptics the recon pictures Fred and I took of the "recycling facility". The Batjack operation and the resulting losses really drove home the point. The other commanders listened intently and shared their information as well. 2nd militia had been able to determine that a few prisons in their area were set up the same way. 5th militia also reported on similar findings in their area, but 4th was different. The 4th didn't have any federal prisons in their district. Whatever plans we considered needed to include the prison system.

Another topic we discussed was church conversions into Community Centers. This seemed to be across the boards except again for the 4th. It seemed the green shirts were bypassing the western part of the state for the most part. Anything west of highway 77 and you were in a fairly free area. 2nd militia operated under much tighter control until you got about 100 miles east of Raleigh. It seemed the green shirts wanted to dominate the major cities in the central part of the state. Then, sometime in the future, expand to the flanks.

5th militia reported on the status of Fort Bragg and Pope Air Force base. The base was definitely being used to ferry in fuel. It looked like the green shirts were getting fuel in somewhere near the port city of Wilmington. Trucks and trains hauled fuel to a staging area at Fort Bragg. We all took notes on that. Fuel would be the key to the green shirts gaining complete control. The military was almost non-existent due to green shirt contract release programs. What few military resources remained, worked to support green shirt police. Unfortunately, the 5th reported that the green shirts had destroyed a lot of the military weaponry. The green shirts decided early on that weapons could be stolen and used against them. I agreed with their thinking.

Another hot topic was gang activity. From all commands, the story was the same. The green shirts had wiped out every gang member they could find. There may be a few pockets left, but not many. That was good, yet concerning news. We all estimated that their new targets would be the militia.

Everyone shared intelligence, but key components were left out just to maintain our individual security. We traded figures for volunteers, weapon counts, estimates of fighting power and so forth. These discussions lasted all day and into the evening. Man, it was good to see all these men from different backgrounds, united in a single fight against the green shirts. It gave me hope. As the day drew into evening, we shared a great meal of kidney beans and cornbread. We stretched our legs outside of the barn and watched the sun setting behind the trees.

After the break, the real topic was next; how to overthrow of the green shirts. I brought up the final topic by reminding everyone that just a couple of miles down the road was a historical site. I explained that the representatives from the North and the Confederate States met in a shed to hash out the terms of Lee's surrender at Appomattox courthouse. Here, we would plan for the overthrow of the green shirts.

"Ok, what are our options?" I asked them.

Several men spoke at once advocating for a combined militia effort before winter set in. Others suggested we continue as-is for now, until spring. Some wanted a general uprising across the state, where others favored a single blow all at once. We debated the pros and cons of each scenario. Colonels traded the dry erase board and scratched out plans. Papers floated around from hand to hand with suggestions. It was organized chaos.

After a while, the 2nd militia Colonel addressed the men, "Men, can we agree on a few key principles?"

Everyone sat listening.

He continued, "#1 We cannot mount any type of coup without fuel to transport the fighters to the fight. #2 We don't have the strength right now. Nor can we expect to in the very near future. #3 We must move as soon as we can before the green shirt hold is too tight, and their numbers increase. #4 Only the force of a combined effort will unseat the green shirts." #5 With the gangs gone, they will focus on the militias next.

Everyone agreed to those points; some reluctantly on the order.

The 2nd's Colonel spoke again, "Then gentlemen, I suggest the following. We take this fall and winter to organize and gather strength. We lull the green shirts into thinking they have pacified the population. We act only to protect our people from threat of death. We gather weapons and ammunition as best we can. In the spring, we strike all at once with all the strength we can muster. By then, we will likely have fuel and transportation, more volunteers, and more fighting power. Whatever we do, it must be by spring. If we try something after spring, the green shirts will have too much control and we will never be successful in overthrowing them."

We took a break and considered the plan. My Colonel was happy with the concept. I thought it was practical, but I was worried how many people were going to prison every day. When the other commands returned from break, they all agreed to the plan's concept. We had a consensus.

We set the planned action date for March 19th and assigned code names for the coup. We had a laugh as we decided 3rd militia was Duke, 5th was UNC, 4th was Wake Forest, and the 2nd was N.C. State. It was only appropriate for the operation we now called "March Madness." It was the perfect cover for our intelligence units. They would have a field day with these names in our respective code departments.

A few more hours passed while we continued to add as many details as possible. Our codes were established and 2nd militia was assigned the task of intelligence gathering on the state capitol. 5th would scrounge military installations for heavy weapons. 4th would continue to organize and grow its numbers. 3rd would support our action with snipers. We had accomplished our goal. The militias all agreed to a central plan, now it was time to get back to our units.

By morning, the teams were packed and ready to make their way home. We had been at the barn now for 3 days and you know the old saying, "fish and guests smell after three days." 4th militia was the first to pack up and head out. I must admit seeing green shirt uniforms on our brethren did shake the nerves a bit. The 5th had stashed their vehicle a mile or so down the road. They headed back the way they came through the woods. 2nd did the same, leaving the Colonel and I in the doorway of the old tobacco barn. I wondered if history would remember those old barns long after we were gone.

The Colonel worked another couple of hours sanitizing the place. We had to make sure if someone came behind us, they would find nothing but cobwebs. We filled the latrine, buried the ashes from the fire, and dirtied the place up a bit. Satisfied, we packed then started for home.

Our route home was dictated by standard operating procedure. "Don't go home the way you came." The first leg of our route turned us south and east toward a place where we could cross I-40 safely. As we traveled, I noticed a lot of housing nearby. That always makes me nervous. You could come across a bunch of kids playing. If they see you, they could alert green shirts even by accident. We found the first leg of the trip to be a royal pain. Creeks slowed us down. Open fields, not on the maps, forced us to alter course. We could never seem to go in any one direction for more than a few minutes. We were in an area that was more grown up than we anticipated. It was likely that our maps were out of date, but we had to press on.

After four hours, we stopped for a map check and rest on a small hill overlooking some railroad tracks. As we sat and got our bearings, the distinctive sound of gunfire crackled in the near distance. It was close to 15:00 as the thumps and pops echoed beyond the trees. The sky was overcast with an ominous threat of rain. You could smell water in the air.

The Colonel asked me, "Which way from here?"

I was intently listening, so I pointed in the direction of the sounds without speaking or looking up.

"I was afraid of that," he said as we stared as if to see through the trees.

As we listened, the sounds grew louder and with more intensity.

I could hear hesitation in the Colonel's voice as he asked, "Are they coming this way?"

I was looking down at the map still listening. "Yeah, it sounds like they are maybe 800 yards out," I told him.

"We have to get the hell out of Dodge then! Quit looking at that map and let's get going," he directed me.

I finally looked up at him and spoke quietly, "Sir we need to know where to go." I pointed to the open map. "If we go south, we run right into a bunch of neighborhoods. If we head any further north, we will be on the wide-open interstate. Besides, there are only a couple of guys with shotguns down there fighting a few more folks with pistols. That used to be a Wal-Mart, and I bet the gunfire will end in a minute or so."

I saw the Colonel working things over in his mind.

"Just how do you know all that, Huck?" he asked.

"Well, I know the sound of shotgun makes a fa-boom sound at a distance. With time, you can tell the direction it's pointed. It makes a different sound if it's pointed at you directly. Pistols are different. They make a crack or popping sound at this distance. If there are no rifles involved, this is most likely a bunch of thugs fighting green shirt police," I told him matter-of-factly.

Within a minute the firing stopped. Ten minutes later, we headed out cautiously. We snaked our way along the original route as we made our way to the railroad tracks. Slowly creeping over fallen leaves was noisy. Every crackling dead branch we broke under a tire, made us jump. The shooting had stopped, but we were too close to the place for my taste. The railroad tracks we traveled offered quick passage, but they were dangerously open. Tracks are to open for daylight travel in my opinion. So, I found us a grove of cedar trees where we waited for night to fall. We were way behind schedule, but I would rather be late than dead.

Night came with a dreary mist making everything wet. With no moonlight, we were in a better situation for traveling in the open. But, it did force us to use some lights. We headed out once again, slowly, and got back onto the tracks. After bouncing along for a mile or so I noticed a roadway bridge ahead. I could see figures around a fire drum under the bridge. I halted slowly. The Colonel rolled up to my position and stopped.

"Who are they?" he asked.

"I don't know, but I bet they are bandits of some sort. I don't see any guns but you better count on them being armed" I told him.

The Colonel stared at the forms under the bridge, "Can we bypass them?"

"Nope, we are going to miss our rendezvous soon, if we detour. If we go any further south, we will most likely run into wide open neighborhoods. I have an idea though. I will find a spot about 100 yards from the bridge and start blasting away as you drive through. You set up 100 yards on the other side and cover me. If we are lucky, they will think we are green shirts and they will run. If not, then we will come up with plan B."

"What is plan B?" the Colonel asked with a dry mouth.

"Plan B is follow me and try to keep up," I smiled.

I edged slowly closer to the bridge and pulled off to the right side. I propped the M-4 on the handle bars and took aim with the red dot.

I sent round after round kicking broken rocks into the thugs. Dirt flew and the people scattered. I could hear the Mule speeding by. The Colonel hit the lights as he passed me. Those guys at the bridge were crapping themselves. They ran in all directions and yes at least a couple of them had weapons. Their fire was erratic at best. I saw the Colonel stop on the other side. He started shooting, so I changed magazines and hit the gas. By the time I made it to the bridge, the resistance was light. There were a few shots from the trees, but nothing close enough to make me worry.

We made our way as fast as the Mule could go onto our next way-point. After two miles, we finally took time to slow. Our little sprint in the last two minutes covered more distance than we had gone the previous five hours. It was hard to cope with the adrenalin rush as I shook from head to foot. The Colonel said it was better than any drug he could imagine.

We made our way to the mid-way rally point, but we were very nearly out of gas. We were wet, tired, muddy, and altogether hungry. The sniper team was late. They finally arrived with supplies, but said we could not rest here. The green shirts had been fighting someone at the old Wal-Mart this afternoon and there was some shooting at a bridge nearby. We chuckled and said, "Yeah, we heard some gunfire."

The last legs of our journey were a bit more pleasant since we were getting away from the larger towns. The country was our home. We relaxed when we could see nothing but trees. Late in the evening of our second day's travel, we re-entered our small community. Our teams were waiting for us as we radioed in our arrival to the sniper bunker. A lot of people were gathered in anticipation of our return. But all I could see was Seven in her pony tail, as she hugged me home.

Chapter 34
My New Career

The day after I returned from the militia conference, I reported for my new work assignment. My sick excuse was successful, but I was being tracked to make sure I reported in. The next morning, the people at the Community Services Center, directed Seven and I to a particular bus that would take us near our office. Seven met me along the way, and we boarded together. The weather was still a bit poor as the bus left town. Cool rain pelted the windows. After several stops, Seven and I were directed to report to a square brick building. I recognized the place as a central telephone office surrounded by security fencing.

A central office is where all your phone calls are processed. Every telephone is connected to every other telephone in the world through the electronic equipment housed in those buildings. Every central office is connected together with a variety of other electronics that use a number of different technologies. Oh it can get confusing. A cell phone talks to a tower, the tower is connected to a central office switch. The switch connects your call through to other central offices, and out to another cell tower or a traditional phone line. Yeah, and that, is just the super-simplified, high-level version, of the telephone systems. It gets crazy from there.

We showed our ID to two green shirt guards at the entrance and were allowed inside. Inside the office, we were greeted by an overweight man with an unkempt beard. Electronic equipment hummed in the background. The lights were on inside the building and the fans were running. The bearded man was not a green shirt, but it did look like he wore some sort of supervisor's uniform. His dark green work shirt was stained at the pocket from whatever he had eaten last.

"Here, put these on," the man said before we even knew his name.

He handed us a couple of light green T-shirts, never looking at me as he stared at Seven. I disliked the man immediately. Seven excused herself to the restroom as I watched this guy follow her with his eyes. When his eyes met mine, there was at least some amount of understanding transferred from my intensity.

"I am reporting for duty too," I told him.

"Well, fine. What experience do you have?" the man asked.

I told him the cover story of Seven and I working as telecom professionals before the power went out. Seven returned from the restroom sporting her new worker's T-shirt. It was right there that I realized how good she was at her intelligence role. She recognized the opportunity of the man's stare and was making the most of his attention. The supervisor quickly dismissed me to the equipment room to learn the system on my own. Seven was ushered into the office by the supervisor for a guided tour.

A few other workers milled about the equipment room, so I introduced myself. The other workers in the office had some, to almost no telecom background. The supervisor seemed to have worked in this office in some fashion before the green shirt takeover. Very few of the workers seemed to know how to even use the hand tools. It was my guess that these poor folks were pressed into service by people that knew even less about the business.

I was able to identify the equipment that was operational and what was still waiting to be restarted. I found the office records and the drawings of the network architecture. My knowledge of the equipment allowed me to spot how much of the telecom network was actually up and running. It looked to me like several of the green shirt offices in several towns already had telephones back up. This was news to us.

When the supervisor returned, he introduced Seven and me to the workers. You could tell he was really getting into his supervisor role. He relished the idea of being important.

He was in control of people's lives, their boss. Under the green shirts, your work supervisor reported how good a job you did to the authorities. If you were a pain to a supervisor, they made sure you experienced real pain, literally. I wondered if this guy had been promoted from janitor.

The day passed without too much trouble. There was a lot of confusion and the workers had no real clue how to run things. Mostly, they sat and stared at manuals trying to figure out what button to push next. I started up some training on how to use common hand tools such as wire-wrap guns and test meters. They were impressed to find out the significance of alarm lights and warning bells. Needless to say, it was a long first day.

One the bus ride home, Seven and I compared notes.

"How was your first day at work Seven? I asked her as we sat in the last two seats of the bus.

Seven looked at me and smiled, "Well our supervisor's name is Bob. Bob is married, which he assures me is very open, and used to be one of the union guys there in the office. I think he was a representative of some sort. The security code for the doors is 3425. Bob's favorite color is blue, like my eyes, and his spare ID card is in my back pocket. Bob has been instructed to get the phones back up and running in all the green shirt offices by Christmas, or else. He has no idea how to do it, but he does not want to fail his green shirt bosses."

I knew Seven was good, but wow.

I told Seven, "Be careful. This guy comes across as someone who loves his authority way too much. But, we are in a great position. I can get things running and set up some ways for us to track phone calls, if you can keep Bob distracted. If you can get Bob to make you an assistant supervisor, it will help us get on the inside of this organization. Our access will get us into a bunch of government offices. But, don't underestimate this guy. He is a bit of nut if you ask me."

Seven assured me that she would be careful. We were both tired and glad to be heading home from the grueling 12-hour shift.

Time passed pretty quickly as we got accustomed to working again. Right before Thanksgiving, I had our central office working close to normal capacity. The green shirts gave us instructions forbidding us to activate any phone lines not on their approved lists. These approved lists, included only government offices and community centers. Cell phones were still outlawed to non-government workers. The green shirts wanted to maintain their ruling status as the only people equipped with the modern conveniences of life.

Our supervisor, Bob, was rewarded by the green shirts for his work to better the public services. He drove to work in a sharp new pickup truck one day. He had been allowed the privilege of driving a government vehicle. Those of us that worked for Bob held our tongues as He bragged about his success at every opportunity. He was really into patting himself on the back for the office's success. I think I saw the man walk into the equipment room a total of twice the whole time I was there.

Seven got herself appointed as a supervisor's assistant, just like we wanted. We were making reports back through our Intel channels on an almost daily basis. That is when we noticed a facility on our green shirt approved reconnection list. This place was labeled top-priority and it carried a bit of clout from higher ups.

Was this the major warehouse we had been searching for all this time? We didn't know, but we were hot to find out. Seven and I made immediate reports to our Intel groups so they could research this place. If our guess was correct, we would have access to items like weapons, ammunition, food stores, as well as the coveted medicines. We knew the green shirts had to be storing this stuff somewhere. But exactly where, had always been the big question.

While we waited for feedback confirmation on the warehouse, Thanksgiving break came. I went to Seven's house where we had a simple meal and observed the traditional giving of thanks to God. Meanwhile the official green shirt edict was to give thanks to the Secretary of the Republic for his leadership and care for the people. They wanted everyone to give thanks for the harvest and the green shirt party and so forth. Green shirt propaganda was never ending and we all wondered what they would do to replace Christmas.

Seven and I spent the majority of our spare time together nowadays. Maybe it was the war, maybe it was the fear of not surviving the green shirts; but we set the date for our wedding. We would be hitched on Christmas, God willing and the creeks don't rise my Dad used to say. Perhaps that was a bit hillbilly of a way to say it, but back then, it was okay.

After the Thanksgiving break, I made a discovery that confirmed a lot of what we suspected. We figured the really top officials in this new government must really be living the sweet life. I was to find out just how sweet as I was ordered to do some remote work on some residential telephone lines.

It was late in my shift as the supervisor called me to his office. He smelled of onions and stale beer as he gave me an assignment.

"I want you to take that line truck, and one of the other workers, to go connect some phone lines," Bob grunted towards me.

"But sir, I thought we were not to connect anything but government offices?" I told him.

"Never mind that," He bellowed. "These people are high ranking party officials. They make the rules. You just do what you're told."

"Ahh, I see. Yes sir I will get right over there and get them up and running in no time," I said. I wanted to see where these people lived anyway.

"You better or there will be hell to pay. I want you to call me when it is back on," Bob threatened me.

I wasn't too worried about Bob and his mouth. Bob knew that if anything were to happen to me, his whole operation would collapse. Bob needed me to keep this place running and he would do anything to keep in the good favors of his bosses. As I packed the truck for the job, I caught Seven's eye. I looked at her and tried to say a lot with just a look. She understood and gave me the, I'll-be-okay-look, and winked. Heaven help Bob if he laid a hand on her.

The worker I choose to go with me was the most experienced person in the office. Raj was from India. He had been an installer before all this crazy stuff started happening. Raj and I left the central office and headed towards the gated community where our work assignment waited. I had been through check points before, but this was crazy. The gated community was one I had known from years past as I passed by it on occasion. Million dollar homes were commonplace. I had worked as a security guard near this place back when I was in college. Boy, they took security seriously nowadays. We had to get through three checkpoints where our IDs were visually verified. They were serious about keeping people out. I saw a small fortress that was the local security office. This community was locked down better than any facility I had seen to date. I wondered if military installation were this heavily guarded.

After gaining entry, Raj and I went about our work. This community had been partially damaged near the outskirts early on in the unrest. Some of the wiring leading to the houses was disconnected and needed to be re-attached. While we worked, night fell and the cool air slowed our progress. Numb fingers are no good for delicate wiring work. We watched as electric lights came on in all the houses. These homes had power and central heating.

I left Raj working on a junction box, so I took the truck. Our security escorts were with us all the way. I drove down to the large mansions near the golf course clubhouse and set up across from a house that was having a cocktail party. What a strange sight to see people in evening wear in a social setting. People in my town were near starvation, and these people were sipping wine and had uniformed waiters. I saw a couple of people using cell phones, but I could hardly believe it. Our office did not support cell phones, so that meant one of the main cell-phone offices in Raleigh was up and running. I made note to investigate that in more detail later.

From the top of the bucket truck's swing arm, I continued to work the fake problem with the telephone wires. The security guy had no idea what I was doing, and did not care. I watched the party for some time observing the faces of the guests.

That is when I recognized him. One of the party guests dressed in a black suit had a face I would never forget in a million years. It was the man that shot our Colonel in the street back in the summer. It was this man that had been sent to our town to demonstrate the power of the state by killing our mayor. If a stare could kill, this guy would have been dead meat. I watched the man for five minutes, before he left the house. When he did, my security escort perked up and started to give me orders. I was instructed to finish my work and get moving. As I completed my fake work, I watched the man get into a limo and leave.

"Who is that guy?" I asked my security escort.

"That is the Chief of Police, you better finish what you are doing here and move along," the security guy told me.

After Raj and I completed our tests, we called back to the central office. Bob wanted to be the person to dial the houses informing them personally how he re-connected the phones. We listened to the gloating Bob-The-Supervisor, as we called him, ring house after house. Bob wanted to make sure all these important people knew he was the one making their lives come back to normal. I monitored everything from the junction box under the watchful eye of the security guards. Once the excitement was over, we packed up for the night and headed back.

That night I had to sleep in the central office because the worker's transportation system stopped for the night. In the morning, an anxious Seven woke me from a deep asleep on the office couch. I awoke to her caressing my face. I could see that she was visibly relieved to find me safe and sound having passed the night in the relative safety of the office. Between our co-worker's entering, I relayed what I had found. She was shocked to hear of the opulent dinner party while people we knew starved. But when I told her of the head of green shirt police attending the party, shock turned to anger.

"That man is a top priority target; we must get him," Seven said determined.

I was with her on that. If that man ever got in my crosshairs again, I vowed to pull the trigger.

Chapter 35
Raid

A couple days after the phone work for the dinner party, our office was assigned to the repair of the warehouse we were interested. I volunteered myself, Seven, and another truck crew to head over to the warehouse so we could repair the lines. Seven was ready to get out of the office away from smelly Bob for a while. Bob was in a fairly accommodating mood that day, and the prospect of another at-a-boy from his bosses, made him approve my personnel request.

We made our way through checkpoints as we drove to the warehouse. This place was guarded almost as well as the gated community. Container trucks interlaced with police cars lined the roads leading to the fenced-in lot. The warehouse itself was massive off-white building with a flat metal roof. After 30 minutes of check-in and vehicle searches, our trucks were allowed inside the parking lot. This was the busiest place I had seen in months. There were fuel trucks off in the corner. Container trucks waited for bays to open up to the warehouse. Forklifts moved pallets. Green shirts with clipboards hustled around directing the work. It was amazing to see.

As we entered the parking lot, we were met by one of the green shirts.

"What are you doing here?" He questioned us.

"We are here to get your phones back up and running," I said smiling.

"You are not supposed to be here till 2PM; its 10:30AM," He said looking at me obviously confused.

"Well, we can come back some other time if you want. I am sure your boss won't mind you denying our entry," I told him sarcastically.

"Come on through then," he waved.

I set our other team to work on the poles leading through the warehouse parking lot. Seven and I got permission to proceed inside from our security escort and headed out. Sure enough, I could see why they wanted to keep everyone out of this place. The warehouse was so massive you could hide a football stadium in one corner. There had been some damage due to riots of months ago. The place was painted, but not 100% repaired. The lights were on in most places, but there were some fixtures either empty or altogether missing. Doorways had been re-constructed, walls had been hastily patched, and there were hundreds of low-level laborers doing any number of tasks.

In one section, normal police cruisers and busses were getting green shirt paint jobs. Giant cooler sections housed food stores. Forklifts carried pallets to and from container trucks. Full pallet racks reached to the ceiling. I saw some of the container trucks labeled 'Recycling Department' and it made my stomach turn. I wondered how many of the workers in this facility knew where these trucks were coming from. Seven and I marveled at the sheer volume of stuff at this place.

"We need to see the office," I told our escort.

We were directed through a maze of hallways and side doors before we got to the main office. There we were ushered into the telecom room. Seven and I worked by ourselves for a half hour before the one of the warehouse supervisors came in.

"We need these phones up and running today," He told us flatly.

"From what I have seen, this will be at least three or four days of work to get you going again," I told him. I wanted an excuse for us to sneak more of a peek.

The man got in my face and reminded me that he was a supervisor and that I should watch what I said.

I thought the man was going to blow a gasket, so I assumed the demeanor of a servant immediately. I gave him a bunch of "yes sirs" and "I apologize" and so forth. He finally relented and left us to work.

Once we were alone, Seven grinned at me and smirked, "You are getting good at this."

I smiled and told her, "Oh, hush."

Our truck crew outside continued to work on the phone lines leading to the building. I continually reported that we kept finding things to repair inside. As we worked throughout the building, there were two sections which seemed to be out-of-bounds. It was not often the doors leading to these sections were opened. However, before we left, I saw one of these sections open up. From a distance, I could see blue barrels with what looked like wood sticks poking out of the top. In the background, I saw wooden crates stacked on pallets. This was a weapons locker.

Jackpot!

With plans to return the next day, Seven and I returned to our central office.

When I finally got home from my day's work, I plopped down for a quick rest. After most everyone settled in for the night, I wrapped up and headed out into the cold. Fall was turning the air cool at night and I hated the prospect of winter already. Our houses were cold, there were no lights, and food was scarce. In a nutshell, it sucked.

I made my way to the headquarters bunker in hopes of finding the Colonel there. As I entered through the trap door system, I saw the Colonel talking with a couple of my sniper squad leaders. Immediately I was recognized as Captain Huck along with the curved finger salute. I planned on getting them back some day.

"Colonel, I have some information you are going to be interested in," I told him.

"What is it, Huck?" he gestured me to sit.

"Seven and I found the big warehouse the green shirts are using to store and distribute their loot."

"Really, where?" he asked as he pulled out a map.

I pointed it out, "The place is secure, like Fort Knox secure, and it's huge. There are weapons, ammunition, food, you name it. But if you ask me, we need to get 2nd militia involved. If we do one big raid we both may get the materials we need to fight these guys. If we try small raids, we risk losing the element of surprise and the place will be locked down even stronger."

"How big is this place, Huck?" the Colonel asked.

I told him everything I saw while drawing out a sketch of the floor plan. I estimated the strength of the warehouse security force. We sat and went through different options and objectives. Rooster and the Captain of Intel were called in to give their opinions. This was going to be the raid to end all raids. The resulting success or failure may influence the outcome of our entire resistance.

We worked late into the night and decided on several key points. Our first objective was weapons and ammunition. We included demolition equipment as much as could be scrounged. Second objective was medicine and medical supplies. Thirdly we needed food, if at all possible. Our plans included some cooperation with 2nd militia and perhaps the 5th as well. Intel teams were woken and activation plans were put into action. Coded radio messages alerted commands all over the state. If possible, we would hit the warehouse on Monday morning. It was the wee hours of Friday morning as we hurried around getting teams their orders and people positioned for the raid.

On Friday morning, I reported to the worker's bus, not having slept a wink. Seven watched over me as I slept in my seat. Man I was tired, but today was our last chance for intelligence gathering on the warehouse. Seven and I reported in for work and waited for our supervisor to arrive. Once he came in, we got his authorization to go back out to the warehouse to complete our work. Bob-the-supervisor was not altogether cooperative today though. He wanted Seven in the office and told me to choose someone else for the truck. His mood had swung again. The man was very unpredictable. One minute he was at least tolerable, the next he was popping a gasket yelling at everyone. So, I choose someone that was a bit lazy and knew very little about telephone equipment. A stooge is useful sometimes.

We packed up and headed for the warehouse. The interstate had lots of traffic for this day and age. But nothing like what it used to be. Upon arrival, we passed through security, and several searches later, we entered the secure parking lot of the warehouse. As the day before, I sent the other truck to work on the lines outside of the building. Our security escort took us to the main office where we found the supervisor in charge. I gave him a whole sales pitch on how we would be finishing today and how much he would like the phones working again. I said we would get the faxes working, and if I could get inside some places, I could repair the internet as well. He was so used to being in charge and irritable that he proceeded to bless me out for not coming sooner. When I think of him, I realize that some people shouldn't be in charge of so much as toilet paper.

After more "yes sirs" and "I'll get to its", he finally let me get to work. My co-worker sat in the telecom room where I instructed him to sit and watch the lights come on. These lights meant little, but I knew the guy would be out of my way for hours. By now, our security escort was accustomed to us going into secure areas. I asked my escort guard to let me in several areas I had not been in the day before. While I pulled wires and worked with hand tools, I noted everything I could see. I actually had to do a little work here and there, but mostly I was doing recon. Finally, I asked to climb to the edge of the weapons storage area. My guard allowed me to go up the ladder and crawl around. While in the rafters and out of sight, I sketched the layout of the weapons and made notes what was available. After 20 minutes, I returned to the main office and started testing the lines.

Again, I gave Bob the Supervisor the opportunity to call into the warehouse and take credit for reconnecting the phone lines. While the two supervisors congratulated themselves, I stood in the background of the office. There I noticed a garbage pail with papers inside. Most importantly, I noticed that these papers were orders for trucks to take containers to various locations throughout the state. I quickly snatched a few of them and shoved them into the bottom of my tool bag. The office workers paid no attention to anything outside their cubicles. Undoubtedly they feared the supervisor to the point where they didn't feel confident enough to look around. I left that day with a fist full of information on how the place ran.

Seven was relieved as we came back from the warehouse. After our work shift, we rode home and I relayed everything I had seen at the warehouse. She reported that Bob chased her around the office and was getting irritable at her unwillingness to cooperate. Bob was getting on my nerves.

I reported once again to the Colonel late in the evening. I was so tired; I barely made it to the bunker. However, my new information gave me a sense of urgency that propelled me on. This new information gave us the ability to make up fake order requests. If we were lucky, we could have the green shirts load the trucks for us and haul them out of the compound. If we were not so lucky, we would have to assault the compound directly. A direct assault had the distinct possibility of epic failure. But, that is always the risk you take.

I finally got some sleep on Sunday night, and was thankful for it as Monday rolled around. Seven and I reported into work as usual to the central office. I made some excuse for working on antennae equipment, while others worked regular maintenance in the equipment room. Once the roof, I pulled out my GMRS radio to listen to the raid. This was the first time I was not a part of a major operation.

In the quiet of the roof top, I listened among the wind.

09:26 *"This is Snake One, go for Betty, six eggs rolled,"* I heard faintly. I knew Snake to be a sniper team setup outside the warehouse. Betty was the operational go-code for the mission. Eggs referred to the number of trucks leaving the compound

09:31 KA-Boom! You could hear the blast from someone's open microphone way off in the distance. Twenty seconds later I heard the dull thump of the explosion from my roof-top, miles away.

09:32 "This is Snake, Fife on the move." Fife was the code for local security. They were responding to the explosion.

09:40 With the rattle of gun fire in the background static I heard, "Bravo Two, go now, I repeat GO now!"

"Two, this is Six. My team is pinned down by the truck to our 2-oclock, I need sniper support."

"This is Snake, wait one. Ka-blam! Ka-blam!"

"Snake this is Six, were good, Charlie Mike." I could still hear rifle fire in the background and lots of it.

I could see the operation unfolding in my mind. The trucks with our goodies had left. An assault force (Bravo Two) from 3rd militia as working with (Bravo One) from 2nd militia to assault the warehouse. Bravo One's goal was to detonate an explosive a mile or so from the warehouse at a major roadway. This distraction would send all available security to their location first. After a brief firefight, 2nd militia would pull back and do their best to disappear. This left the warehouse to Bravo Two. Our sniper teams were covering the assault and keeping the green shirts off balance.

09:50 "Bravo One this is Rattler, Wilma, I repeat Wilma." I knew Wilma was the code for pulling back and disengaging.

09:51 "Rattler, this is Snake-Three, Geese, Geese, eta six minutes." Snake-Three was a sniper team assigned to watch the airport helicopter gunships at the airport. Geese referred to helicopters themselves. Rattler was our Colonel.

09:52 "Bravo Two, Rattler, two minutes. Op status Go."

"Rattler this is Bravo Two,....roger 2 minutes. 50%, over.

09:53 "Snake this is Bravo Two, cover the west gate! They have blocked the gate!

"Roger Bravo Two, sending now." Ka-Blam! pow,pow,pow.

The gunfire could be heard in the background of every transmission. From my roof, I heard rotor blades from helicopters off in the distance.

"Bravo Two, Rattler, Wilma."

"Kingpin roll, I repeat Kingpin roll."

"Daisy roll, Daisy roll."

"Snake units, Wilma. Snake units, Wilma."

"Snake-Three roger; geese flying North from position alpha."

As I listened to my radio on the roof I was barely aware of the access door opening. I was so in the zone listening to the operation that it was almost too late for me to conceal the small radio into my coveralls.

"What are you doing up here?" Bob demanded.

"I came up to reset the GPS antennas. Then I heard gunfire off in the distance after that loud boom," I told him.

Bob looked off towards the declining noise then said, "You have been gone for half an hour, now get back downstairs and make yourself useful."

I was more than annoyed at this jerk by now. I didn't know how long I could stand this guy.

The rest of the day I was just about useless. My mind kept racing back to the operation. I was more than anxious to find out how successful it had been. Who was alive and who had died, making this daring daylight raid?

That night, after we got back to our town, Seven and I snuck to the operations bunker. As we passed through our secure doorway, the interior was packed with people. The mood was exuberant. I went over to the Colonel who was in the mass of camouflaged militia.

"Huck! It was great! You should have seen it. We got so much stuff, it will take a month to hide it all," the Colonel gasped.

Rooster chimed in, "Those green shirts are still wondering just what the hell we did to them. Good luck finding us," he sneered.

"How did you guys get away from the gunships?" I asked with a smile.

"Oh, that was great. We used six decoy trucks loaded with some cadavers."

"You mean, you guys drove around with dead bodies in the cab?" I asked.

"When the green shirts realized that we had stolen their trucks just outside the gates, the trucks became targets. They came looking for six container trucks and that's what we gave them. Our drivers took the real trucks to several old IBM buildings a mile or two down Alexander drive. The prop trucks with the corpses were parked on I-40, just off US-1, where the green shirts had traffic blocked. When the helos came over I-40, they saw our six decoy trucks and didn't look any further. The green shirts assumed we had gotten blocked on the interstate, and we let them do the rest. While our drivers escaped under the bridge, the helicopters rocketed the trucks," Rooster explained grinning from ear to ear.

"Holy cow, guys that was brilliant," I told them.

The Colonel continued, "2nd militia made a getaway after they stirred up the hornet's nest. They report only a few men wounded."

"Do we have all the stuff we need then?" I asked hopefully.

"You bet we did, Huck. The teams started reporting the trucks at their unload zones a couple hours ago. We made away with four entire truck loads. The other two was sent to the 2nd militia. Captain Bullet reported that his command had buried a whole truck, cab and all, five minutes after it arrived at his location." Everyone cheered.

Others chimed in with their stories. The logistics Captain said it would take more than a week to go through the stuff and distribute it among the bunkers. The sniper teams were not all back yet, but some were already reliving their shots for the people gathering around the bunker's tables.

I could not believe what a stress reliever this mission had been. It actually worked. A few of our people had been injured, but nothing too serious. The green shirts lost a bunch of people, but had nothing to show for it. I would hate to be the one left trying to explain how six truckloads of weaponry and ammunition disappeared. I did not expect to see that irritable green shirt warehouse supervisor any time soon.

Maybe they will call again and want me to fix their phone lines.

Chapter 36
Nothing Fancy

The weeks that followed were busy, but not as bad as before. December was getting cold and winter was plowing into full gear. Almost no leaves were left on the trees, and woods seemed that much emptier. A lot of us had moved in with friends who had houses with wood stoves or fireplaces. My parent's old house was older and had a fireplace. During the fall, I managed to remove my small cast-iron stove from the garage and put it into the kitchen. With both the fireplace and stove burning, the house was livable. After much persuading, begging, pleading and threat-of-force, I convinced Seven and her folks to move in with me. No, Seven and I did not share a room. We waited for our honeymoon.

With Christmas around the corner, I was getting nervous about getting married. Seven was feeling the same way from the way she acted. I think for her, it was a problem with logistics. There were only a couple of ministers in hiding and finding one was going to be difficult. She and I had always imagined getting married in the church. But that looked unlikely. We talked about the arrangements several times, but it seemed like we were better suited to running militia operations than planning a wedding.

That is when it dawned on me how to prepare for the whole matrimony affair. We would have our closest friends help prepare everything. Yep, I got Rooster as Captain of the sniper teams to find me a minister. We fixed up the sniper bunker with drapes and took the cross down off the ceiling. With the cross hung up on the end wall and we made a short stage out of wooden crates. As long as we did not have to dance on it, we were okay. The teams really got creative and spruced the place up really nice.

Seven was kept in the dark and was not allowed to see the arrangements. She told us "nothing fancy" because that was not her style. What was funny to watch, were sniper teams coming back from recon missions and finding wedding decorations.

"What the hell have you guys been doing in here?" as one team came in.

"Are we having church or something?"

After they grounded their rifles and packs, they pitched in to hang draperies. My, what sight to see, those guys all decked out in camouflage hanging draperies.

The day before Christmas, a minister was found nearby. After a bit of begging, he was persuaded to perform the illegal, un-authorized, religious ceremony of marrying Seven and I. Oh yeah, the illegal wedding was to be performed in an illegal secret bunker, run by hard core militia types to boot. The minister would have stories to tell someday. What was funny was how the bride's family, as well as the minister, had to be blindfolded and led through the woods just to attend the wedding. It was a necessary security precaution though.

I had been in the bunker for a day or so getting everything ready. You don't know how anxious I got an hour before everyone was supposed to arrive. All sorts of things played out in my mind. Where was Fred, my best man? Would the green shirts stop my bride on the way to our wedding? Would today be the day someone gets spotted coming into the bunker? I would have rather been out on a mission than waiting here on pins and needles. Once everyone arrived, I was better. After a bit of clamoring, all our blindfolded guests made their way into our bunker. The place was cleaner than I had ever seen it. I hoped it would be approved by my mother-in-law to be. She looked around and did not gasp, so I figured we were okay.

Fred arrived late, "Sorry, Huck. I couldn't get away."

"Thanks Fred, it's not important or anything, just getting married here," I scolded him.

"They had me cooking down at the Community Center," he whispered back at me while people shuffled us around. We were lined up where we were supposed to stand for the ceremony.

"Cooking? They had you on the late shift? How did you get out of it?" I asked without thinking.

Fred paused for a second, "I told them I was sick."

"How did that work out, Fred?" I asked.

Fred responded quietly, "Let's just say, we are going to need a new coffee pot in the kitchen."

The preacher and I nearly busted out laughing. Fred grinned mildly as we got several looks of, "Will you guys shut up already?"

The wedding started right on cue with most of us holding back tears. I and the minister waited up front, while Seven and her father made their way from the other side of the room. We had a small aisle between chairs to make the place look like an actual little church setting. The music started, and our guests rose to see Seven. I turned and saw Seven for the first time in her white dress. I knew she was good looking, but I was in shock. She was stunning. Even in the dim light, she glowed. Her hair was down and she wore a graceful veil. My thoughts immediately went to my suit. Was I dressed nice enough? I was really worried that I my suit had not been dry-cleaned in more months than I cared to think. Wow! She was marrying me? As she got closer, all thoughts of my suit drained away. Nerves hit me for real. I stood rigid without being able to hear more than the pounding of my heart.

The ceremony was traditional, yet brief. The minister was well versed in wedding ceremonies and ours went smoothly. I almost stumbled my vows because Seven looked so deeply into my eyes. I got through without passing out, but it was close.

Our reception consisted of a handful of friends back at my house. We wanted to celebrate with people not in the militia, as well as club members. Some of Seven's friends had no clue she was involved in the resistance, and would never understand if they ever found out. The minister was thanked and offered an M-4 for his troubles.

He looked at me and asked, "What's and M-4?"

Half the people in the living room laughed, while the other half smiled blankly wondering what was funny.

Christmas was a blur as our lives seemed to be going at light speed. I was married and could hardly believe what was going on. Memories of those days gave me hope when it seemed there was none.

Seven's parents tried to give us as much privacy as possible in my parent's little house. We managed well enough. The temperature was dropping outside, so we could not let her folks freeze in their unheated home. It seemed we had to make a lot of these changes in our thinking just to cope with current living conditions. Little did we know just how much our lives were destined to change.

Winter

"Valley Forge"

Chapter 37
Deep Freeze

Green shirt offices made the point of being open on Christmas day. All workers were bussed to their regular green jobs. We mostly sat around and did nothing, but the point had been made. The green shirts would not allow any outward observance of a "religious" holiday. Outward religious ceremonies were prohibited in order to promote tolerance. At least, I think that was the official line. I think we all snuck out some decorations and celebrated in our own way. Most people were too scared to even whisper "Merry Christmas" to one another as they passed on the street. Fear of persecution is a powerful tool in shaping the behavior of the individual.

A day or two after Christmas the weather took a turn for the worse. The fall had been mostly sunny with some scattered rain. As November led into December, we had high hopes of a mild winter. Those hopes were dashed right after Christmas. North Carolina gets snow sometimes, but it usually does not last too long. The problem we have is ice. Sometimes North Carolina gets good and cold for a mid-Atlantic state. The jet stream arcs down over North Dakota and curves east towards us and Tennessee. When you mix the cold jet stream with mild moisture from the Gulf of Mexico, we get some serious ice. The temperature of the day may get above freezing, but when the night comes, the temperature drops and everything re-freezes.

Houses without power, without heat, froze. Houses without some form of heat like a wood-burning stove became unlivable. People huddled in their houses trying to stay warm. When temperatures drop in the teens, it gets real hard to cope without power. I had heard of people out west sleeping between the mattresses, but I never tried it until that winter. This was our first winter without the creature comforts we had become accustomed to in those days. We thought we were tough as the summer sweated us. The warm fall gave us a false sense of hope. But, the frigid winter temperatures humbled us.

Pipes that are uncovered have problems in these southern cold spurts. However, since we had no running water there was nothing to freeze. Yet the problem quickly became getting enough water to keep hydrated. That is where the green shirts were yet again playing a role. The church, now turned Community Services Center, offered warmth and light. The high school opened up and took people in. These seemed to be great at first; but only at first. People were forgetting already that the green shirts were the ones denying them power, heat and water.

To some, the promises of green shirt jobs and housing looked better and better. As part of the emergency-housing, came an opportunity for more "educational programs." These classes were a lot like the ones we had taken before the new green jobs initiatives. Although now, everyone including kids were being instructed. Family groups were split up. Adult programs focused again on "Public Duty", "Saving the Environment", and "How capitalism almost killed us all." Some of these classes did not even pretend to hide the fact that their origins came from Carl Marx or Chairman Mao. Kids were divided into different age groups and taught according to their level of understanding. During class, the children were quizzed on their parent's activities.

"Did your Mommy decorate for Christmas? Does she ever leave the house at night? Who are Daddy's friends? Does Daddy have a gun at home?"

Meanwhile praise sessions thanked the new Secretary of the Republic for his leadership and kindness in this time of crisis. The people ate the state's soup and drank from a state's cup; their liberty paid the bill.

Those of us healthy enough to live on our own did so. Those that had heat or water, tried to help others the best we could. We formed little cliques where we could share houses with wood burning stoves. We cut fire wood whenever possible, but gas for chain saws was long gone. This meant cutting trees by hand axes when the green shirts were not watching. They didn't want us to hurt the environment by killing trees. We wanted to survive the cold and plant trees later. The elderly again took the brunt of the poor weather. Older folks are cold even when it is warm outside. Now that temperatures dropped, sickness spread its ugly head again. Coughs became pneumonia. The green shirts only offered housing to those healthy enough to work. The militia supplied a few doses of medicine, but we had nothing able to really fight so many cases of pneumonia. Again, people died and there was nothing we could do but watch helplessly.

One night right before New-Years, several of us were huddled around a wood burning stove in a friend's cold house. By candlelight, the owner of the house pulled out a history book and began to read aloud the accounts of Washington's Army wintering at Valley Forge. It was incredible to hear the hardships of those times and see the same things happening again. The soldiers at Valley Forge were 11,000 strong and only 22 miles from a major city. We were in the hundreds spread out and trapped in our own small towns with no means of escape. After a while, we joked how this seemed more like the Alamo around here. Fred wished he was in Texas right now.

Seven and I worked during this time, but it was sporadic. The green shirt busses often had problems in the cold and sometimes there was simply no transportation. Restrictions on private vehicles on public roads kept us at home. The state had to hold its breath until the weather relented.

Chapter 38
New Years

When New Year's Eve rolled around, the green shirts again called for a community-wide town hall meeting. Brutally cold winds ushered in the town as the hour of the meeting arrived. Seven and I showed up and unbundled from our shabby coats coated with ice. Inside the former church was warm and inviting. Looking around, we noticed just how pale and sickly we all looked. Those of us willing to live on our own contrasted to the people submitting to the green shirts. As usual, I started looking at the number of green shirt police in the building. It was in my nature to always count the threats in any given situation, and I was not allowed to let my guard down now.

A woman I knew as one of my neighbors, Pam, had gone to the school several days ago when the cold spurt began. She was now dressed in what appeared to be a grey worker's uniform. I recognized these uniforms from our visits to other facilities while we fixed phones. Anyone that was a low level worker for the state wore these outfits. She addressed Seven and I while greeting us to the Community Center. She had known my parents and I had played in her yard as a kid. Now she looked at Seven and told her that she needed to come on over to the high school to the women's shelter. According to Pam, living on our own was ridiculous in this cold.

Seven looked at her and smiled saying, "But we just got married and we want to live on our own for now."

Pam looked left and right and was outwardly nervous. "Sweetie you can't be married unless you get approval." Her last few words were almost whispers. Pam looked like we had just told her we were eating people in the basement. She looked at us and smiled away her anxiety while she ushered us to the former sanctuary. I wondered if Pam was trying to help us, or if we needed to run.

We sat in the pews while greeting people and shaking hands with our friends. Everyone was at this meeting. Coughing could be heard throughout the building. We were in pretty bad shape. Our green shirt community-organizer-in-charge got the crowd's attention and called the meeting to order. Again we sat listening to a bunch of communist viewpoints on the citizen's duty to the state and adherence to its laws. After about 45 minutes of the speech, the speaker directed our attention to the drop-down screen. We watched as the screen lit up, and the house lights went dark.

The screen showed a cover page with the People's Planetary Revolution logo. As we watched, the screen flipped over to what appeared to be a live internet broadcast. We sat amazed at what we were seeing. There had been no TV or radio or internet for six or seven months. In appearance, the broadcast seemed like a presidential news conference. No U.S. flag hung behind the podium. Instead the PPR logo and what looked like a variation on the United Nations logo were shining silver emblems against an emerald green background.

A man dressed in a nice suit began the presentation by introducing himself as the secretary of broadcasting. It was his pleasure to announce the return of internet services and how this was the first broadcast on the new People's Information Network. The P.I.N. was now the sole source of broadcasting in all mediums. Tonight's broadcast was the first demonstration of the newly rebuilt internet. In order for us all to be an informed citizenry, they had to create this new ......blah....blah.

This continued for another 20 minutes, but it seemed like hours. After this PIN-head finished, I perked up again. The benevolent Secretary General of the Republic, Ronald Jones, was introduced. This was the first time any of us had seen this man.

The secretary general approached the podium and began his speech. There were a lot of things we did not understand as he spoke, but we listened. His message was full of self-gratifying accomplishments on how he reformed the broken American system and reformed it to a more fair and equitable society for all. There was no more rich and poor class. No more poverty, unemployment was all but wiped out. The state would care for everyone's needs, but there was also personal responsibility. The people had to work. Every citizen had to contribute his or her own skills and be rewarded for the same. Everyone was encouraged to do their best and work hard to rebuild the country in this new year.

The Secretary then continued as he pointed to a picture of the globe where most countries had been highlighted. These were the countries with agreements for mutual cooperation in the new era of civility. The former U.S., most of Europe, Russia, China, India, and the Middle East were now a part of a global cooperative. This league-of-nations shared the same laws and a new rate of exchange. Each nation would trade with the resources it had and share with partner nations less fortunate. Any nation not in the collective would have no means of trade with the civilized world.

And as he finished, he reminded everyone that disobedience to the state meant punishment. He would not allow the people to slide back into the old ways of self-fulfilling greed and laziness. Every man woman and child would need to get-on-board and follow the path to social justice and prosperity. No exceptions.

The internet feed concluded a short while later. We quietly discussed what we had seen. We were amazed at the outward appearance of control these people seemed to have across the world. It was shocking to see all those countries signed up as part of the collective. How in the world were they able to get all this done in such a short period of time?

Just when we thought we were about to be dismissed, our local speaker got everyone's attention. He announced that our area had been approved for 25 beds in the new medical center some 30 minutes away. Anyone needing medical care could go see a person designated in the back of the sanctuary. The rest of us were invited to stay for a reception where we would be fed in honor of the new year.

I noticed several of the militia leadership head towards the sign-up for the medical services. I knew they had the same questions as me. Where is this medical facility? When will people sent there, get back? We wanted to make sure these people were actually going to a hospital somewhere and not a prison. After a lot of questions and talking some of our folks got on the transport bus. We were worried, but we could not voice our concerns too heartily and risk reprisal. If we resisted now, it would only reflect badly on those of us refusing to get sick people the medical help they needed. We had no choice.

Chapter 39
Wanted

We made our way to the fellowship hall where some coffee and soup awaited. This was a pleasant gathering as we mingled around and talked with one another.

Fred came to where Seven and I stood, then quietly said, "Look over there by the door on the billboard."

Seven and I recognized his tone and casually made our way to the wall. On the wall were the normal public messages about the typical nonsense, but then a picture caught my eye. I recognized the scene in the photograph. This was the main street of the town where our militia teams had fought the gangs. This picture must have been taken a half hour after the fight from what I guessed.

I pointed to the picture and told Seven, "I was standing by that tree maybe 30 minutes before this was taken. The green shirts are going to blame this on us?"

She looked at the photo and read the caption below it. "Anyone with information on the vigilantly group responsible for the massacre of the citizens of...so forth and so on. "The criminal known as, Huck, with his criminal circles of violence....so forth and blah, blah." In essence, I was being blamed for everything from the beginning of time, or close to it.

Instinctively, we moved back to where we were standing before.

Fred asked, "Don't that kick you in the head?"

Seven responded, "I can't believe they are actually using picture of dead gang members to set up the militia this way."

I looked back and said, "It works for them quite nicely, don't you think? The green shirts allow the gangs to do their dirty work. When they are done with the gangs, they allow us to help wipe them out, and then blame the violence on us. We become the only threat left to a civilized world."

Seven looked worriedly into my eyes, "They know your code name."

"Yeah, I know. Maybe they will forget all about me some day," I smiled. Seven did not look amused.

As the night wore on, we mingled around and got a feel for the place. We had not been here for a while and the building had been going through a lot of changes. The wanted posters were spread out among all the walls between signs for new public jobs and what not.

There were a couple of computers along the wall, which seemed to be running. I watched as several of our older youth quickly sat down expecting to get on Google or perhaps download some music. As they went through the obligatory green shirt entrance page, they found only one web address available. It was the state information page. There was no access to anything else. You should have seen the disgusted face of the kids when they clicked music and all they got were new era patriotic songs praising the state. They were being taught a hard lesson in freedom, or lack thereof.

It was then that one of the local green shirts approached me from the crowd. He looked at me and asked "You are one of the workers in the communication facility right?

I told him I was.

"Your skills are required in the office," He directed me; pointing the way.

Seven held my arm for the briefest of moments to let me know to be careful. The man led to one of the back offices and knocked on the door. After a moment or two, he opened the door slightly and poked his head through. Once satisfied, he opened the door fully and ushered me in. Inside sat two men. Neither were in any kind of uniform. However, they were definitely green shirt. I guessed they were police and tensed up ready for a fight.

One of the men said, "We are having problems with this power system. Can you look at it and see what you can do?"

I breathed again and said, "Sure."

The men watched me for a minute or so, and then gradually went back their business. Even though their PC screens were blank, I knew what they were doing. The equipment I was working on was a data storage device for video equipment. As I worked the power problem, I noticed a lot of new coaxial cables coming from the ceiling. These guys were using too many surveillance cameras and it was crashing their system. I tried my best to keep the data storage device from operating properly, but there was no way to know for sure. After I restored the power, I told them it was something common for these systems.

"Nothing to worry about guys. If it happens again, just flick this switch, press this button, and you will be good to go," I told them.

I was escorted back out to the crowd where I joined an apprehensive Seven.

"Everything okay?" she asked while looking the other way.

"Oh yeah, everything's fine. Now go over there to that little boy of the Parkers, and get him to pull the fire alarm in the hallway," I told her between bites of soup.

Again, to her credit, she did not blink or ask me any questions. She casually made her way over the boy known for being one of the town's most infamous little rascals. After a couple of minutes, I noticed the boy leave the crowd. Right on cue, the fire alarm sounded and the crowd left the building in near panic. While leaving, I told several key militia members to get out of here as quietly as possible and spread the word to the others.

Seven got her folks out, and we made an excuse for leaving early. Most everyone left for the night after the fire alarm. Some reluctantly stayed to enjoy a few more minutes of warmth, before returning to their frigid homes.

Yet, more people signed up for training and the promise of a warm place to sleep that night. The green shirt public works programs were at least warmer than the cold houses waiting in the dark.

We left the parking lot and started our icy walk home. As we walked, I shared my discovery of the security cameras as well as the new green shirt men in the phone closet. I told everyone to pass the word that we were under surveillance.

"Don't underestimate the green shirts now, they control all the technology," I told them.

Chapter 40
Refugees

For about a week we did nothing but try to survive the cold. It wasn't till about mid-January when the ice cleared enough to allow traffic into our small town. Just seeing a bus gives me chills to this day. When I see two or three of them together, it makes me shudder. I remember how they used to arrest people and ship them off on busses. Seeing the faces of entire families trying to be brave as they looked back on their homes for the last time was something you never forget.

At least this time, when the busses came, they were full of people. That was a relief, but definitely not expected. About 10 in the morning, the busses pulled into the Community Services Center and started unloading dozens of worried, slow moving people. From the looks of it, they were carrying everything they owned in their hands. Seven and I had been in the area for some odd reason or another when they arrived. She insisted on finding out as much as she could. I watched as she helped usher the people into the building and pointed directions as if she were running the place. Man, she was good.

After a couple of hours, Seven returned home. I had lunch on the stove as she came in through the door.

"Hi sweetie, come on in," I told her as she closed the door.

She looked around the room, "Are my folks here?"

"No they are out; what did you find out? I asked.

As I served her some lunch as she told me her story.

"Let's see where to begin. The people from the busses today have been all over the place in the last few months. Most of the folks come from Chatham County somewhere. Some are from Pittsboro, some from Siler City, and everywhere in between," she began.

"Holy cow those folks might know something about 1st militia," I thought out loud.

"Well you can ask the gentleman I talked to about that," Seven smiled. "Once he gets settled, I have arranged for you two to meet."

"What do you mean, settled?" I asked perplexed.

"'Well, that's the second part. I looks like the green shirts have taken note of all the empty housing around here and they intend to settle these people permanently. From what I gather, the green shirts have been using this group as a mobile labor force and now that winter has come, they want to go ahead and assign them housing."

I interrupted, "Do you know, this could work to our advantage? These people have been carted around seeing things most of us in Intelligence could never sneak our way into. They may know all sorts of useful stuff."

Seven looked at me and said, "Well yeah, that's why I spent the last two hours in the Community Center wiping kid's noses," She had a way with words.

She only pecked at her lunch. She didn't seem to be real hungry. I was immediately taken aback. "Are you sick?" I asked.

"No, I just felt a bit queasy this morning and it seems to have lasted."

"Are you sure? You aren't running a fever are you? I felt her forehead. Nope, no fever. "You haven't been coughing have you?

"No, I just got up this morning and felt bad."

I looked at her blankly, "You couldn't be....a well...uh."

Seven looked at me in shock, "No, I mean can't be that.....uh well it would have had to be...let's see.....err, hmm."

I could see the gears turning in her head, calculating, "Well I could be, but I think it is just some bad potato or something. I am sure it will pass in a day or two."

Over the next few days the symptoms did not go away, they got a bit worse. Yep, we were going to have a baby. Our world had flipped upside down enough for one lifetime already. We were in no condition to be thinking about a baby. My life flashed before my eyes as I stared out of the window. How in the world could I provide for a family in these times? Would the green shirts end up getting us all?

Lucky for us, I had my meeting with one of the gentleman from Pittsboro and that got my mind focused on something else for a while. I left the house and walked over a few blocks to where this gentleman and his family were housed. I knocked on the front door as the sun blazed behind me in a cloudless sky.

"Hi, I believe you spoke to my wife the other day when you came into town?"

"Oh, yes come in please," the man greeted me.

I noticed his eyes dart left and right over my shoulder to see if anyone was watching me come in. This was a man accustomed to being on the defensive. He was a survivor. He looked to be in his mid to late forties with the definite air of a determined man. I sat in their living room as the kids were sent to play. We exchanged names and got to know each other for a while. We traded pleasantries on weather along with all the polite talk of getting settled in a new house and so forth.

After several minutes I asked, "So you are from Pittsboro?"

"Yes I am," He said non-committal.

"I hear there was some fighting down your way back in the spring."

"There was fighting all over back in the spring," he lobbed back at me.

"I heard that some tanks rolled in from Fort Bragg and really did a number on your town. They said Pittsboro downtown was half destroyed; a lot of people died."

I had to let him know I was in-the-know without being too overt. This guy might be a spy, for all I knew.

"You hear a lot of things up here. They're right about Pittsboro though. The town will never be the same," he said never looking away from me.

I could just about see the man's mind whirring in the background. He didn't know if he could trust me or not. For all he knew, I was a spy or informant. I had to be the first to approach him, so I did.

"I met a Colonel from your area back in the spring. I think it was on the *first,* if I remember correctly."

The man's eyebrows jumped when I said, *first.* Of course, I was meaning 1st militia who had been wiped out as they attempted a stand at Pittsboro.

"Ah, yes I think I know who you are talking about. I heard you guys up here lost a Colonel on the *third* a few months ago. I was sorry to hear that," the man lobbed back at me sipping his cup.

I knew we were good to go. He was referring to the 3rd militia's first Colonel who had been killed at the end of summer.

"What can you tell me of the green shirts where you come from?" I asked.

The man paused only for a second then decided to tell me. "After Pittsboro was reduced to smoking rubble, the green shirts left us alone for a while. It wasn't until late summer when they came to call. It's my guess that the green shirts were just getting organized about that time. They had enough gas to start transporting work-crews all over the place. We worked on roads, churches, farms, any labor intensive job they needed done. We moved from one job to the next."

"Have you been to any prisons?" I asked.

The man glared at me and said, "You don't want to go to no prison, son. I haven't seen anyone come back from one yet."

"I know. That was a lesson we learned too," I told him. I couldn't tell him more. "What do you know of the capitol? What is going on there?" I asked.

The man looked at me, "Back in the fall we worked several big projects in Raleigh. The green shirts had stuff going on all over. We dug tunnels and underground parking garages all around the capitol complex. Nobody ever works there long. They keep the projects under wraps because they don't want any one person to know too much."

"What do you mean tunnels?" I asked intrigued.

"Oh, they have all the buildings connected from the municipal building all the way down to the Governor's office. It took months of ripping up the streets and digging out the trenches. They would bring us in and work for a week in one place, then move us to another place the next week."

He gave me every detail possible. We sat in his living room and drew out maps according to his memories. He directed my drawings and filled in details from his first hand perspective. This information was pure gold for our upcoming operation. I was itching to share this with 2nd militia as soon as possible.

"Oh yeah, the buildings were re-dedicated to the green shirt movement and the People's Planetary Revolution. The Parks and Recreation building is now the Department of Recycling."

That tidbit caught my attention and held it, as I looked at the man in the face. In all seriousness that would scare most people I said, "I have an appointment there, and I intend to keep it."

He understood at some level. I meant the place was to have its reckoning and I wanted to deliver it. He simply took me at my word, and did not ask any further. I bet he would like to have a bit of payback after working in mobile labor camps for the last few months.

After several hours of talks, I thanked the man for his information and wished his family well. As I walked home my mind raced with all the possibilities this information offered. I was hoping this would be our big break.

Chapter 41
Fired

As the weather finally broke, we were able to start up what little normalcy we had left. Seven and I went back to the central telephone office where we worked. That day spelled the beginning of the end of my career as a phone man.

As per normal, Seven and I made our way to the bus stop and got on board. The busses took forever due to the remaining ice, but we got to work safely, although a little late. Upon arrival, Bob-the–Supervisor greeted us angrily at the door.

"Where have you two been? You have been gone for ten days!" Bob screamed red-faced with veins throbbing in his forehead. I didn't want a fight with this guy, this was a facility guarded by green shirt police. I did not want to risk arrest just now; I had too much to lose nowadays.

I responded calmly, "The busses have not run the whole time we were gone. We had no way to get here."

Smelly Bob blared, "We have been given reconnection assignments and things are running too slowly! You need to be here come hell or high water."

"The high-water was frozen," I joked in complete deadpan.

Seven started to laugh and covered her mouth with her gloved hand. Bob was having none of it and quickly reached out and grabbed her hand away. As I stepped forward to thrash Bob, he stopped dead in his tracks. Seven was holding her breath and genuinely looked fearful.

"What is this?" Bob demanded as he felt through her glove.

Seven looked at him, "It's my wedding ring."

"You cannot be married. I haven't given you permission. I was not given the form, so you CANNOT be married."

Seven looked at him, "I am not asking permission from you to get married."

"I should have you two arrested," Bob threatened towards me. He must have instinctively known it was me that she married.

I shouted at him, "Then where will you be, Bob? I do all your work around here. I was the one that got this office up and running. I trained the people how to do the job. You need me to do your work for you," I told him in a forceful way that I had never taken with him before.

Bob sneered back in a menacing, "I don't need this! I am going to fire you mister. You cannot be married, period!" And he stormed out of the room.

The rest of the day was pure tension at best. The other workers cowered in the furthest corners of the office and hardly spoke. They did not want to give Bob any excuse to get going again. That night we rode home in the back of the bus as usual. Seven was devastated that wearing her wedding ring caused so much trouble. Our nerves were on edge, and the evening passed slowly in the cold.

The next day we returned to work as normal. We were fearful on how Bob would react today. He may have us arrested as we walk through the door for all we knew. We expected a fight of some sort. But what happened took us all by surprise. Bob had a thing for Seven from day one. That was plain for everyone to see. As such, I didn't expect his rage from the day before to go away any time soon and everyone anticipated a fight.

Bob didn't seem to be anywhere nearby, so we tried to get to our regular duties. Seven headed to the office while I got my tools and went into the equipment room. I worked for maybe 15 minutes with a piece of gear before I heard Bob cursing at one of the other workers. They were behind some equipment racks on the other side of the office. I was genuinely surprised to hear him in the equipment room. This was only the second time I actually saw him in there.

"You stupid @$!#, you don't have any idea what you are doing. Do you?" Bob yelled at one of the workers. Bob ranted on, "You are just some stupid slut that has no idea what is going on around here, do you? I am going to have you all arrested. See how you like that."

In the background, I heard equipment being slammed and the woman crying. I saw Bob march off towards the office with tools in his hand.

This is the behavior I feared most from Bob. He was becoming mentally unhinged. Unfortunately, Bob was a green shirt approved supervisor for this facility. He could have any one of arrested for any reason. I was having none of his physical abuse though.

I headed to the other side of the office to find my coworker cringing in the floor. Bob had given her a gash across her face and temple. Until now, I didn't know Bob had hit her. I got pressure on her wound and tried to calm her down. Sounds of a commotion came from the office and my heart stopped. In near panic, I realized I needed to get to Seven NOW!

I ran through the equipment room and raced into the office. The desks were knocked sideways and most of everything was in the floor. Lamps hung by their cords over the side of chairs. Papers were strewn everywhere. Seven was backed up against a file cabinet trying to fend off the 350 pounds of smelly Bob. I ran full speed catching him under his right arm football tackling him against some shelves. Bob's right hand had a large torque wrench we used for tightening bolts. He smashed the hilt of the wrench down onto my back knocking the wind out of me. As I fell, I saw Seven give him a left side kick she learned in self-defense class. Even though her kick caught him solidly in the side, his massive bulk soaked up all the power of her blow. He once again reared back to hit her, my wife, my child, with that big chrome handled wrench.

I did the only thing I could do. I reached under my jacket and drew my concealed Glock 19 with all the speed I could muster. I lost count after the fourth shot from point blank range. Blood splattered all over the place. Crimson red splotches turned to running drips down the wall. Bob slumped until he fell over dead. He was nothing more than a heaping pile on the floor. Seven was frozen in place. Blood smeared her pretty face. A shocking amount of pain in my back and shoulder persuaded me to lower the Glock's muzzle to clink it on the floor. Bob must have broken one or two of my ribs just under the shoulder blade. I could hardly breathe. After what seemed like forever, but was likely seconds, Seven leaned down and hugged me crying.

In a few more seconds, I heard the back door of the building open. The other workers were getting out of the door with the injured woman. They had heard the shots, but did not know who was doing the shooting.

Seven looked around shaking and said, "We better get going."

I looked at her and got to my feet, "No, I am the wanted man. I shot Bob. Our baby does not need a fugitive mother."

"You are not leaving me here; I am coming with you," Seven protested.

"I have to go now, Seven. You have to stay here and continue our mission. You are next in line to be supervisor. Stay! They will not blame you for what I did," I pleaded with her.

Then I heard the sound of one of the security guards coming into the equipment room looking for the gunfire.

"Stay here! We cannot afford to have you on the run with our special delivery due in October. I will meet you in a couple days at the sniper bunker," I told her as I made my way to the side door.

Seven kissed me quickly and told me she loved me.

Chapter 42
Escape and Evasion

I headed out of the side door of the office as a police cruiser pulled into the secure parking lot in the front. The police were busy at the door as the workers milled around not knowing what had happened. I slipped into the rear parking area where we kept the trucks. For a moment, I considered taking one of the trucks, but I realized how quickly I would be caught. Instead, I holstered my Glock and flung open the driver's side door of the nearest vehicle. Inside the truck, I scrounged for anything useful. I found a set of coveralls, a cheap lighter, an old metal coffee cup, and a small spool of lacing. Lacing is a wax-coated string used to tie down cables in phone offices.

Twenty seconds later, I was scrambling onto the cab and climbing onto the top. I walked down the side of the square utility body and turned to the face the fence. This truck was parked right next to the outside chain-link fence. I used the coveralls as protection from the razor wire strung along the top of the posts. Without fear of being cut, I hauled myself over the fence and jumped down to the other side. I yanked the coveralls off the wire and headed for the adjacent ice-covered parking lot.

My adrenaline had not stopped all morning. I was sweating even though the temperature outside was close to freezing. I felt like I had already run a marathon. Before long, I would need to rest, but not until I was far from here. I heard a siren in the distance heading in my direction. I rounded a couple of corners and took stock of where I was. This was once a nice neighborhood in the 1960s. Now it was a bunch of small homes with flaking paint and bad roofs. The places were a dump for the most part. Old lawn mowers sat beside broken lawn chairs. Trash sat in the yards poking out from under what remained of the snow and ice. Every icy footstep I took made an enormous crunching sound. I worried that each step would give me away. I walked on as fast as I could without running or leaving tracks.

I walked a block or two north, then went a couple of blocks east. I had to get as far away as possible before the green shirt police could corner me. About 20 minutes into my escape, I saw a patrol car crossing a side street. As quickly as possible, I ran off the sidewalk and into the backyard of a house. This place had no cover, so I ran towards the nearby wooden fence. I jumped over and saw a place to hide. It was an old dog kennel that was thankfully un-occupied.

I crawled inside and curled up to stay warm. Luckily this thing actually looked like an igloo and it offered a perfect hiding spot. From my backyard hide, I watched the patrol car slowly pass by on the street. There were two cops inside. Each man looked out of his own window scanning the yards and houses. I stayed put for another five minutes and decided to poke my head out. Slowly I made my way towards the side of the nearest house where I caught sight of another patrol car. I quickly scrambled back to the doghouse and climbed back inside.

For the first time in 20 minutes, I felt the cold. As I lay there in the dank kennel, I noticed my leg shaking. Either from the adrenaline leaving me or the actual freezing cold setting in, I sat there shaking uncontrollably for several minutes. I was still clutching my rolled up coveralls with what few treasures I had scrounged from the truck to keep me alive. My back burned like fire making me wince.

I lay there thinking about what had occurred that fateful morning. Bob was dead. My new wife was hopefully alright, but I had no way to know for sure. I was on the run for real this time. I had almost no supplies, the weather was freezing cold and I was 15 miles from the nearest militia bunker. My back hurt like you would not believe. The neighborhood I was in looked something close to downtown Beirut. I had to get out of the green shirt dragnet soon, or risk being snatched before the sun went down. If I survived the day, the sub-freezing temperatures tonight may surely kill me.

After several minutes, I made a general plan of action. I had to keep moving or else the green shirts would catch me sooner or later. My community lay north, so I knew I had to make my way there as soon as possible. As I looked towards the street, I saw a single dark curtain move sideways. A young boy's face showed through the frosted glass of a window right in front of me. He must have been three years old or so. His eyes and mine locked. I knew I was in serious trouble. It was only a matter of time before a parent would discover me hiding in their back yard.

While the child watched, I crawled from the kennel once again and made my way around the house. I quickly crossed the street and headed through the next row of houses. I looked for houses that appeared to be boarded up or else had undisturbed snow in the yard. Undisturbed snow meant nobody was outside on a regular basis. Tracks, meant people regularly passed through the area.

After an hour of dodging patrols and people walking down the street, I found a burned out house that still had a few intact walls. I crouched in a blackened corner and put on my coveralls. Quickly, I took stock of what I had left. My Glock still had 9 rounds, a crusty lighter, a dirty coffee cup, and a roll of string, were my all I had to get me home. Why in the world did I leave my knife at home that morning? While I rested beside the burned wall, I kept turning my head in all directions. Once or twice I saw a police cruiser in the distance, but none were on this street.

Freezing air whistling through what remained of the house helped me decide to keep moving. Just moving was keeping me fairly warm, and kept my focus on getting out of town. Moving had several advantages as well. The green shirts were less likely to find me if I left no traceable path, and got beyond their patrols. A couple of plastic bags with trash made good props for my impromptu camouflage. I wanted to look like a workman running an errand or going home from the store. People are less likely to stop you if you look like you belong there.

I turned east trying to get out of the rows and rows of houses. How could so many homes be in such bad shape, I wondered. How bad were the first few months of power outages here? Was all this destruction due to gang violence?

My easterly direction took me towards a large roadway I knew I would eventually have to cross. This area was less residential and more oriented towards garages, old fast food places, and contractor yards. Most of the buildings were completely deserted or destroyed while a very few remained open for business. I walked along the sidewalk with only a few people taking mild notice of my presence. During that time, you didn't know who is walking down the street. That stranger could have just shot his boss that morning for all you knew.

What a weird sense of humor your mind creates when you are under so much stress.

Killing Bob weighed on my mind. It didn't have to be that way; but he forced me. Yet, I wished it had turned out differently and thoughts of guilt ran through my mind. Afternoon grew into evening as I walked. The pain in my back was severe. But the cloudy grey day was getting darker and soon it would be night. Clouds kept the air warmer during the day, but after the sun went down, the temperature would drop below freezing again. I had to find shelter for the night, and soon.

The last cinder-block building, before the overpass, looked like an old tire and radiator shop. One garage door was ajar with another hung sideways out of its metal track. Most of the windows were completely broken out or at least missing large pieces. Derelict cars sat with hoods open in the parking lot. I saw nobody around so I headed in that direction. At the door I dropped my bag of trash and pulled out my Glock 19. I cleared the rooms quickly to make sure nobody was still hanging around. I was alone.

Very few usable things remained in the garage. This place had been picked over many times throughout the months. Empty shelving covered in cobwebs lay broken and scattered. Trash of all kinds littered the floor. Empty oil cans, broken grinding wheels, chunks of wheel weights offered me nothing of value for surviving the night. This building would not offer me shelter either. There was no cover in case someone came looking around and police would be sure to visit before long. The walls would hold in the cold and freeze me to death by morning. I noticed a fire pit in the rear of the garage where someone had taken refuge long ago. All the firewood was gone. It was then that I noticed a piece of canvas covering one of the rear windows. I tore it down and looked for more. I found only a fragment of mirror from the bathroom and stuck it in my plastic bag. After lingering as long as I dared, I headed back to the front of the bay.

As I walked towards the garage door, I noticed a small hand held tool or something under the remnants of a workbench. Reaching down, I grabbed the duct-taped handle and discovered a true treasure. This had been a hunk of steel about eight inches in length and quarter inch thick. One side was ground down to make a sharp edge and other was covered in tape to make a handle. This had either been a knife for cutting sections of rubber hose or else been a make-shift weapon. It was exactly what I hoped to find. I tucked my new knife in my belt and shoved the canvas along with some loose cardboard into one of my plastic bags. I now had everything I needed to survive.

Briskly, I left the old garage after ensuring nobody lurked outside. No road traffic was in sight, so got back onto the side of the road. Continuing east under the bridge, I walked along the white line trying to look as if I belonged there. As I walked, a few trucks passed as well as a few busses. I wondered if Seven was on a bus heading home right about now. These thoughts kept my mind racing in the background. Was she safe? Had she been arrested? Did I make the right decision by leaving her behind? More than once tears ran down my face as I trudged along.

It was about dark when a squad car passed me on the road. The sight caught me off-guard to say the least. I watched horrified as the car slowed to a stop and started to back up. Instantly I weighed my options. If I ran, they would surely chase me. Almost surely they would catch me and find out who I was. A gun fight was not much of an option, my back was killing me and I didn't know if I could out-shoot the police with my broken ribs. The cops pulled alongside of me and rolled down the window as I stood there.

"What are you doing? The passenger cop asked.

"I'm just heading home, sir," I replied as light heartedly as I could.

"Where are you going?" he asked.

"Oh, I am just dropping off a sack for my supervisor," I said as I approached the car and lifted the bag slowly to show him.

The green shirt cop looked at me and paused briefly. The driver leaned over and looked at me through the passenger window and sat back up. "It isn't him. Let's go."

The passenger cop looked back at me and said, "Get going, you know you are not supposed to be out after dark."

The patrol car pulled out as I responded, "Yes sir."

I had no idea there was a curfew. It didn't matter though; my nerves were shot as they went out of sight. I would have thrown up if I had anything left in my stomach. Nerves with a lot of pain can cloud your thinking, but I had to press on. It was time for me to find some shelter or die from exposure.

I had several choices, but none of them were good. I could try one of the houses where smoke rose from the chimney. But I had no way of knowing what kind of reception I would get. The place might be a home of a green shirt cop or something just as bad. I could force my way in, but then I would have to hold the occupants at gun point all night. I was not willing or in-shape for that kind of nonsense. The last thing I wanted right now was more bloodshed. I chose the old-school approach to make camp in the woods.

The light was failing fast as I finally found an acceptable place to spend the night. Off to the right of the road there was a tract of wooded property with no houses. Five acres of woods was perfect to get off the road and stay hidden. I headed off the pavement among the oak trees, trying not to make tracks in the snowy patches. I looked over my shoulder, but nobody was paying any attention to me. Nobody wanted to outside in this freezing weather. I jogged through he leafless trees looking for the darkest part of the woods. I could barely see without a light, but I knew the cedar trees would be the darkest blobs in the woods. Small tree limbs snapped my face as I plodded along. With my face stinging like crazy, I reached the cedar trees some 250 yards off the road.

I dropped my shopping bags and marched in place trying to get feeling back in my legs. The temperature was dropping rapidly. My clothes were wet with sweat from all the walking that day. Wet clothing might prove to be fatal if I could not build a fire or get into some shelter. I pushed my way into a clump of cedar trees and picked out a small one in the middle. With my make-shift knife, I started cutting at the trunk about 30 inches off the ground. I hacked and cut and swore at that tree for quite some time before I was able to push the top of the tree over on its side.

The cedar tree had no snow or ice under it, due to its evergreen branches providing cover. With the top of the tree touching the ground and the trunk partially attached, I hollowed out the branches facing the ground. The area under the fallen trunk protected me on three sides. I cut several handfuls of branches from other nearby cedar trees and tied them to the side of my tree using the roll of lacing. More branches made a sleeping pad. Heaps of leaves insulated the sidewalls from the wind and would keep the light from my fire from shining too far. The nasty oil-covered canvas from the garage closed the open side of my make-shift shelter. I left a hole off to the side and top of the tree trunk to let the smoke out. The cardboard was laid on top of the cedar branches to make my bed.

Now it was time for fire. Again, I went to the cedar trees and collected the stringy flakes of bark for tender. I gathered a couple of handfuls of bark and several oak tree branches that were suspended in nearby trees. I did not want branches under the snow; they had soaked up too much water and would not burn well. I clumsily went about my work doing most of it by feel in almost pitch black. I was getting tired and colder by the minute, but I had to get enough supplies for at least a few hours. Once I holed up for the night, I did not want to come out again until morning. Once satisfied, I got inside my shelter and closed the canvas door. Everything depended on that old lighter from the telephone truck working. If it didn't work, I was in real trouble.

I felt for the cedar bark and rolled it in my hands making it like a ball of yarn. I pulled the lighter out of my pocket and flicked it. Nothing happened. I flicked it again, nothing. I was getting frantic. I started hashing out plan B in my head, but there was no plan B to be had now. I was committed to this place. I thought for a minute in complete silence in the black frozen woods. Then I remembered that some of these lighters have push-button safeties. I felt for the button with my numb hands and punched several things not knowing if it had worked. Again I flicked the lighter and it hissed out the most beautiful yellow flame. I quickly lit the cedar bark and added small dead branches slowly. The warmth and light of the fire was overwhelming.

I reclined on my cardboard mat and relaxed while the fire snapped and cracked to life. My muscles ached, my back protested profusely, and my stomach growled. When I felt I was able, I peeled off my coveralls and took off my hiking boots. In the light of the fire I removed my disgusting socks and wrung out the cold sweat. I remembered what I always told my Scouts. "Dry is warm and wet is cold." I was never gladder to have been a Boy Scout than right at that moment.

With the broken shard of mirror from the garage, I looked at my back. I could see a large nasty looking bruise swelling up from the impact of the wrench. It was already a multi-colored mess under the skin and it hurt just like it looked, bad. I laid out my clothes and started to dry them by the fire. Fatigue hit me as I lay on my left side thinking of Seven.

I awoke during the night a few times when the fire died down. The cold air alerted me every time the flames became small embers. In the morning, I woke at my regular time and poked the fire back to life. My clothes were dry, but smokier than ever as I dressed and opened the door of my shelter. Man, the air was cold this morning. It must still be sub-freezing temperatures outside. Back inside the shelter, I pulled out my old coffee cup and wiped it with fresh snow. I then filled it with clean snow and placed the cup at the edge of the fire. I added snow until I had a full cup of warm water ready to drink. My new enemy was dehydration as much as a green shirt cop right now.

I needed to be on my way, so I doused the fire with dirt and snow. Once I was sure I had everything, I grabbed my plastic bags and headed out. For the rest of the morning until perhaps mid-day, I kept to the woods as best I could. I figured I was about a mile east of the main road leading home, but it was kind of hard to tell. I had no map and I had to keep far enough away from roads to not be spotted. I tried to avoid houses because of the security risk they posed. These philosophies made my trip further, but it was the only way to keep safe.

As afternoon passed into evening, I once again started searching for a place to pass the night. My progress was already slow from lack of food. It was not like I was well fed or anything from the start. Now I had not eaten in two full days and my energy was draining quickly. My brain started to wander and I made mistakes while I trudged along. I could not afford any more injuries right now, so my focus was more important than ever. An image in the edge of the woods caught my eye. It must have been an old hunting cabin along the gas pipeline easement I was following. I stopped and watched the place for several minutes before I decided to check it out. No lights shone from the outside, the doors and windows all seemed to be intact. No smoke from the chimney; this place looked deserted.

I cautiously made my way around to the front of the cabin. There was an incomplete screened-in porch covered by a tin roof. With darkness falling fast, I quietly made my way onto the steps and stood by the door. Looking left and right I drew my Glock 19, and worked the door knob with my left hand. To my surprise, the knob turned and the door opened.

I took a step through and instantly realized I was not alone. The interior of the rustic cabin was dimly lit with a couple of candles illuminating stuffed ducks, a squirrel, and a white-tail deer's head hung on the wall. An old picnic table with a battery radio on top sat beside an ancient couch in front of a massive fireplace. I stood frozen; listening for the inhabitant, not daring to breath. The kitchen was sparse to say the least. Interior walls looked as though they had not been cleaned in decades. The wooden floor had a few rugs that had long since been worn out.

A door opened from my left as a black man in his mid-thirties walked into the room. He was completely unaware of my presence, or the open door.

Chapter 43
In Hiding

I closed the cabin door getting the man's attention. He froze, as he stared back at me in disbelief. He looked at me as if I were a grizzly bear that had snuck in. We continued to stare; nobody daring to move first.

"I am not here to hurt you," I tried to reassure him, while staring into his eyes through the Glock's sights.

His posture didn't slacken, "What do you want then?" he asked.

I told him, "I would just like to share your fire for a while, if you don't mind,"

The man looked and pointed at my gun and asked, "Okay then. Are you going to shoot me later then?"

"Maybe" I said as I walked around the two rooms to see if we were alone. There were no signs of anyone else living there.

He watched me go from room to room, "I see. So, who are you then, mister?"

"You can call me, Huck," I said without thinking. In the back of my mind I regretted the mistake instantly. I forgot how *wanted* I was at the moment.

I could see the recognition in his face. He played it off, but I could tell he had heard the name before. I was betting that I was pretty close to being portrayed as Jeffry Dommer or someone just as bad.

"What's your name then? I asked after finishing my security sweep.

"I'm Richard Pate," he said flatly with his hands still in the air. He had not moved from the spot or twitched a muscle since I came in.

My mind raced for a moment. I knew that name. I had seen it somewhere before. But where? While I thought, he moved to sit by the fireplace in a reclining chair. I walked over and patted down the chair to make sure he didn't have a gun in the cushions; then stepped back. He sat calmly without saying anything after I moved away.

Then it dawned on me, "I know where I heard that name before. You were a reporter for the newspaper, right?"

"Yeah, that's me" he replied.

I sat on the cruddy old couch, and faced Richard while holstering my Glock. My back made me wince and take a deep breath as I sat against the cushions. I never took my eyes off him though.

"I thought all you newspaper guys were dead and buried by now," I smirked.

"I might be the last of the writers before the green shirts took over management. I heard *you* have been busy lately, though," he gestured to the radio on the picnic table.

"Yeah, trouble seems to find me somehow. It's a long story. Maybe you will have to write it some time," I joked coldly.

"I don't think my services are required anymore," Richard replied. "You see, I might not write exactly according to *the new Department of Broadcasting standards.*"

I added, "I know what you mean. I wouldn't let my supervisor kill my wife with a torque wrench, and here I sit," I said in perhaps too much honesty.

Richard looked at me and leaned forward, "You are not here to kill me then?"

"No, I'm not," I told him as I blinked for the first time. I knew this man was not a threat; he was in hiding as much as me.

We both relaxed as I admitted, "In fact, I hate that I have disturbed your evening. I thought this cabin was abandoned when I came in."

I think Richard breathed for the first time in ten minutes. I don't know how, but we both felt as if we were not a threat to each other.

"Would you like something to eat?" Richard asked pointing to the stove.

"I could eat a horse, thanks Mr. Pate. But I know how hard things are right now, so if you don't have enough, don't worry about me."

Richard went to the stove and dipped out a couple of bowls of some great smelling potato soup, "You know this is the first time I have sat down with a mass murderer. Would you like some salt and pepper?"

I laughed and took the bowl he offered. There was no hiding my appetite as I devoured the contents. Between slurps and gulps I thanked him profusely for the food. He watched me in near amazement as I finished the food inside a minute. Richard ate slowly, still unsure of me.

"Has it been a while since you've eaten, Huck?"

"Yeah, I have been on the move for a while," I responded kind of sheepishly. "You have a nice setup here. How long have you been on the run?" I asked.

Richard ate his soup and said, "About two months now. I have a couple of friends that bring me food from time to time. They have been most helpful since my…departure."

"Have you been on the run ever since the green shirts came into power then?" I asked.

Richard looked onward with his eyes slightly out of focus, "Yes, it has been almost a year now."

I think this was the first time he realized it had been so long. "What was it like for you Richard? How did you get out after the revolution?"

Richard paused for a minute, and looked my way. "I was on assignment in Raleigh, reporting on the riots when the green shirts arrived. The power was still on back then. cell phones still worked, things were still normal. All the field reporters were out there covering the protests. The last thing I expected was for it all to come crashing down."

I could see his emotions were intense on this subject, but I wanted to hear it from someone that was there. "Go on," I prodded him lightly.

Richard continued, "The police, at the time, were overwhelmed with the riots. Things were getting out of control quickly. I was outside the senate chambers in Raleigh, when I first saw the green shirt uniforms. A couple of state senators came towards us and said there were new officials taking over public safety concerns The old Chief of Police was supposedly fired that morning. Some new green shirt captain was put in charge during the interim. We naturally scrambled to get the story."

I asked, "So you were in the senate building when all this happened?"

Richard looked at me, "I was outside covering the police reactions when the stand-down orders came over the radio. The other reporters had already been ushered inside the municipal building. A few minutes later, I saw the busses parked outside on the street. But at the time, I thought nothing of it. I watched from the walkway above while the reporters and certain public officials were escorted onto the waiting busses. My police Lieutenant, and friend, had his radio listening to the staff channels. He let me hear the stand-down messages to the other officers. The rioters were allowed to overrun the state offices everywhere. I asked the lieutenant what the busses were for. He said they were arresting terrorists on some list. By then, we were separated by the masses of protestors rushing our area. By then it was all I could do to get back to the home office in Durham." Richard took a breath and ate a bit of his soup as I digested what he shared.

Nobody from my town had heard any of this and it was a shock to hear it from somebody that was there, "So they labeled people terrorists and just arrested them? Nobody knew what to make of it during a riot then, did they?" I asked Richard.

Richard sat back and continued, "Once in Durham, I walked through the door heading straight to my editor's office. I was pretty sure I had Pulitzer all but wrapped up. For some reason, I took the stairs instead of the elevator that morning. That is what saved me. As I started to pull the stairwell door on my floor, I noticed a strange scene through the door's glass. My editor lay on the floor with three or four green shirts standing over his body. They were demanding all reporters to immediately submit to questioning. Anyone that had ever submitted so much as a recipe in the paper was arrested and bussed off to who-knows-where. I backed out of the building and stayed with friends, fearing to go home. By the time the power went out, I could not find any of my co-workers. I tried calling my desk for messages, but someone picked up the phone and started asking me questions. My house was ransacked and my car was impounded. I realized I needed to go into hiding immediately," Richard recounted bitterly.

I listened to his story intently. We in the militia had never come across anyone who had actually been there. It was amazing to hear his first-hand account.

Richard continued, "I guess they are all still in prison. I have not seen anyone from my paper since the spring. I kept moving around until I finally ended up here, in my Dad's old hunting cabin."

I doubt Richard had never told anyone else what he had witnessed. It was amazing to see things from his perspective. I didn't know what to say. However I chose to give him a bit of information about the prisons.

"Richard, I'm afraid to tell you that I doubt your friends are still in prison."

"What do you mean?" Richard asked.

"Some friends and I *visited* a converted federal prison and found that the place had been set up as a one-way facility. By the time we got there, all our friends were long since *gone*." He recognized what I meant.

Richard expression was one of shock. He most likely suspected the dark secret I just revealed to him, but my story was confirmation. He was upset for some time.

"I was afraid of that," Richard confided.

I decided to tell him more. For some reason, I wanted him to know that I was not the deranged killer he had learned about on a wanted poster or green shirt radio.

"Some friends and I decided we were not going to take the communist overthrow of our state and we decided to resist. When the raiding gangs came, we were ready and we ambushed them. When they raided our neighbors we stopped them again. We have been running operations since the power went out. I was working in the mandatory green shirt work programs when my supervisor tried to kill my new wife. I shot him, to save her."

The investigative reporter in Richard asked, "I heard you planted a bomb under the street in one of those battles and killed a lot of townspeople."

I looked at him, "Yeah, we did set off a pretty big bomb in the street. The civilians had been out of town since the day before though. The bomb was used to disable the gang's armored dump trucks they were using as tanks. After we left, the green shirts wiped out the rest of the gang. You see, the green shirts would come into a town and disarm everyone. Their gang puppets would follow behind in a day or two, rape, pillage, and plunder the defenseless people. The loot would then be collected by the gangs and delivered to the green shirts for re-distribution to the compliant citizens in other towns. The recipients didn't know they were receiving stolen goods from their dead neighbors."

Richard sat in awe, "I never knew the green shirts were so organized. It's hard to grasp it all."

We talked for hours about many topics as night descended on us. I got up asked for the restroom. As I did so, I drew the Glock and laid it on the table. The magazine was in my pocket, but he didn't need to know that. Richard smiled and knew I meant him no harm. When I got to the bathroom, I looked in the mirror. I was horrified at the mess I had become. I looked like a limping train wreck. My face was covered in dust, dirt, and grime from my travels. I cleaned, but there always seemed more. My back looked worse than ever, and it felt like I had been shot. Lucky I had not, but it felt about the same.

I returned to the den where the Glock lay untouched on the table. A blanket and pillow sat on the couch waiting for me. Richard told me that I had better stay the night and I could sleep by the fire. I thanked him and slept like a dead man the whole night. It was one of those sleeps where you don't even dream.

The next day I awoke and dressed. I thanked my new friend for his hospitality and gave him a way to find me if he ever made his way to our town. With all my gear in-hand, I shuffled off towards home. My journey was only halfway complete, as I started out. Now, I was in a rural area where I could make more of a beeline towards home. I still avoided houses as I walked through patches of ice and snow. Lucky for me, the sun was out today and the temperature was relatively balmy compared to the last two weeks. The snow was melting, but the resulting mud slowed my progress. I continued along making my way between fields and crossing creeks mile after mile.

It was late in the evening, and nearly dark, as I found the place I was looking for. When I was Captain of the sniper units, we used certain remote hide-outs where teams could go on long patrols. We would often store food and ammo in these hides to supply our teams. A team needing groceries in an emergency could stop in and get what they needed. Sometimes, a sniper team in training would stop by one of these places and rest for a night. I rummaged around and found the hidden stash of goodies. Night fell while I sat and ate. Until then, I had eaten only a single bowl of soup in the last three days.

I sat in the dark eating, when I heard two men approach the old shed. They were talking a little too loudly as they walked through the door with their sniper rifles slung across their backs. They entered the shed single file and nearly fell over themselves to see a strange man barely visible in the darkness.

"Who the hell are you?" demanded one of the men while clumsily drawing his pistol.

Between crunches I said, "You guys had better watch what you are doing. When I was Captain of the sniper teams, I taught all recruits to approach a building with their weapons drawn. You two Marys walked right up here chatting away like a couple of school girls on a Sunday stroll. I'm going to have to talk to Rooster about standards. Now get over here and get some food."

"Yes Sir Captain Huck, we didn't know it was you. We uh were not expecting......uh, sorry sir."

We spent the night in the shed and I had the men help me back to the sniper bunker the next day. Four days since I left for work, I finally returned to my home town. My mind raced with questions over Seven as I hauled myself into the sniper bunker. I was more scared than when the green shirts stopped me on the road.

Rooster met me with a hug that I had to stop because of my back. As I peeled off my shirt to examine my wound, Rooster called for a medic. When the medic arrived, he sat me on a chair and started working on me.

"Where is Seven?" I asked Rooster with a knot in my stomach.

Rooster looked at me and said, "She's fine, Huck. She's okay. I left a message for her to come here tonight."

I nearly threw up from the relief and the medic probing my back.

Rooster continued, "She snuck here every night waiting for you. The green shirts searched all over town for your sorry butt and ransacked your house. They posted new *Wanted* posters for you in the Community Center and called you by name. So, I'm afraid you're going to be in hiding for quite some time," he finished.

It was the longest six hours of my life until Seven came through the entrance of the sniper bunker that night. We hugged, cried, and kissed our greetings. My world now consisted of her and the militia movement. I couldn't even walk down the street.

Spring

"Emerald City"

Chapter 44
War Plans

The remaining weeks of winter challenged my spirits. I was in near isolation with only militia operations to keep me company. Seven visited every chance she could. But as I guessed, she had been put in charge of the central telephone office for the time being. New greens shirt political officers from a local union were in charge of taking the credit for all the work she directed though. Between work and tightened green shirt security in town, Seven could not visit me very often. Luckily the green shirts did not blame her for Bob's shooting. For that, I was grateful. I guess Bob assaulting the other worker in the equipment room was proof of his mental instability. No matter how instable Bob was, there was no forgiveness for me. Green shirt police wanted the resistance sniper known as Huck pretty bad.

It seemed too much of a coincidence that the green shirts had miraculously linked Bob's killer, me, with my code name in a matter of hours. The green shirts were really focused on the militia groups. This was no time to be careless.

But of course, there were a few things to keep me busy while everyone else got on with their life. We had cases upon cases of ammunition, rifles, machine guns, and some explosives from the raid to catalogue. You see, back when we stole all the stuff, there was no time to do anything, but hide it all. As the trucks rolled into designated temporary hides, they were offloaded by hand. Then the loot was carted by hand to various bunkers and weapons caches all over the county. The empty trucks were then returned to the various places from where they had been stolen.

Until I went into hiding, nobody had organized all that stuff. The bad weather nearly stopped our operations completely with the main concern of leaving tracks in the snow. We could not afford to have our footprints lead right to our most secret hiding places. But, as the weather broke and the snow melted, we had our first chance to get the weapons organized. By the second week of February, I had a pretty firm idea of what we had and how much.

We had always been a bit short on rifles until now. After the raid we had plenty of magazines, M-4 carbines, M16s, and a mixed bag of civilian AR-15s. Our armorers and gunsmiths fixed up all the rifles and made sure they were in working order. Each rifle was then carefully bore-sighted and assigned to a volunteer. As the volunteer went about operations, he would sight-in the rifle properly out to 100 yards. In a perfect world, you could work these issues on a range over several hours. But we didn't have that luxury. We are issuing hundreds of rifles spread across our entire territory. It took us weeks to do the basics in preparation.

One thing that really got us excited, was finding the machine guns. Until now, we had never had any real firepower other than the Barrett .50 cal. Morale took a big jump when I uncrated six M240 machineguns. Holy cow, those things were cool. Gunny was with me that night. We talked at length about how to employ them in combat. Luckily, a few of our former military had operated the weapons and could help cross train volunteers who had never shot one before. We immediately started organizing a training program. After several more sessions in other caches, I found a couple of M249 machineguns. I was really excited until I realized that we had almost no linked 5.56 ammo. We had loads of linked 7.62 for the M240s, but we not gotten more than a case or two of linked 5.56.

Our pistol ammunition was in a lot better shape. I found we had many cases of NATO spec. 124 grain 9mm. That was further good news when I uncovered a case of five MP5 sub-machineguns. We didn't have enough magazines for them in my opinion, but those guns are always cool. I also discovered a couple of cases of the giant .50 caliber ammunition. The only problem was that it was standard ball and not sniper-grade. I hoped for more armor piercing incendiary rounds; but we could have to make do.

Our explosives guys were excited to find we had secured several cases of C-4. The next big find was two cases of electric detonators with various spools of wire. Unfortunately, there was not as much detonation cord as we hoped. I knew our guys would make the most of what they had. But, my philosophy is to have three times as much as you think you need. Just in case.

I found six police 40mm grenade launchers. Also to my extreme pleasure, we had four M-4s with M203 grenade launchers attached. Again, we were less than pleased with the amount of ammunition that was scrounged. Several cases of the ammunition were only tear-gas. We did manage a case of high-explosive rounds, but that was not very much in the greater scheme of things.

We did however come up with several cases of hand grenades. I had hoped to find a bunch and was pleasantly surprised. We also had a variety of smoke grenades in various colors. As I intended to be a part of the sniper teams, I knew the value of smoke in an urban environment. You never know when you have to cover some movement. I would prefer doing it under smoke rather than out in the open.

After I completed my survey, I scheduled a meeting with the Colonel.

The Colonel was anxious to know how we made out, "So, what does it look like, Huck? Do we have enough to overthrow the green shirts?"

I told him, "According to all the departments, it looks like we have met the minimum standard for the operation. But in some areas, we just barely came in over that minimum standard." I passed him my report.

But I also added, "That is according to the overall plan as we know it. When do we get the actual detailed plans?"

"We should get the March-Madness plans delivered via courier sometime in the next three days. I've got Rooster's people on it," the Colonel informed me.

"Are we going to coordinate an action in town to route the local green shirts?"

The Colonel told me, "No."

"Really?" I asked, quite surprised.

"I know some guys around here are anxious to give some payback for all the people this town has lost. But, we need all our people on this action. We can clean up the green shirts when we get back," the Colonel looked at me.

"Shouldn't we keep a squad here to protect our families just in case our operation takes a while?" I asked while the Colonel looked into my face.

"We will make sure Seven is safe. It's you, I am worried about."

"What do you mean?" I asked.

"I am going to make *you* tell her she cannot go on the operation. Good luck with that, Huck," the Colonel grinned.

Yeah I was afraid of that. It had been on my mind for a while. I could see no way for her to go on this mission three and a half months pregnant. This was one conversation I was not looking forward to.

By the end of February, we had the detailed plans for operation March Madness in-hand. We were well equipped and training was underway on the new weapons. The problem we had was road traffic. Yep, after so long without fuel, it was hard for us to get used to traffic on the roads again. Even with restrictions on personally owned vehicles, there were lots of buses and trucks on the road nowadays. Our teams had to resort to crossing roads in the dark, or under bridges, in order to stay hidden. This put a serious crimp in operations.

It looked like fuel was now flowing through the green shirt controlled part of the state. We all knew the re-introduction of fuel was the warning sign that the green shirts were consolidating power. It was looking more and more like the success of operation March Madness would be the harbinger for our whole movement. If we failed, everything may be lost and resisting militarily might prove to be fatal.

We called all the leadership of 3rd militia to the operations bunker to hash out the plans for the overthrow of the green shirts. Seven sat beside me as we awaited Rooster. We were all sitting around the strangely clean table with the lamps lit. You would have thought we were expecting Santa Clause or something. We were all itching to see the plan. Rooster was the last to arrive. He dropped the case on the table with a thud. For an instant we looked at the package and stared. Our lives depended on the contents of that box. If the contents were good, we had a chance. If the information was incomplete, we were in trouble.

Finally, the Colonel unlocked and opened the lid of the black pelican case. He pulled out paper after paper and they just kept coming. We unfolded maps and hung them. There were maps with overlays, operation plans for each militia, target buildings, estimates of police forces and troops, a code book, as well as timetables for the operation. There must have been three pounds of documents inside. We took notes and discussed the plan until morning. The amount of data was massive. 2nd militia had done a great job.

The genius of the plan was the flexibility. Each militia was assigned a separate set of goals and targets completely independent of other units. The plan did not hamper us by trying to coordinate our every move down to the second. And better yet, the plan only spelled out our objectives. It allowed us the flexibility to decide how to maneuver, how many people to assign to a target, and goals once on target. The only inter-militia cooperation was the timing of events and the initial transportation. It was up to each of the commands to accomplish our goals set by the plan.

A unique form of transportation was selected for 2nd militia and 3rd militia to get into the city. A set of railroad tracks would lead a train full of us right into the heart of downtown Raleigh. We would board the train several miles south of Raleigh in a remote area. The plan was to travel along the tracks leading into downtown in a captured passenger train. We would stop the train just short of Peace Street, allowing militia to exit only three blocks from key government buildings. If all went well, the speed of our arrival would confound any defenders and give us the all important element of surprise.

The outer perimeter plan was pretty straight forward in concept, yet quite brilliant in its own right. We had a natural perimeter of downtown in the bypass of I-440, called the beltline. Each militia was assigned a list of roadways we would block in order to limit green shirt reinforcements reaching downtown. This also served to deny the green shirts the opportunity to escape. Roadways, too large to defend with just our small-arms, were planned for demolition.

Our department heads went over every aspect of the plan, inch by inch. We drafted warning orders to all the other commands, planned for movements in company formations, and started to estimate what it would take to accomplish each objective. The discussions and debates lasted for hours on end.

One thing stood out to me in particular. As our Intel department flipped through 2nd's report, they came across something special.

The Intel Captain looked up from the file, "Hey Huck; you gotta see this. The Intel report from 2nd militia has you in it by name."

"They do?" I asked as Fred and I read over a map.

"They say the green shirts have been tracking your exploits for some time. In fact they have heard a bunch of your stories from way back in the summer. Looks like the green shirts have had their eye on you for a while. Until you shot Bob, they didn't have a clue of your real identity."

"Yeah, I noticed. I didn't get a Christmas card," I told them without looking up.

Fred snickered while Seven made a sound that I knew meant I had better listen.

The Intel captain continued while he flipped through the intelligence report, "It looks like 2nd militia has confirmed some of our suspicions. Here is the report on the fuel and oil embargo. They confirmed that the PPR orchestrated the embargo. They also confirmed that the new Department of Recycling was directly linked to releasing the prison convicts. The roving gangs were directly run by the Department of Recycling and the head of green shirt police. Finally, they included a list of names of their operatives that lost their lives getting this information."

The Colonel looked the rest of us who sat in silence. He told us that he was more determined than ever to route the green shirts. And here is how we are going to do it. 3rd militia is assigned the following targets, The Department of Recycling building, the Revenue Dept., Legislative offices building, the Legislature Building, and the PPR/Green Shirt office complex between Jones and Lane Street. "From now on start using the code names assigned for this operation. We don't want any leaks. Our plans cannot get out."

It was time for Seven to talk about communications, "Gentlemen, as you know we have people inside the telecommunications facilities and have been monitoring the green shirt phone system and internet for some time. The most important thing I can tell you is this. You cannot use any form of electronic communication associated with this operation. The green shirts are monitoring everything. If you were to search a map on the computer, they can track exactly where you looked. They read every text, every email. Every phone call runs through their analysis programs; EVERYTHING electronic is being monitored."

Seven continued, "With a minimal number of volunteers, I can gain access to the central telephone office in Raleigh and take down the network from the inside. We can attack the power supply and leave the equipment intact. Once we are successful, we will have the phones at our disposal."

Everyone sat in silence knowing what was coming. It was time for my conversation with her.

"Seven, I cannot let you go on this mission with you three months pregnant," I told her as gently as possible.

Gentlemen if you have ever heard of the "hormone fairy" in regards to pregnant women and don't know what that means; pray you never do. Seven was so upset I thought she was going to explode right there in front of us. Half of what she said was incoherent, thank goodness. I learned new swear words I had never heard before. It turns out my parents were sons of motherless goats according to her. I think most of the men in that bunker had to check their underpants after the meeting. All of them were glad not to be married to her. Let's just say she took it poorly and go from there.

However, her idea to strike the Raleigh central office was sound. If we could disrupt the phones, internet, and cellular phones, all in one strike; it would be a good tactical advantage. I was able to give a briefing on how to accomplish the mission according to plan. Seven was able to give information on access codes to the target building while I gave directions on how to identify and disable the power equipment.

Seven forgave me after much consoling and more than a few pickles. She reluctantly conceded that her condition was not the best for conducting raids, assaults using high explosives, and general overthrow of a government. However she was determined to do as much as she possibly could to get everyone ready. She was as determined as anyone else.

In the final weeks leading up to March Madness we conducted training exercises in all kinds of weather and all terrain conditions. We studied the intelligence reports. We practiced room clearing techniques. Equipment was checked; then checked again. We memorized the code words and made mock-ups of the target buildings to get a feel for street layouts. We honed our skills and prepared the equipment to move out at a moment's notice.

Every night by the radio we waited to hear the militia broadcasts. There was a delay of 24 hours, but then on the night of March 20th, the code words "Tiger, Tiger, Tiger" came over the radio's speaker. Yes, this was from the movie where the Japanese used "Tora,Tora,Tora" for the go-code attack on Pearl Harbor. Tora means Tiger, so you get the idea. We were about to pounce on the green shirts, and I thought it was fitting.

That night, I snuck into town and spent the night with Seven and her folks at their house. My house had been confiscated and boarded up by the green shirts after I shot Bob-the-Supervisor. Knowing what was about to happen, I got Seven's dad off to the side where we could speak privately.

"Sir, I know with your military background, what I am about to tell you has to stay with us here in this room," I whispered as Seven and her mom were in the kitchen.

"Okay?" He answered cautiously.

"You know Seven and I are involved in the movement to unseat the green shirts. What you may not know, is that I am the one they call, "Huck." Your daughter's code name is, "Seven".

He father looked at me in disbelief, "You are the one in the wanted posters? The sniper they call, Huck? Oh my, I had no idea," he said with his eyes wide open and his mouth ajar.

"Sir, we are about to take on the green shirts head-on. Our chances are good, but things can always go wrong. If they do go bad, I want you to take the backpack under the stairs, get Seven, your wife, and go into hiding. Inside the backpack, there are a couple of pistols, ammunition, food, and directions to some hideouts where you might escape. Just promise me that you will fill in for me if I don't make it back."

He looked me in the eyes and said, "You know I will, son. You make those green shirts pay for what they did to our country."

Chapter 45
March Madness

Operation March Madness technically started on Tuesday March 19st at 07:00, in the western foothills of North Carolina. The peaceful town of North Wilkesboro was the first to hear gunfire as the 4th militia took out the local green shirt office. About 15 green shirt offices along highway 77 were raided that morning. Green shirt offices from Mount Airy, North Wilkesboro, Winston Salem, Statesville, Hickory, and as far south as Charlotte, were destroyed. 4th militia just slapped the sleeping tiger of the green shirt war machine and told it to come and get me.

The rest of us in the militias checked our watches and waited until our turn. As the day wore on, we listened for the reports of green shirt police and military units moving west. By late afternoon we heard of several convoys of troops and equipment heading towards Charlotte and Winston Salem via I-40. The bait had been cast, the hook was set, and we were about to haul in the catch. If all went well, we would have our objective under our control within 24 hours. I hoped the 4th militia well. I knew what a risk they were taking by providing the rest of us the necessary distraction.

I spent the last few hours of that day in the sniper bunker. Seven was at work in the telephone office and would not likely be back before I was scheduled to leave. My rifle and gear waited for me on the edge of the briefing table. Men were finishing the last minute details of packing gear and loading backpacks. Maps were stored in pouches and code books reviewed one last time. Sporadic radio chatter hummed in the background. Teams were busy all over the county stealing busses, tractor trailer trucks, and dump trucks. Other men were carrying the ammunition and supplies from secret locations to their staging positions. Teams gathered to locations waiting to be picked up by their designated transport. Everything was going well, it was just the kind of busy you get right before a big event.

With the last few men in the sniper bunker, I strapped on my load bearing vest. My trusty Glock 19 rested in my Blackhawk SERPA holster off my right thigh. The left side of my pistol belt was filled with magazines for the Glock as well as my flashlight and Seal Pup knife. My load bearing vest had two fragmentation grenades, two smoke grenades, my AR15 ammo, a laser range finder, map case, radio, spare batteries, first aid kit, and who knows what else. The thing weighed a ton. In my day-pack I had the rest of my ammunition for my AR15, more 9mm pistol ammo, more batteries, and a few highly prized energy bars that had been saved just for this occasion. All these things I put on over my Multi-cam field shirt over my last pair of 5.11 pants. Lastly, I grabbed my freshly cleaned AR sniper rifle.

I looked back on the sniper bunker, thinking how special it had been to have played a part in the resistance. What a set of memories I would have. I wondered if the men that fought with George Washington realized how much of a historical event they were participating in. I wondered if they had the same fears as I did. Would my men come back heroes? Or would history see us as failures?

I didn't know things would turn out, but I was determined to play the hand I was dealt. We walked out of the empty corn field under the cover of darkness. The air was cool, but not cold. The early spring leaves had early night's dew on them. That allowed us to walk quickly through the woods without too much noise. The hike to the departure point was uneventful. Upon arrival, the scope of the operation surprised me somewhat. Some 60-80 heavily armed militia volunteers were crammed in the woods behind a church that had long since been boarded up. I had never seen so many of us in one place on one operation. It ran through my mind that there were nine or ten of these rally points. All of them were busy loading trucks and busses right now. Dozens of these sites were pulling men from all over our territory.

We quickly loaded the gear onto the waiting trucks and got everyone onto the busses. I was glad to hear there had only been minor problems obtaining busses. So far, we were right on schedule. I hoped all the other units were faring as well as we were. The ride to the next rally point took forever. We must have spent almost two hours in those busses. But it was necessary to use only the back roads that were not monitored by green shirt patrols. I would have hated to be a green shirt cop that stopped one of our busses. Could you imagine anything worse for one of them?

It was about 02:00 in the morning of the 20th, as our lead bus pulled up to a remote section of woods along a straight stretch of two-lane blacktop. A quarter of a mile forward was two more busses sitting in the middle of the road. I could see they were doing the same as us, unloading. Our people scrambled off the bus and headed for the cover of the woods. In two minutes, we were off the busses and heading east through the trails in the underbrush. The busses left as soon as we were clear. I knew this would be happening here every few minutes for the next two or three hours if all went well.

I followed a trail that had been tramped down through the fairly dense woods. I could hear the hushed voices of hundreds of men passing the time. While my group sat down, I went in search of the leadership. The woods cleared as I stepped onto the gravel embankment of the railroad tracks. There was a figure close by with a clipboard and small flashlight.

I reported, "Captain Huck, 3rd militia, with departure station five. All accounted for."

A familiar voice came back from the dark outline of the man standing in front of me, "Good to see you again, Huck."

It was the Colonel from 2ⁿᵈ militia I had met way back in the conference.

"How are you sir? I asked shaking his hand. "Any trouble?"

"There have been a few glitches in getting enough buses; but we will manage. You group is assigned to car 1, you will find your other 3ʳᵈ guys up there," he pointed.

"Good Luck" he told me.

"You too, sir" I replied.

I walked back to the group I rode in with, and told them where to go. As we moved into position, the sounds of buses stopping every few minutes echoed in the cool night air. I knew this was 2ⁿᵈ militia's backyard, so I was only slightly apprehensive and not downright worried. There were so many of us here in one place, you could not help but feel a little overwhelmed. We had never operated in groups of 100, 200, or 500. I went out alone or in pairs, on some rare occasions with eight or nine men at most. This collaborative effort among militias was reassuring. Seeing how we were willing to risk everything to unseat the green shirts, let me know that I was not alone.

By 04:30, the buses and trucks were few are far between. If you didn't know any better you would think it was going to be a peaceful dawn. We sat on the edge of the railroad track embankment in the cool night air trying to stay warm. Even though hundreds of men waited by the tracks; there was little sound. We all knew the dawn at 07:00 meant the day of our revolution. There would be a lot of blood shed before nightfall.

In the distance, thunderous sounds from a locomotive's diesel engine could be heard. Over the din you could hear 500 pairs of boots get to their feet in unison. A light shown from the southern end of the tracks as the engine rounded the bend. The roar of the diesel engine got my adrenaline pumping throughout my body. I shook from both nerves and the cold, as the engine slowed and stopped near my position. I looked down the tracks at the rest of the train to see hundreds of armed men climb aboard.

Once on board, a strange sense of relief swept the men. I don't know why, but we all felt like we could talk for the first time all night. The passenger car lights were turned down low allowing us enough light to see. But they were not bright enough for a passerby to see inside the car's tinted windows. In the first car, I met up with my Colonel and most of 3rd's leadership. 3rd's Alpha company, and some of Bravo company sat around me. From the looks of things, most everyone had made it this far. A few men were unaccounted for, but not many.

While we waited in the train, we organized the men. Anyone not in the right car was moved. Anyone missing equipment or needing additional supplies was straightened out as team leaders fussed over their men. The Amtrak train sat still on the tracks where it picked us up. Our attack was still hours away. Some rested, while others re-checked equipment.

Right on schedule, the train's engine changed from its idle speed hum and began to rev up. A moment later we felt a slight bump in the cars as we slowly started on our way. At 09:30 hours, on a slightly overcast Wednesday morning, our operation began. Our train was still several miles south of Raleigh, so we expected to be at our disembark-point in about 20 or 30 minutes. As the train chugged along, several of the militia leadership gathered in the first passenger car. I saw the 2nd' Colonel to the porter's station and pick up the intercom phone. In a second, I heard the train's intercom system click on allowing the whole train to hear.

"Ladies and Gentlemen, thank you for traveling militia Amtrak this morning. There will be no breakfast served and there will be no movie, but at the end of this trip there will be a show!"

Every man on the train cheered.

"I don't need to tell you what lies at the end of these tracks for us. We are going to forcibly remove the green shirts from power once and for all. Our reports from 4th militia are as follows: They engaged several green shirt military columns around Charlotte and Winston-Salem overnight. Several more green shirt offices have been raided since yesterday morning. The 4th has taken out 20 or more facilities so far. It looks like we have successfully lured the bulk of the green shirt's fighting force away from our objective, Raleigh, also known for this operation as Emerald City."

Again there was a cheer from the men.

"A reminder on the rules of engagement. Remember, the majority of the people we are going to run into are government employees, forced to work for the green shirts. They are not our enemy. In fact, they may be able to help us identify the people we are after. Our objective is to eliminate the green shirt security forces, and secure the green shirt leadership. When you take a building, cover all the exits and search room to room. Don't let anyone out until you are sure of who they are."

The 2nd militias Colonel continued, "Leaders. Remember to refer to the Intel reports in your packets. Review the timetables and maps with your men. Go ahead and turn on your radios and check frequencies. Make your weapons hot. Set your sights. Good luck and good hunting!"

For the next few minutes, the train was filled with the flurry of metallic ratcheting sounds. Bolts ran home rounds of ammunition in rifles, while pistol actions cycled. Meanwhile, the train reached the outskirts of Raleigh. As we passed over the I-440 beltline, I squinted to see the major intersection of Highway 401 and 70 only a half mile to the east. I could just make out two tractor trailer trucks seemingly broken down on the side of the road. I was relieved. I knew that each truck contained a platoon of men whose job it was to close off that roadway. I knew the drivers of those trucks were watching the railway bridge to see our train pass by.

A mile before our objective, the train slowed and came to a halt. Everyone was anxious; this was not our designated drop off. We waited in silence as an unarmed militia ran forward of the train. It was okay though. He was manually switching the tracks to keep us on the right route. No doubt some railroad controller miles away was confused as his track indicators did things of their own accord.

The train started again in a few minutes, and we proceeded down the tracks. By the time I could see the Highway 70/50 underpass, my heart was pounding in my chest. As weird as it seemed at the time, I wondered what those people waiting at the Hillsborough Road railroad crossing would think in five minutes. Would they even understand what was happening? Would they freak out? I was betting on pandemonium.

The train's locomotive slowly crossed the overpass along with the first and second passenger cars. The rear of the train stretched out beyond sight south towards Hillsborough Street. When the train came to a complete stop just before 10:00, the doors opened and hundreds of militia poured out.

I looked to my Colonel and quoted, "Cry havoc and let loose the dogs of war."

He smiled and said, "Good luck, Huck."

Chapter 46
Retaking the Capitol

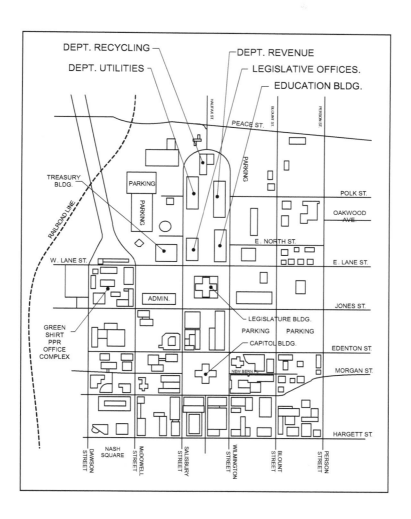

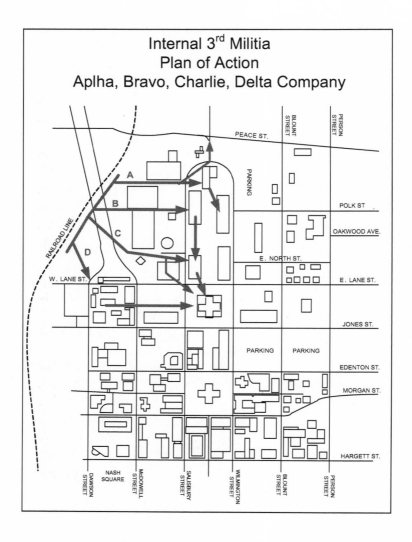

Internal 3rd Militia
Plan of Action
Aplha, Bravo, Charlie, Delta Company

Once out of the train, units quickly assembled, then headed to their objectives. I followed Alpha company on the northern most route towards the Department of Recycling building. Bravo Company headed for their staging area in the parking decks, just opposite of the five-story Dobbs building. I watched as our security groups took green shirt trucks from the government lots and headed out to their designated security checkpoints. The Colonel, with

282

Charlie company, moved onto the 401/50 highway and stopped what little traffic passed under the railroad bridge. They continued towards the ten-story State Treasurers building which was the 3rd militia's planned operational headquarters. Delta Company crossed Dawson Street and made their way to the Days Inn motel at West Lane Street. That is when we heard the first gunfire.

Even though we expected the sounds of fighting, it was none the less a bit shocking to hear. Delta company had run into a hornets nest from the sound of it. I could hear the sound of an M240 opening up. Rifle fire crackled and popped as green shirt and militia engaged each other in a street brawl. We knew speed and maneuver was the key to success, so we pressed on to our objective.

Bravo Company quickly passed through the parking decks and began a hasty assault on the Capitol Police building. The office was a small brick building with a paved lot on both sides. Empty squad cars provided cover for the fighters clearing the building inside.

I saw lead elements of Bravo Company engage the fortified doorway leading to the massive five-story Dobbs building. The Dobbs building was quite the modern granite exterior with dark rows of windows looking formidable across Salisbury Street. Someone was hammering the concrete structure above the sidewalk with 40mm grenades and rifle fire. I doubted the green shirt security could resist for long.

Alpha company headed for the Recycling building while the security element and my team headed for the intersection of Peace Street and Salisbury Street. Intelligence gave us a heads up about a green shirt roadblock at that intersection. They were not kidding. The green shirt police had constructed an elaborate concrete guardrail maze to control the roadway. Any car passing through would have to slowly turn several times in order to continue. Inside the barricade, were about a dozen uniformed traffic cops intently listening to the firefight just two blocks away.

The Alpha company security element engaged the green shirts at the intersection with all their might. From my vantage point, it was hard to see more than the eastern most side of Peace Street. I maneuvered back to the parking deck and found a stairwell. Once on the second level, I crawled over to an inner parking lane, and got on top of a nearby SUV. From the roof of the SUV, I was still deep inside the covered parking deck and not exposed. I set my bipod legs facing the intersection while my team formed a quick perimeter. Even from my new vantage point I could only see half the intersection. My first target appeared from behind a concrete K-rail to shoot his riot shotgun. I put my crosshairs directly over him and squeezed the familiar Jewell trigger. Pow! My first target was down. I saw a man run from one K-rail to the other. When he poked his head out to shoot, pow! My second target was down.

From the corner of my vision I saw a blur of white as a small pickup truck screeched though the intersection heading west. I knew it was green shirt police trying to get out of our kill zone.

"Huck, target heading west," one of my team called out.

I reached with my hand and drug the bipod to the left. I picked up the truck in my scope as my peripheral vision matched my scope's view. As the truck sped down Peace Street, I trained my crosshairs on the truck's pillar and started shooting. My first shot broke the driver's window and cracked the windshield. My second or third shot hit the driver, sending the truck veering towards the sidewalk. The truck flipped as it hit the guard-rail partition near the entrance of the gas station on the other side of Peace Street.

After a few more minutes of fighting, the intersection was secure. I could see Alpha Company's security detail setting up defensive positions. My team and I headed out of the parking deck and continued towards the Recycling building. As we crossed the elevated and wide open

Salisbury Street walkway, I looked right towards the Dobbs building. There was a slightly smoking hole in the first floor entrance with chunks of concrete littering the street. I saw militia security standing guard, so I knew the Bravo Company made it inside. Just as I continued down the walkway, a third story window blew out, spraying glass over Salisbury Street. Someone must have just used a hand grenade in that office. I could hear rifle fire coming from the same window.

My team and I made it to the entrance of the Archdale building, now called Department of Recycling. The building seemed taller and quite a bit larger than I had anticipated. The white concrete walls stood out at the northern end of the grassy mall. All the other buildings surrounding this block were granite and had dark windows. I was betting a lot of green shirt officials had offices here. We made our way into the lobby where I found a squad leader from Alpha Company.

"What's the situation?" I asked.

He looked at me and said, "We have the building's perimeter secure. About 25 office workers have been identified and escorted out. But the teams hit a road block at the eighth floor. The green shirts constructed a secure barrier, unlike anything I have seen. Our teams have tried to blow it, but with no luck so far."

I ordered, "Get your Captain on the radio and tell him to cut the power and phones to the entire building. If we can't smoke them out, we will crash the building down on their heads. Now go."

The squad leader rushed off down the hall relaying my message to his Captain. I could not allow the green shirts to control one of the highest buildings on the whole northern end of downtown. I watched through the lobby windows as office workers from the adjacent Dobbs building were ushered outside into the courtyard. About the same time, the stairwell door opened behind me as more office workers poured out. Alpha Company's men searched them and checked their IDs.

"Where is the director of Recycling?" one of our men asked an office worker.

"I don't know, his office is on the 12th floor, but I did see him come in today," the worker looked around at all of us and asked, "What are you doing here? What are you going to do with us?"

I heard him tell her that we were here to fire the green shirt`s. The workers were told to escape through the parking lots off to the east. In a day or two, it would be safe for them to come back.

Even inside the lobby, I could hear sounds of gunfire and small explosions back towards Delta Company. The amount of fighting worried me since we had not anticipated such a firefight near their first objective. Delta had been assigned the PPR complex three blocks west of the Legislative building. The entire block was all PPR and green shirt headquarters. Intelligence reports said security was tight, but nothing too extensive. The sounds of sustained machinegun fire suggested differently.

My team and I ran over to the Dobbs building where we found the Captain of Bravo Company in the lobby.

"How are things going over there, Huck?" he asked.

"It looks like they have fortified the upper five floors and there does not seem to be a way in. Most likely all the key party officials are holed up in there. If we can't get to them soon, I plan on blowing the whole damn building," I told him.

The Captain looked at me in shock, "Do you really think that is necessary?"

I reminded him, "If you had seen the prison system they set up and calculated the number of people they killed, you wouldn't wait another five minutes to blow the place."

He looked at me for a moment, "We are almost finished in this building. I have several units standing by to take the

Legislative office building next. How about Alpha company?"

"They are ready to take to take the Department of Revenue building in a few minutes," I told him. "But I hate leaving half the Recycling building only half secure to our rear. I am going to make my way down to the Colonel's position and see what we can do from there."

My team and I jogged along the outside of the building until we came within site of the Treasury building. I could not believe the extent of the underground structures in the area. The buildings above ground were already massive to behold. But from the looks of it, the entire grassy mall between buildings was one giant underground parking area. I radioed the Alpha and Bravo company commanders to start sending teams down there immediately.

We waited for the assault on the Legislative offices building to start before we proceeded. I was able to support the action with a few well-placed shots, but overall we just held on to our position and found cover.

As we waited, I heard the distinctive sound of the Barrett .50 cal rifle booming from the other side of the Treasury building, just south of my position. It was my guess that a sniper team was set up to support the fight for the PPR offices. Occasionally, I could see bullets strike the glass windows off offices as machine gunners missed their marks causing the damage.

When it was clear, my team signaled the security detail on the first floor of the Treasury building. We proceeded to the side entrance as bullets ricocheted around us. My team and I headed to the sixth floor where we found our Colonel and his team of radio operators in a corner conference room. All were busily talking on their radios and updating maps while being able to see things from their high vantage point. When the Colonel finished, I walked over to him.

"Sir we are going to need a demo team over at the Recycling building."

"Are things that bad, Huck?" he asked.

"Yes sir, they have some sort of barrier on the eighth floor that we cannot penetrate. If Alpha Company can't breech it soon, I see no other way. It looks like most of their senior level officials are above the eighth floor. Most of the office workers are out already."

I continued, "Bravo Company has taken the Dobbs building and the legislative offices are underway. Alpha company has assaulted the Dept. of Revenue, but I don't have an update on their progress. The northern intersection of Peace Street is under our control."

The Colonel said, "Well that's good....."

A distant BOOM, followed by a shockwave, rattled the windows before the Colonel could finish. I got off the floor and looked south towards the direction of the massive sound. I could hear incredible amounts of new rifle and machinegun fire in the distance.

The Colonel looked towards the sound, "That would be 5th militia attacking the old Wake County Sheriff's office, now Green Shirt Police headquarters. They are in for one big fight down there. That explosion was just to breech the outer perimeter wall of the place."

"Anyway, like I was saying. I will send a team to demo the Recycling building. In the meantime, the PPR offices over here have bogged down Delta Company. We had no idea there were so many of them or how well they were entrenched. Delta Company is going to be there for a while."

One of his radio men broke in and asked a question then returned to his radio.

The Colonel continued. "Our outer perimeter is holding along I-440. We knew there would be a few gaps, but nothing too substantial. A few of the larger intersections require more men than we hoped. The team at the airport has successfully blocked the green shirts from using the National Guard Apache gunships. As long as they hold out, we should not have any aircraft to worry about. The phones are down, by the way."

That was good news. If the phones were out, the green shirts could not call for backup or give any information to the outside world.

"Alright sir, where do you want me?" I asked.

"Huck, I am going to need you to support the assault on the Legislative building. If Delta Company is tied up Alpha, Bravo, and Charlie companies will have to do the assault themselves. They will need as much sniper support as possible. 2nd militia has formed their perimeter North to South along Person Street. They will be assaulting the historic sites like the old Governor's mansion in the next few minutes.

"Roger that Colonel. I will contact Rooster and coordinate a sniper blanket over these four square blocks."

The Colonel looked at me funny, "Huck, I just got word before you arrived. Rooster was killed supporting Delta Company. I'm sorry. I am putting you in back charge of the sniper units from here on."

I was shocked to my soul. "Roger that," I told him with a large lump in my throat. I saw Fred look over at me from maps he was updating for the Colonel. For the first time in his life Fred didn't know what to say. Rooster was a good guy, losing him was real hard. But, I had no time for sorrow just now. There was fighting to do.

I collected my team and changed our radios to the sniper frequency, "Sniper teams of the 3rd listen up! This is Huck, I am taking command. Captain Rooster was killed so I need to make sure you have current orders. Report in."

Once in touch with the teams, I gave them new directions to support the assualt. As I reached the lobby floor, I remembered all the tunnels that had been constructed over the last few months. Perhaps we could use them to get into position. I directed my team to head to the basement. We searched around and finally found the entrance. The heavy steel door swung open leading down the dim tunnel. I didn't like this tunnel-rat business for nobody.

My team of four men consisted of one other sniper and two fighters with standard carbines. I let the carbines go first down the rabbit hole, and I followed. You could still smell wet cement as we walked down a long corridor some 300 feet long. As we headed north, I noticed several tunnels heading off to the east along the way. I wasn't sure, but I thought I heard distant sounds of people talking. My team used all hand signals, so I knew it was none of us.

At the end of the tunnel we made a turn to the east where we expected to see the basement of the Legislative offices building. Instead, the lead man of my team rounded the corner and nearly bumped into a handful of green shirt police. The resulting gunfire was ear shattering. My point man was on full auto spraying down the tunnel. The green shirts had machineguns and pumped lead back in our direction.

The noise blinded the senses and made you want to assume the fetal position. Seconds seemed like hours. Rounds were bouncing off the interior walls. Shrapnel from copper-jacketed bullets struck everyone causing nasty little wounds. After a few seconds of this, I grabbed for a grenade in my vest and pulled the pin. I bounced the grenade off the angled wall and yelled, "Grenade out!" Everyone clamped their hands over their ears and closed their eyes. Blam! The corridor finally fell silent after the echo diminished.

I checked my point man. He was dead. His body had blocked most of the green shirt's fire. His front looked like ripped hamburger. I had never seen anyone so torn up. It was horrible. We made a mental note to come back for him when this was all over, and we left.

The green shirts we had encountered were special police or some security detail. We grabbed their MP5s and spare magazines then stuffed them in our packs. You never know when you might need a little extra firepower. I kept an MP5 in hand because it was so much easier to use in the tunnels than my sniper rifle.

The noise of our firefight alerted Alpha Company. We were met with rifles pointed in our faces as we exited the basement. After telling them our story, we advised them to secure the tunnels before we moved out again. I could not hear for several minutes. I am sure I was yelling at the Alpha company guys based on the way they looked at me. For the next 15 minutes, an alpha medic patched up our wounds and okayed us for action. During that time, I looked at my watch for the first time. It was 12:20. How in the world had it been that long already? Then again, it felt like when we got off the train only a few minutes ago. It is weird sometimes when you lose all track of time. Nothing makes sense.

We finally made our way to the Education building on the west side of the Lane and Wilmington Street intersection. There we met elements of Bravo Company waiting for the big assault on the Legislative building. Another sniper team reported in, and I directed them to the southwest corner of our building. We were located on the same floor, but overseeing the southwest corner. I could see the old Governor's mansion two blocks east and one block south of my position, but just barely. From the looks of it, 2nd militia had taken those streets and was moving south. We were nearly ready for the big push on the senate building.

We busted out the windows of our hide, not trying to conceal our position. We needed the ability to shoot quickly and rapidly without the hindrance of glass. MP5 machine guns are good at breaking glass by the way.

I radioed the sniper teams and made sure we were all in place. After a few minutes, all teams reported in. I radioed back to the Colonel that his cover was ready. Alpha, Bravo, and half of Charlie Company, assaulted the Legislative building from the north and west. The green shirts had been preparing for the last two hours to defend the building, and it showed. The amount of fire coming from the building was impressive. They had machineguns at all the entrances and rifles out of every window it seemed. Lucky for us, we had snipers covering almost every angle of the place. The roof of the Legislative building is covered in windows and odd pyramid shaped roof-tops. Every time their forces opened up, we let them have it.

After a while, they backed away from the windows trying to hide from our fire. This allowed the assault units to get close enough to use grenades. An hour and 30 minutes later, all three levels of the building were secure. This was the one place that nobody could deny being a green shirt, or a PPR representative. You had to be one just to walk in the door.

I took a look around as my watch read 15:00. Everything north of Jones Street was under our control. The only exception was the Recycling building, which had been isolated and surrounded. Most everything east of Blount Street was under 2nd militia control. The fighting in Delta Company's sector was finally winding down. The sounds of a major battle still echoed from the south, where 5th militia fought for the headquarters of green shirt police. 2nd militia had taken the Department of Transportation, Administrative Buildings in the surrounding blocks, and the Capitol building itself. Hundreds of prisoners were being processed and identified. Informants were giving descriptions of green shirt officials and pointed them out.

Not all office workers were helpful. It was quite shocking to come across a former U.S. citizen who was perfectly fine with communist rule. They loved the power of their position as a government official. When we interviewed them, it was striking to see their condescension for the common working-class person. They made threats that our rebellion would suffer for these transgressions against the state.

I heard one of my guys tell her sarcastically, "You're now free; you're welcome."

Others gladly spilled the beans on their government co-workers. Stories of arrest, harassment, and brutality in the workplace were plentiful. PPR officials were pulled from masses of common office workers. Records and files were collected for what we were sure to be lengthy trials. I left sniper teams in overwatch positions to make sure we were safe.

I walked down Lane Street towards the Treasury building with empty rifle magazines rattling in my pockets. As I stopped to secure the magazines, I looked over to our casualty collection area. We had a lot of casualties. Too many were from Delta Company. The assault on green shirt headquarters had been more costly than we anticipated. I wondered how many of these men would recover from the more serious gunshot wounds. Charley Company had suffered badly as well. Luckily, Alpha and Bravo Company were relatively whole.

Chapter 47
Wounded

I walked up to the Colonel's floor of the Treasury Building, and reported in. While the Colonel organized fighting units to process prisoners, I talked with some of the other leaders. I sat my relatively small AR15 beside the giant Barrett .50 cal. sitting in front of a broken window facing the train. I walked over to the sniper in charge of the Barrett as he talked with Fred. From the background, the Captain of Logistics reported that we were almost completely out of hand grenades. There was no more 40mm ammunition, and the explosives were all dedicated to demolition projects already underway. Medical supplies were running low and most of the machinegun ammo was used.

I looked back over to Fred and said, "It's a good thing we're about done here."

The sniper using the Barret .50 looked at me and said, "The magazine in there has my last 8 shells."

I directed teams from the Treasury building for another hour or so as operations changed from assault to police mode. I heard reports from 5th militia that the southern end of downtown was secure. The green shirt police headquarters was partially destroyed. It was on fire, and expected to collapse within a day or so. 2nd militia reported their sectors all clear. All units were processing prisoners and calling for intelligence people to help sort through everyone.

Our operation was a military success. The green shirt police forces had been subdued, their leadership was being arrested; we had won the fight!

Someone in the background wondered how things were going for 4th militia in the western part of the state. My thoughts shifted to those foothills and I thought for the first time all day about Seven. It would be nice to have place in the foothills all alone out there away from this big concrete jungle. I looked west to the sun as it shifted towards the horizon. As if from the back of my mind, I heard the radio crackle and frantic voice call out, "tanks!"

Everyone that heard the radio stopped what they were doing. The hum of the office ceased in a second.

The Colonel looked at the radio like he didn't understand, then walked over to the radio and turned up the volume.

The Colonel's radio operator said, "Repeat last, repeat last."

The voice on the other radio yelled into the handset, "I have tanks coming in from my northeast. I see maybe four or five, no wait, now six. They have the green shirt logo on the side."

The operator glared into the handset and spoke quickly, "What do you mean tanks? Do you mean dump trucks with steel plate or armored buses?"

"No sir, these are the big Abrams tanks like in the gulf war. They are cruising right down the road towards my position, maybe three-quarters of a mile out. I can see them coming down the hill beside Mayflower restaurant."

The Colonel grabbed the radio and asked, "What is your location, son?"

"Sir, we are blocking the roadway where the 440 beltline meets Capitol Boulevard.

The radio operator turned to the Colonel and said, "That is only three miles from here sir."

The Colonel stood back with a look of utter confusion, "There are no M1 Abrams tanks stationed anywhere in this state. How can this be?"

Just then another radio cracked to life, "Sir, this is the security element holding the 264 East interchange. My squad leader told me to radio in that we are knee deep in tanks over here and….," static echoed for a second, then nothing.

The Colonel looked around and asked, "Just what the hell do we do now?" The rest of us were silent not knowing what to think. The Colonel walked over to the window and looked out to west, deep in thought.

As the Colonel turned to face us, the roar of a jet airplane whooshed overhead. We all looked in complete surprise as an F-15E banked and turned to the northwest and out of sight. A second or two after the jet passed, the most thunderous explosion I had ever witnessed, pounded the ground on the west side of our building. The outer walls of our corner office seemed to explode inward. That was the last image I remember before the scene changed.

I awoke what must have been quite some time later. What happened? How much time passed, I don't know for sure. Fred was leaning over me trying to get my attention. I sat up slowly trying to get my wits, but my body was slow to respond. The world seemed to just hum in the background. Glass and office debris covered every surface. Papers floated in and out of the windows, maps were in shreds, tables were gone. Men lay all around us in pieces. I was 10 feet from where I remembered standing last. Fred was bleeding and cut, but not too bad. I hurt all over. The nice conference room looked like a complete wreck as lights hung from wires. Debris cluttered every inch of the floor. The ceiling tiles were broken and hanging. It didn't even look like a room any more.

With Fred's help, I got to my feet. As I propped myself up, I looked out the hole where the windows and outer walls used to be. The remains of our train lay on the tracks below. There were two distinct craters where the engine used to be. Another crater was all that was left of the two-story Archives building previously next door to the Treasury building. Little fires burned in all directions for hundreds of yards. I stumbled around trying to get my balance through the fog in my head. They must have dropped 2,000 pound bombs to do all this damage. My sniper rifle lay miraculously intact on the floor. Two other men were alive, but everyone else in the room was dead. The Colonel's body was by the window with an obviously fatal wound to the back of his head. The room was something close to horror film, but worse.

Fred directed us all to the stairwell where the door hung sideways on its hinges. The wind now freely blew through the building making the stairwell door creek. We stumbled down the stairs until we made it to the lobby entrance. By the time we got there, another incredibly loud boom was heard off to the south. Even 10 blocks from the impact, the ground trembled and loose pieces of windows fell onto streets already full of debris.

I reached for my radio on my vest. My hand found half the radio which fell into pieces as I touched it.

"We have to get to a radio," I stammered at Fred.

Fred looked around, "Let's go over here to the Education building then we will make our way to 2nd militia headquarters."

"No, we have to consolidate forces here" I said through a bloody nose and God knows what else.

Fred and I worked our way to the main floor of the Treasury building. Our casualty collection area had been behind the building in the loading dock area. Unfortunately this was right beside the Archives building, which lay in ruin.

"Looks like they've had it; I don't see anyone alive," Fred gasped in awe.

The blast stacked dead bodies against the far wall of the bottom loading dock. People were mixed in with remnants of cars and trucks from the nearby motor pool. Nothing could survive that blast. We turned east towards the Education Building. Small fires burned the debris. The contents of the building were scattered everywhere.

Militia and office workers scrambled from building to building trying to find cover or medical help. Fred and I made our way across the grassy courtyard between buildings. Once there, we met a security detail from Alpha Company.

"Captain Huck, sir, are you alright?"

"I'm hurting, but I ain't out of this yet" I told him through gritted teeth. "Where is your company commander?"

"He was at the casualty collection area when the bombs fell, I don't know where he is now."

I asked, "Do you know where Bravo's commander is?"

"No sir, I last saw him heading towards the treasury building about a half hour ago."

I was about to tell him something as more planes flew over. I watched as the block south of the Treasury building erupted in an incredible series of explosions. The shock wave took us off our feet and slammed us into the Education building's granite exterior. At that point I wished I was dead; but I wasn't. By the time I could sit up, I saw the treasury building gradually start to shift to the south, and then gradually pick up speed until the entire building collapsed across Lane Street. Dust and thick black smoke blocked parts of the sky. Fred and I huddled by a concrete planter trying to survive the chunks of flying building raining down around us. The sheer noise was enough to make a fighting man a coward.

After several long minutes, my hopes of reconstituting 3rd militia faded. All I could think of was the Recycling building and not letting the bad guys get away. Fred and I stumbled and fell our way to the northern end of the courtyard. Dust blanketed our clothes to the point where I felt grit in my underwear. The familiar sounds of gunfire could be heard popping off in all directions. Small to medium explosions thundered in the not so far distance.

The lobby of the recycling building was a collection of glass and wrecked counters. Bodies lay here and there all covered in a thick layer of dust. For the first time in a while, I thought of my security. I reached for my Glock 19 and drew it. I didn't realize my sniper rifle was strapped to my back until I banged it going through the stairwell's doorway. I unslung the rifle and handed it to Fred, who was unarmed. He and I cautiously went down the staircase as quietly as we could. The hallways were clear of people with only a light dusting. It seemed that Alpha Company was nowhere to be found.

I led the way to the basement in hopes of finding the demo team still hard at work prepping the building for demolition. I saw the team had been there, as I followed wires from packs of explosives on load-bearing steel girders. I knew the wires led to the detonator, so I followed them into a series of hallways. In the inky darkness, I saw something faintly in front of me. The building's lights were out, but the distant corner of the basement shone dimly. Among a clutter of storage crates and cardboard boxes, a group of three men huddled around a hard-plastic Pelican case, I knew to be the detonator. They were shining the light down onto the box and examining it thoroughly. Fred and I got closer making no noise whatsoever. We took a side path towards the men where they could not see us approach. With my side against a crate, I stopped to let Fred catch up.

In an instant, I knew these were not Alpha Company men. These were green shirt special security most likely. I bet they came from the tunnels between buildings. They could have sneaked from the eighth floor, but I couldn't tell yet. I looked at Fred and signaled 1, 2, and nodded my head for three. Fred blasted away with my sniper rifle while I blasted the men with my Glock 19. All three men went down. Their flashlight dropped to the floor and went out.

Now, in complete darkness with my ears ringing once again, I reached into my assault vest and pulled out my flashlight. Fred and I made sure the men on the floor were dead. The first two were dead. The third one was still conscious, but bleeding out as I shined my light into his face. For a moment I thought I had shot someone I knew, but I could not place him. Where had I seen this man before was a mystery to me, for a whole minute. Then it dawned on me. The memories of that face would forever be etched in my brain. The last time I saw this man was through crosshairs. This was the head of green shirt police that had executed our mayor, 3ʳᵈ's first Colonel, back in the summer of last year.

I looked at the man and considered putting another bullet in him for sheer spite. I never expected to see this man again. Oh, I had hoped, but I did not expect it. Now I was faced with a choice.

"Fred, Do we shoot him? Or do we give him the Wizard-of-Oz-treatment?"

Fred looked at me puzzled by the light of the flashlight.

"Should we drop a house on him, like Dorothy did the witch in the Wizard of Oz? I mean, we call Raleigh, Emerald City as a code name, so I think it's only fitting," I mused.

Fred looked at him and said, "Give'm the Oz."

Fred checked the detonator and said we were good to go. The timer had been set for ten minutes to give us a chance to get out. I told Fred to push the button.

Fred and I ran by flashlight back towards the stairwell. Once back up to the lobby, we looked around. The dust had settled a bit. Gunfire cracked all over the place. What could only be tank shells, were hitting buildings almost non-stop. I could hear the whine of turbine tank engines off to the north. They were really close.

Fred and I headed back down towards Lane Street where the Treasury building once stood. Machinegun fire out to the east splintered the trees lining the street. Parked cars burned out of control. A few scattered militia and a few lost office workers scrambled in the dust trying to find cover but there was none from tanks. Fred led us south down Salisbury Street towards the Judicial building. In the distance, we heard another muffled boom of an explosion and turned around. We saw the Department of Recycling building tumble down in sections as it crushed everything on Peace Street.

We turned west on Edenton Street trying to get out of the target zone. We were completely cut off. No radios, nobody to link up with, we were on our own. We made our way cautiously to the railroad tracks building by building. Heavy machinegun fire could be heard in all directions. It sounded like it was just on the next block everywhere you turned.

Fred and I crossed the tracks by a long section of one-story cinderblock buildings, only to find ourselves 150 yards from a tank. The tank's turret was pointed at the corner of the building as we scrambled for cover. The tank fired.

I remember Fred looking into my face but not being able to hear him. The sky above him was cloudy with streaks of smoke passing above the trees. I remember pain. Pain like I had never felt before gripped my right side. At one point I remember spitting blood onto a smooth sidewalk, somewhere. Fred's voice echoed in my ears without my recognition, as he supported me through unknown streets. It could have been hours, or it could have been days between memories, for all I knew.

Chapter 48
Until Next Time

My next memory was blurry at best. I opened my eyes surprised to be alive. Or was I? I could not feel my body or hear anything. All I could see where white ceiling tiles. I assume I was lying down. When I closed my eyes, I drifted back to oblivion.

Again, I awoke to the dull white ceiling tiles, but it must have been night. I saw the tiles as if they were lit by electric lamp light. A strange woman's face looked down into my eyes but her voice was distant like in a barrel or underwater. Her lips moved, but I didn't understand what she said. I drifted back to nowhere.

I awoke in daylight. This time I awoke to a sound. I heard what sounded like a church bell way off in the distance. When I opened my eyes, I saw the same strange woman's face beside a man that looked oddly familiar. They were speaking to me, but I could only process so much. After a few minutes, I regained enough brain power to try to speak. It was then I noticed a tube in my mouth. I coughed and gagged until they removed it. I don't remember any more than that. I was out of it.

I awoke again in daylight with the sun shining on the ceiling tiles. I stared at those tiles for hours, trying to feel my body. I felt pain all down my right side. My right arm hurt, my right side stung like fire, I cried out. The nurse, I now recognized from previous mages, leaned over me and spoke words I understood. She told me to settle down and to breathe. I did, and the pain became manageable.

I asked, "Where am I?" I didn't recognize my own voice though.

She responded, "You are in the People's Hospital of Dorothea Dix, now, why don't you tell me who "Seven" is?"

"You call out that number in your dreams," She said softly but unwaveringly.

Thoughts raced through my mind. Two plus two was equaling five or something. I faked dozing off and lay motionless. I heard the nurse walk away with her shoes clicking on the tile floor. I opened my eyes and moved my head slightly. I was surprised I could move when I did. The hospital ward was lined with twenty or so other people all bandaged up like me. After a few minutes looking around, a familiar face stood at the foot of my bed looking to make sure we were alone.

He spoke quietly as he sat beside my bed and put his hand to my cheek, "They don't know who you are. Don't tell them anything and you might be okay," he got up and walked away.

I nodded slightly. His voice was familiar......Darin.

How could it be? Darin, my minister, had been gone for so long. He was alive? Questions of *how* and *what* clouded my brain to the point where I could not think anymore. We had long since thought Darin dead. Here he was telling me to keep my identity a secret. That must mean that our coup was a total failure and I had to be a prisoner held in a hospital somewhere. The rest of the day, I tried to regain my memory and focus on where I was.

Days blurred together as I healed from my wounds. Every couple of days, a doctor or least a person in a white jacket, looked over my chart. What I was really needed, was pain medicine. However, I got nothing to dull the pain. My whole right side had what seemed like hundreds of lacerations. Some were larger than others. During a bandage change, I managed enough consciousness to see a series of crudely stitched wounds all over my arm and upper right side of my body. Pain was my only full-time companion.

Darin would pass by on occasion and give me bits of information. I found out that Fred was the one that brought me here after the tank shell nearly killed me. Fred was not hurt severely, and the last Darin saw of him was the day of the capitol battle.

Alone one evening, I asked Darin, "What happened? We had the green shirts beat. Then came the tanks and aircraft shredding us to bits."

Darin looked around to make sure we were not overheard, "From what I hear, the PPR already had an army group mobilized and was passing through the Southern states. It's hard to say from here, but it sounded like they wanted to make sure all the former states had their allegiance. From here, they went on down to South Carolina, Georgia, and so on." They just happened to be close by when you guys attacked.

"We had no idea," I said looking blankly into the wall. "We always focused on our own state, thinking that if we could just free it, then we could help others."

"How did *you* manage to survive? It's been a year and we all thought you were dead," I asked Darin.

He told me about the early days of the green shirt takeover. How all the ministers were rounded up and most of them sent to the prisons. A few were spared to work in certain "caretaker" positions in hospitals after intensive re-education. He resisted the re-education, with only a few physical scars to show for it. But after time, he realized that God had spared him to be a servant to those of us persecuted by the green shirts. He had been here for four months now.

Darin explained that I was in a ward reserved especially for severely wounded political prisoners. Our allocated resources were next to nothing. He further explained that the 20 of us in the ward were all that remained of an initial 40 or so brought in. The others had been allowed to succumb to their wounds. He guessed that I might serve some purpose in propaganda television shows that covered the attempted coup. I didn't want to be a spokesman for the crippled resistance fighters, turned wards of the benevolent state. But, I doubted I had much choice in the matter.

Time passed slowly, and I recovered the best I could. Darin was right. I was paraded around and interviewed several times by the People's Broadcasting talking-heads. The interviews were pathetic rah-rah sessions on how soundly the criminal counter-revolutionary resistance had been quashed. Between interviews, my recovery continued in true green shirt manner. During painful physical therapy sessions, I was questioned about what I knew and what I remembered. I claimed a lot of memory loss mixed in with a lot of bull-crap about being a local shopkeeper. But that was all they got from me. My chart showed that I suffered from a concussion, which likely shielded me from more serious interrogation. Thank goodness. They must have believed I was either suffering from memory loss, or I may have been a lower level resistance fighter.

The whole time, I thought of Seven. I wondered what had become of her and if she had kept safe out of the fighting. I doubted she had been arrested though. She was smart enough to get well hidden. She knew to keep her relationship to me a secret. I am sure if the greens shirts knew about Seven and me, they would have used it to break me. It was maddening to not know anything though.

Late one night Darin came to me in the ward. Darin looked left and right as he sat down by my bed, "I have a message from Fred."

I sat up in bed and listened over my pounding heart.

Darin continued looking at the note trying to make sense of it, "Seven okay, Batjack underway, you are Rooster."

"That is all it said. But I have no idea what it means," Darin said looking at both sides of the paper like it was written in a foreign language.

"It's okay. I know what Fred is trying to tell me," I told him as I sat upright in my hospital bed.

"Well, as long as you know what it means. By the way I have something for you. You know to keep this out of sight," as he passed me a small object wrapped in a white towel.

I took the towel and tucked it under my blanket.

Darin looked at me and asked, "How are you holding up? I noticed they have been a little rough in your physical rehab."

"Oh, I am getting along," I told him. "What about you? I know your wife and family searched for you for a long time. We all thought you were dead. Based off everything we found out the prisons, we didn't expect to find you alive."

Darin paused, looking off down the hall, "They are still with me here." he said pointing to his heart. I could tell it was hard for him to think about his family who he had not seen in a year.

"Perhaps I can get you back to your family," I said quietly.

"What can you do? You are bandaged up from head to toe. You have more stitches than the pillow under your head. We cannot simply walk out of here, you know," Darin exclaimed. His voice was mildly heated due to his frustration.

I could see he had wrestled with the notion of escaping, but I could tell he wanted to protect the rest of the men in the ward. I had to give him hope without giving away too much information.

"Darin, there might be an opportunity where we can all get out of here. You need to be ready to go at a moment's notice. The green shirts are still recouping after our attack; you must be ready to move quickly," I instructed him.

Darin looked at the ward in silence for a moment then said, "Do you think we can get everyone out? Will they be in any shape to move or will we kill some just by moving them?"

I assured him, "I don't know all the details, but I guarantee you that we will do everything we can to save as many as possible."

Darin left a little while later. When nobody was watching, I looked at his present. Contained in the towel, was a small pocket copy of the New Testament. The pages were dog-eared and warn from use. It was amazing to think someone had kept this Bible from confiscation and hidden for a year. It was amazing to see. Only the sight of Seven herself walking through the door would have been as comforting to me.

Over the next two days, I walked through the ward whenever the nurses weren't looking. I got familiar with the men and their condition, so that I could direct the rescue team when they got there. I knew from Fred's message that he was going to attempt another covert extraction like we did in the Batjack operation. Rooster had gone into the prisons for three days to collect the people and get them ready to move. Now it was my turn, but I hoped I could manage a better outcome.

To my surprise, there were only a few men from 3rd militia in the ward. Everyone else was a mixture of 2nd and 5th militia whom I didn't know. Luckily there were only two injury cases that had me worried to move them. But given the generally poor conditions of our ward, I was betting that they would have as good a chance with our medics as here. That is, *if* we still had medics. I knew only of our defeat and had no idea of how many our people escaped. How were we equipped for casualties?

By the morning of the 3rd day, I was beside myself with anticipation. It had been four weeks to the day of our failed coup attempt. I was ready to get out of this place and away from the dragon woman of a nurse overseeing our ward. She was kind of like one of those mixes of personalities like Attila the Hun meets the Bride of Frankenstein. But she was worse.

Darin dropped in on me right before lunch. I told him to make an excuse to stay in our ward as much as he could today and gave him a knowing look. He obeyed and did what he could for us as he came and went several times.

Then late in the afternoon, I heard a slight commotion from the hallway. Several of the caretakers and nurses from the ward marched through the double doors followed closely by three uniformed men. I recognized the second man immediately. He was from 3rd militia's intelligence group. The nurses in the ward looked onward with a mixture of fear and obedience. The head nurse looked outwardly happy. A strange thing to behold, since I had never seen her smile and was quite surprised to see that she was physically able to do so.

The uniformed men came striding down the row of beds, followed closely by the nurses. When the Intelligence operator stopped by me, he squared off in my face where he said, "You criminals are hereby transferred to the reformed prison authority of North Carolina. There, you will be punished for crimes against the state."

I looked at him as if surprised to hear that I was in prison. I calmly walked back to the pillow of my bed and reached underneath. I saw surprise as they watched me pull out the small Bible and hold it up.

I pointed to Darin, "This man is a former minister and has passed me forbidden propaganda literature. He should be arrested."

The look on Darin's face was worth my injuries. He had no idea we were in the process of being rescued. He must have thought I had lost my mind to betray him like that.

Darin pointed his finger at me and yelled out, "God help you!"

The uniformed men took him by the arms and handcuffed him on the floor immediately. The rest of us watched, along with the nurses, in near shock. The head nurse was spitting mad. She called Darin all sorts of rude names as they forcibly removed him from the room. She was livid and I knew she secretly feared for her own safety. She knew being guiltless in this government, didn't equal freedom.

The rest of the wounded were ushered outside onto a waiting bus with all the proper markings of a prison transfer unit. While being led out, I overheard the head nurse being told off for having such an obvious usurper of the state, right under her nose. She was speechless as our Intel operator blessed her out some more with a few threats of investigation. She was as pale as a ghost when our man climbed on the bus.

After about five miles down the road, I turned around to Darin who sat behind me.

"Welcome to the revolution," I said with a wry smile.

You could have knocked him over with a feather as our Intel operator walked down the aisle of the bus and unlocked his handcuffs. After releasing Darin, the Intel operator looked at me.

"Captain Huck, Sir, I'm glad to see you made it."

Darin looked at me in utter amazement, "You mean....this is our escape? I thought we were headed for prison for sure," he sat back in his seat and smiled like no man I had ever seen before. He was finally free after a year of captivity.

This had been some year indeed. Our country had come apart at the seams. When it was rebuilt, it looked more like the old Soviet Union than the America we knew. Our resistance had gotten strong, but our attempt to free ourselves had succeeded for about 20 minutes, before being crushed. Many of us were dead, and who knew how many more, would follow before it was all over. All we could do was trust in providence to see us through. God willing, we would someday win our freedom.

As the bus bumped along the roads leading to wide open country, I looked back to Raleigh fading in the distance, "Until next time."

Epilogue

"Grandpa, I had no idea you were *so* involved in the war," Jake said as he sat looking over the reams of notes from my stories.

I looked at Jake, "The stories I have told you for this book haven't been shared in decades. Most people in the resistance didn't even have all this background. Maybe your generation will have a chance to learn from what happened back in those days, and learn from it."

Jake thought hard for a few moments, "That's an amazing story Grandpa. I'm sure there will be loads of people wanting to read your stories, thanks for sharing them with me."

This time I paused, "Jake, it didn't end there. That was only the first year of the resistance. There was plenty of fighting before it was all said and done."

Made in the USA
Columbia, SC
02 September 2019